MW00579141

Praise for
New York Times and USA Today Bestselling Author

Diane Capri

"Full of thrills and tension, but smart and human, too."
*Lee Child, #1 New York Times Bestselling Author of Jack
Reacher Thrillers*

"[A] welcome surprise....[W]orks from the first page to 'The
End'."
Larry King

"Swift pacing and ongoing suspense are always
present...[L]ikable protagonist who uses her political
connections for a good cause...Readers should eagerly anticipate
the next [book]."
Top Pick, Romantic Times

"...offers tense legal drama with courtroom overtones, twisty
plot, and loads of Florida atmosphere. Recommended."
Library Journal

"[A] fast-paced legal thriller...energetic prose...an appealing
heroine...clever and capable supporting cast...[that will] keep
readers waiting for the next [book]."
Publishers Weekly

"Expertise shines on every page."
*Margaret Maron, Edgar, Anthony, Agatha and Macavity Award
Winning MWA Past President*

FATAL BOND

by *DIANE CAPRI and*
NIGEL BLACKWELL

Copyright © 2017 Diane Capri and Nigel Blackwell
All Rights Reserved

Published by: AugustBooks
http://www.AugustBooks.com
ISBN-13: 978-1-942633-03-7
ISBN-10: 1-942633-03-3

Original Cover Design: Cory Clubb
Digital Formatting: Author E.M.S.

Fatal Bond is a work of fiction. Names, characters, places, and incidents either are the product of the author's imagination or are used fictitiously, and any resemblance to actual persons, living or dead, business establishments, events, or locales is entirely coincidental.

Published in the United States of America.

Visit the author websites:
http://www.DianeCapri.com
http://www.NigelBlackwell.com

ALSO BY DIANE CAPRI

The Heir Hunter Series
Blood Trails
Trace Evidence

The Jess Kimball Thrillers Series
Fatal Enemy
Fatal Distraction
Fatal Demand
Fatal Error
Fatal Fall
Fatal Edge (*novella*)
Fatal Game
Fatal Bond
Fatal Past (*coming soon*)
Fatal Dawn (*coming soon*)

The Hunt for Jack Reacher Series
Don't Know Jack
Jack in a Box (*novella*)
Jack and Kill (*novella*)
Get Back Jack
Jack in the Green (*novella*)
Jack and Joe
Deep Cover Jack
Jack the Reaper
Black Jack (*coming soon*)

ALSO BY NIGEL BLACKWELL

CAST OF CHARACTERS

Jessica Kimball
Gary Hadlow
Henry Morris
Carter Pierce
Mandy Donovan
Alex Cole
Debora Elden
Claire Winter
Rafa Lopez
Vanna Sánchez
Ethan Remington

FATAL
BOND

CHAPTER ONE

Gloriana Island, Angola
After Midnight

RAFA LOPEZ FOCUSED HIS sharp eyes on his workers as a starving wolf attends his dinner. The lights in the control room were low. Rows of LEDs blinked. Lines traced readings across monitors. Books and coffee mugs held down papers, combatting the ever-present blast of air conditioning.

In the corner behind him, Vanna Sánchez leaned against the wall. Tall, austere, and platinum blonde with deep blue eyes and the long-limbed muscles of a distance runner, she was easily the most attractive woman in any room. A cell phone in her hands held her full attention. At her feet was a small backpack.

At regular intervals, a tinny and distant voice came from a small speaker in front of a large, thick window. The glass revealed six transparent glass-walled laboratories on the floor below.

In the middle of each laboratory was a circular stainless-steel drain. Around the clear walls, stainless-steel benches held complex looking glassware and machines protected with thick seamless plastic covers.

Each room had its own class III biosafety cabinet, a large structure with built-in rubber gloves for conducting experiments inside a hermetically sealed environment.

Only one of the six rooms was occupied. Two workers, both in full protective suits, breathed air through a hose that connected to a panel on the wall. The suits were constructed of material as transparent as the lab walls. The first worker was a bald, heavyset Texan. The second was female, half the Texan's weight, with Asian features and thick black hair trimmed short.

The Texan stood at the biosafety cabinet. His hands were deep in the rubber gloves, pipetting liquids into a multi-well sample tray like a miniature ice cube tray.

The Asian woman divided her time, alternately operating a high-power digital microscope and a liquid chromatograph to monitor reactions.

Results were fed to the control room where a young man categorized them before they were displayed on two massive television monitors in front of Lopez.

The televisions displayed graphs and images side by side in squares. The graphs portrayed biochemical changes taking place in the visual image.

The Texan's pipette appeared in the corner of one image. He had a steady hand. A single drop of clear liquid formed on the end of the fine glass tube and dripped onto a pinkish sample in the multi-well tray.

The pinkish sample was a sliver of muscle. It contracted to half its size in a single convulsion. Had it been the complete muscle, such a jolt would have been powerful enough to tear tendons from bone.

"This is hopeless," said the Texan with the pipette. His electronic voice grated through the speakers. "The electrochemical transfer process will have to be thousands of times slower."

Lopez keyed a microphone. "Lower the molarity. Move down a decade."

"A decade won't do it. We need a different solvent. A lower ionization constant at least," the Texan said.

Lopez pressed the microphone switch again. "Move down a decade, please." Cool and calm, as if the researcher's advice had not been spoken. Lopez combed back his salt and pepper hair with his fingers while he waited.

Knowing he was being observed every moment of the experiment, the Texan at the biosafety cabinet suppressed a sigh and simply nodded. He stood the pipette in a holder and placed the multi-well tray on a rack in a metal box.

The box was for the destruction of biological samples. It met all the international standards for safety considering its contents.

When the experiments were completed, an automated system would lower the box from the biosafety cabinet into an oven. For thirty minutes, the box would be subjected to temperatures beyond anything a living organism could withstand. The box would then open, and the charred inert remains would be disposed of.

In order to maintain the biological integrity of the box while it was being lowered into the oven, there was a stainless-steel door. The door was opened and closed by an electric motor, which applied enough torque to compress a silicone gasket around the edges and ensure a hermetic seal.

The Asian woman pressed a switch down, and the door began to close. The tray wasn't fully seated, and the door impacted the wells. There was a momentary grinding noise, the motor winding tension into the door's gear mechanism. The Asian woman flipped the switch up, and the motor stopped.

The Texan pushed on the tray. It didn't move. He pushed harder. The tray scraped a fraction further into the box. The door kept its pressure on the rear of the tray. He placed both hands on the tray and pushed. It moved with a jolt. He lurched forward, banging against the cabinet glass.

The door's mechanism released. Even without power, the precision gearboxes acted as a coiled spring and spun in an instant. The door snapped down.

The fingers of the Texan's right hand were inside the box. The door scythed down. Debilitating pain shot through his nerves. He screamed long and hard.

A raging fire grew from his hand up his right arm. The door had trapped the tips of his left glove. He yanked the glove free, ripping the ends of the fingers.

The Asian woman rammed the operating switch to the open position as hard as it would stand.

The door lifted.

The Texan stumbled back, screaming as he dragged his shattered fingers from the thick gloves. The Asian woman shoved a chair behind him, and he collapsed squeezing his right wrist to control the pain.

The safety cabinet's gloves bobbed in the air, inverted and pointing outward from the Texan's rapid and agonizing exit.

It took only a fraction of a second for the Asian woman to realize why the gloves had gained their jaunty bounce. "Breach, breach," she screamed.

Sánchez looked up from her phone. Lopez started a timer and moved closer to the window. The Texan's hand was bloody.

The biosafety cabinet's gloves had been ruptured.

The young man in the control room slammed his hand on a large red button. Yellow lights flashed, and a woman's voice calmly announced an emergency had occurred.

In Lopez's opinion, the announcement was pointless. There were only five people in the building, and they were all well aware of what had happened.

Sánchez picked up her backpack.

The Asian woman pulled the air hoses from the panel on the wall and levered the Texan to his feet.

"What concentration level were they using?" Lopez said.

The young man stared, his mouth open. "We've got to get them out—"

"What concentration level were they using?" Lopez repeated, precisely as before.

The young man turned to his monitor. "Um, er…ten ppm."

The Texan stood still, coughing.

"Move!" the Asian woman said.

"I'm going to open the next lab," the young man said.

"No," Lopez said.

Sánchez held her backpack in front of her.

The young man shook his hands in the direction of the Texan and the Asian woman. "But they're exposed. We have to get them into another chamber, or they won't stand a chance."

"Wait," Lopez said.

"Wait?" The young man screwed up his face. "Are you crazy?" He crossed the room in two steps and flipped the red safety covers off two large switches. "I'm opening lab 3," he said into a microphone.

Sánchez took a pistol from her backpack. In one smooth motion, she stretched her arm out straight, looked down the gun sight, and fired. The sound from the small gun was a harsh pop, not the deafening boom a larger caliber weapon would have produced.

The young man yelped as he snatched his hand away from the switches and clutched it to his chest. He gaped at Sánchez. "What—"

Sánchez lowered her gun and put a bullet in his knee. He collapsed, screaming.

She stepped beside him.

He used his good leg to slide back a couple of feet. His wounded knee left a bloody trail across the floor. Panting with pain, he sat up. "You can't do this!"

Sánchez took a step forward. A lunge. The heel of her foot crashing down on the man's ruined knee. He screamed and swore.

"Enough," Lopez said quietly.

Sánchez thrust the gun in the young man's face and fired three times. The blast shoved his dead body back. His legs caught under him in a mangled heap.

She chose a blood-free patch on his shoulder and leaned on it with her foot. His body twisted and his legs popped free. He lay flat on the floor in a growing pool of blood.

Sánchez stood beside Lopez, watching through the Plexiglas windows.

Lopez opened a metal door that covered a series of electrical breakers. He ran his finger down the list of circuits and found the one marked *chamber doors*. He had to push hard to move the heavy-duty switch to the *off* position.

A muted thump struck the window. The Asian woman stared up through the transparent lab walls, still secure in her airtight suit, pounding on the glass.

Lopez turned back to the breaker panel. He hefted the breakers for the HEPA filters and oxygen supply to *off*.

The Asian woman hammered on the glass, her eyes wild. Her mouth moved, but two layers of bulletproof glass and her own safety suit muted her screams.

The Texan fell to the floor, twitching, and retching.

The Asian woman ran to the oxygen panel and reconnected her hose. A moment later, she jerked her head around to stare up at Lopez.

Realization dawned.

Her choice was to suffocate or expose herself to the contaminated air.

The Texan's twitching stopped. He remained still.

Lopez checked his stopwatch and wrote in a notebook, *Forty-nine seconds from exposure.*

The Asian woman mouthed obscenities. At two minutes she struggled for air and sank to her knees. At three minutes, she cracked open her helmet, eyes filled with burning hatred. She panted and gulped.

Exposed.

Lopez pressed the button on his stopwatch. He watched until the Asian woman's body stopped moving. He recorded the time in his notebook. *Fifty-three seconds from exposure.*

He shook his head. The Texan's prediction had been wrong after all. "Forty-nine and fifty-three seconds," he said. "Reducing the concentration isn't going to improve that."

Sánchez kept quiet.

"I need a new strain."

"The American one?" Sánchez asked.

He nodded and sent a message. It was the middle of the night in the US, but the reply arrived within seconds.

Everything was planned and ready. He nodded with satisfaction. "We will be back in business in a couple of days."

"What about more scientists?"

"I have that covered as well." He picked up his notebook. "Get a cleanup crew. The next shift will be here soon."

Sánchez offered a warm smile that reached her eyes. "My pleasure."

CHAPTER TWO

Four months later
Monday, August 15
6:30 p.m. MDT
Denver, Colorado

JESS KIMBALL'S OFFICE WAS on the top floor of the *Taboo Magazine* tower block, situated in central Denver at Broadway and Colfax. The view from her floor to ceiling window swept from the State Capitol, across the Civic Center Park to the District Courts.

When she finally glanced up from the article she'd been writing, shadows had lengthened and faded into the dark as the sun set. Street lamps had come on. The Art Museum was a beacon of sharp corners and odd angles bathed in spotlights.

Bright squares set in the side of tower blocks marked the late-night office workers.

Like her.

People who lived alone and had no reason to go home to an empty apartment. Jess had lived alone a long time, but she'd never get used to her son's absence. She'd find Peter one day. When she found him, then she'd go home earlier, with joy in her heart every day.

But for now, she stretched her arms over her head to work the kinks out of her neck. Which was when she noticed the small red light flashing on her desk phone. Voicemail.

Invariably, messages this late in the day were the most difficult.

Morning calls came from people who knew what they wanted. They'd spent the night agonizing over worst-case scenarios, real or imagined. In the cold light of dawn, they made the decision to reach out to the media. To call Jess Kimball.

But late messages often came from people who had suffered for many hours that particular day. Pressure weighted their uncertainty until they could wait no more. Not much could be done after business hours, no matter what the problem. They knew as much before they called. But they wanted to hand off the worry. Move the relentless pressure from their lives to hers.

Jess was a lifeboat for such people. She depended heavily on *Taboo Magazine's* readers to support her constant search for her son. And for many of them, she was the lifeboat they clung to when life's uncertain seas became overwhelming.

She leaned back in her chair, stared unseeing through her office window, and pressed the play button on the voicemail.

The recording's time and date were announced by the machine, and then a woman spoke. Jess recognized the voice immediately.

"Jess, this is Marcia McAllister. I'm sorry to disturb you, but I didn't know who else to call."

Marcia McAllister's daughter, Melinda, had been living in Paris when she disappeared a while ago. Jess had reported the

FATAL BOND | 21

case, but the crime was never solved, and her daughter was not found.

At least, not yet.

Jess never gave up on the families who came to her for help. Giving up on their cases would be too much like giving up on Peter, and she simply would not do that. Not ever. No matter how long it took her to find her son.

Marcia McAllister was no exception. Jess had worked hard for Marcia, and she'd keep working hard until Marcia's daughter was found. She had no plan B. No alternatives. She simply would not quit.

Jess hoped that Marcia was calling with new information on the case. The situation was, like so many others, heartbreaking. But through it all, Marcia had been a rock. She'd suffered the torment of not knowing what happened to her child, a torment Jess understood all too well. Marcia McAllister handled everything with more grace than many others Jess had helped over the years.

Marcia had pushed and cajoled and encouraged US and French authorities to investigate her daughter's disappearance, but never once had she publicly lost her equanimity. She was a woman to be reckoned with as well as the kind of determined female Jess always admired. She simply didn't have it in her heart to fail.

She leaned forward and turned up the volume.

Marcia cleared her throat. "I...well, not me, but a friend of mine. Nicola Cole. She's worried sick. It's her son. Good kid. Not that he's a kid anymore. Ph.D. and all that. But he's got himself into some trouble. Well, it's not right, of course. He wouldn't do that. A good kid. Oh, did I say that?"

The message rambled in a way that Marcia never did in

person. Which was enough for Jess to conclude she must be completely distraught.

"Anyway, I'm sure it wasn't Alex. Really." Marcia coughed before she continued. "He's a scientist working at that insecticide place here in Chatham. The one in the news." Her voice became shakier with each word until she reached the end of what she was determined to say. "And, well, they're blaming him for that explosion."

Jess knew what she was referring to. The Kelso Products bombing had been all over the news around the globe since it happened Thursday afternoon. She'd have had to be living on another planet to be unaware of events in Iowa.

She'd worked with Marcia closely every day after her daughter disappeared two years ago. The case was cold, but still open, and they'd stayed in touch. Simply put, Jess trusted Marcia implicitly. Alex Cole could very well be innocent if Marcia believed it so.

She also knew the law had its own momentum and wasn't easily swayed from its path.

Jess's experience had proved time and time again that justice for crime victims depended on action.

Jess felt more than a little guilty, too. She'd hit a wall in Marcia's daughter's case. She'd let Marcia down. Maybe she could help now and make up for it, at least a little bit. The very least she could do was try.

She pulled up two large monitors covered with articles and pictures of the explosion and subsequent fire at Kelso Products before she returned Marcia's call.

Explosions like this one were too often caused by terrorism, and the big news outlets covered potential terrorist attacks like ants covered picnics. Which meant there was plenty of video reporting already available over the past five days.

CHAPTER THREE

SHE WATCHED THE KELSO Products security camera footage first. The time stamp in the corner of the images established 12:42 p.m., Thursday, August 11, as the moment so many lives were changed. The images horrified her.

Five days ago, a massive powder storage tank exploded. The kind of explosion that didn't happen out of nowhere.

The deafening pressure wave fanned out, smashing windows for hundreds of yards.

The explosion's force rippled through the pipework to another tank. From there, it ran swiftly into the half-mile long production facility.

Flames burst from windows.

Sections of roofs collapsed.

The second tank split along one side, spewing burning contents over a line of trucks parked too close to the side of the building.

Jess moved to the next series of videos covering the new information as it became available.

Three workers at the plant had died. Each face was displayed in photos from family members during happy times, which made the losses more poignant.

Thirty-seven employees were injured. Most were treated and released, thank God.

Seventeen remained in Chatham General hospital.

Three were in critical condition, not expected to survive. If they died, Marcia's young friend could be charged with no less than six murders. He would be sentenced to death. No wonder his mother was distraught. How could any mother cope with that?

The explosion and its implications brought FBI power to work alongside the local Chatham Police Department and other state agencies.

Ethan Remington was the lead FBI Investigator. Jess watched his most recent press conference. He told reporters the bomb had been planted in the first storage tank. The valves between the tanks were opened, and the bomb was detonated remotely, he said.

The FBI hadn't formally released details of the explosive material, but the media had figured it out themselves.

The bomb had been small, which ruled out a fertilizer bomb, and the explosion massive, which meant it had to be a powerful material. There was only one common explosive that fit. Triacetone triperoxide, or TAPT.

Jess knew that terrorists used TAPT in bombs across the United States and Europe, including Paris and Manchester. But the Kelso Products bombing probably wasn't a terrorist incident. Terrorists were quick to claim responsibility and grab publicity for their twisted causes, and no group or individual had claimed responsibility for this one.

A reporter was explaining now that ingredients to make

TAPT were easy to obtain. TAPT didn't burn like most explosives, either. The molecule simply burst apart and expanded fast, from a dense solid to a gas occupying a couple of hundred times more volume. Which caused a massive explosion and propelled a pressure wave comparable to dynamite.

"The ingredients to make TAPT are readily available," an expert said, "but preparing TAPT is extremely hazardous. TAPT is detonated by shock. Sometimes even the stress inside the crystals formed during the production process can detonate the compound. Only someone with experience can make enough TAPT for a bomb as destructive as what we've seen at Kelso Products."

The last video news report Jess found announced that one man had been charged today with detonating the bomb. Alex Cole. The same Alex Cole that Marcia McAllister had pled with Jess to save.

But could Jess really help? The evidence against Cole sounded formidable.

Remington's sound bite said the bomb's triggering command had been traced to Cole.

Corroborating evidence located thus far included emails, internet search histories, even the computer records from a coffee shop Cole frequented.

Jess shook her head. The media scrutiny was intense. Until something more exciting came along to fill the twenty-four-hour news cycle, they weren't likely to let up on the pressure, either.

In response to questions, Remington said Cole had the means and the opportunity to commit the crime, but he admitted they'd found no motive for the attack. A motive wasn't necessary to convict Cole, but in Jess's experience, a missing motive was certainly odd.

Most people had reasons for the things they di[?] those reasons were more than a little crazy.

Marcia was convinced the police had arrested the wrong man.

Jess needed nothing more to check things out. She owed Marcia that much.

She picked up the phone and dialed her favorite G-man, FBI Special Agent Henry Morris.

They'd met and worked together on one of Jess's investigative cases that evolved into kidnapping, extortion, and murder. A tough case that led to significant trust became an unbreakable fatal bond when Morris killed a man to keep her alive.

Over time, she'd learned that Morris was solid in every way that mattered. He was physically and mentally strong enough to be a good match for her, unrelenting in the pursuit of justice, and brave, too. Not too old, not too young, and good looking as well.

A while later, after she'd learned that he wasn't married, she no longer had any reasonable excuse to reject his invitations. As he'd continually pointed out.

And he gave her all the space she needed to do her most important job—finding Peter.

She grinned. How's a girl supposed to resist a hero like that?

Despite his work ethic, Morris had a knack for keeping life in perspective and a sense of humor that didn't solely consist of sarcasm. Later, after Morris transferred from the FBI's Dallas Field Office to Denver, Jess found herself in the first serious relationship of her life.

There had been another relationship she'd thought was serious at the time, with Peter's father. She'd been wrong then, which made her wary now.

"Jess," Morris said when he picked up. She heard the pleasure in his voice and felt her face warming uncomfortably.

"I've been looking at the Kelso Products accident."

He laughed. "And it's really nice to hear from you, too."

She smiled again, although he couldn't see her. "I've got a few questions."

"Who doesn't?"

"Something about this whole situation doesn't pass the smell test, Henry."

"What do you know that you're not telling me?"

"Nothing yet. But so far, Alex Cole has no motive for blowing that place up."

"No *known* motive," Agent Morris corrected.

"Fair enough. But people who know Cole well say he's not capable of violence like that."

"People who know the accused always say that, and it means nothing."

She nodded to herself. "Which is why I need to go to Kelso Products."

She heard him sigh through the wireless connection, but he didn't object. As always, he respected her decisions.

"I'm leaving tomorrow. First flight out of Denver. I called because I need some help."

He paused. "I'm not involved with the investigation, but I'll do what I can."

Jess put the gratitude that sprang to mind into her voice. Dating an FBI agent had its advantages. "Can you get me thirty minutes with the lead agent?"

"That I can do. Ethan Remington. Omaha Field Office. Good guy."

"Thanks, Henry."

"I guess this means dinner tomorrow night is off?" he asked.

"I'll make it up to you," she replied. "Look on the bright side. It was your turn to pay."

She disconnected while he was still laughing.

She found *Taboo's* travel website on her computer and booked a ticket to Chatham, Iowa. She continued scouring the wire services for anything and everything she could learn on the Kelso Products bombing before she saw Marcia McAllister tomorrow.

CHAPTER FOUR

Tuesday, August 16
10:00 a.m. CDT
Chatham, Iowa

CHATHAM WAS A SPRAWLING medium-sized industrial city in the middle of farm country. People worked hard there. But what Jess saw as she flew into the international airport were mostly gray skies, grayer buildings, and dirty gray concrete.

Her rental stood out against the gray like a beacon. A cheerful red Chevy Malibu sedan with less than a thousand miles on the odometer. She put the address for Kelso Products in the car's navigation system and pushed the button to start the engine and rolled out.

The rental's GPS guided her onto the interstate that looped around the city. The sedan was surprisingly quick. She eased off the accelerator.

The radio was tuned to a local talk station. The Chatham Cubs, the local minor league baseball team, was suffering through a losing streak. The explosion at Kelso Products came up next. A rehash of what she already knew.

The newscaster moved quickly through the national news and finished with a brief reference to the continuing effort to track down the cause of an outbreak of sepsis in Botswana about three months earlier. Jess tuned out as she arrived at the Kelso Products plant.

The employee parking lot was only half full. Jess pulled into a space near the center in the back where she had an unobstructed view of the facility.

A police car blocked the driveway that led from the employee lot to the management lot. His lights weren't flashing, but the officer's expression declared that no one would enter without authorization.

A television crew was staked out ten feet from the cruiser. A broad-shouldered man Jess didn't recognize spoke earnestly into a large microphone.

Several floor-to-ceiling windows in the main building were boarded over. At the steel and glass revolving front door, four workmen struggled to replace the damaged panes.

Clusters of flowers and wreaths and handwritten signs covered the pavement around the entrance. On the roof, Kelso's flag hung at half-mast.

Behind the management offices marched enormous industrial buildings. Pipes of all diameters wound their way in and out between storage tanks.

One of the tanks had split open. Thick steel walls were peeled back like an orange. The tubes and pipes around it were twisted and mangled.

Before the explosion, buildings, tanks, and pipes had been painted white. Now, the area's blackened scars testified to the force of Thursday's explosion and the ensuing fire.

The most severely damaged areas were cordoned off with yellow tape, the words "Do Not Cross" emblazoned in thick black font along its length.

Jess's phone buzzed with an incoming message from Henry Morris. The agent in charge of the investigation, Remington, would meet with her for thirty minutes at noon.

She checked her watch. She had time to meet Marcia McAllister first. She texted her thanks back to Henry.

She walked across the main road to the bus stop. Marcia arrived a few minutes later, wearing jeans, a windbreaker, and a lime-green baseball cap emblazoned with the Chatham Cubs logo. She looked exhausted.

Furtively, she glanced across the road toward the Kelso Products plant, as if she was worried about being spotted.

"Hello," Jess said, to capture her attention.

Marcia nodded. "Thanks for coming."

"I thought Mrs. Cole was joining us."

Marcia shook her head. "A pack of reporters are camped out at her house. Nicola can't go anywhere. They hunt her down. She's fraying at the seams, frankly. I'm worried about her almost as much as Alex."

Jess glanced around. She saw no obvious amateur surveillance. If Marcia were being watched by the FBI or other professionals, neither she nor Nicola would ever see them.

"Let's walk." Marcia led them away from the police cruiser, turned left two blocks south, and found a park bench under a tree. She plopped down heavily. "Nicola wanted to be here. Really. But…well, let's just say local emotions are running high."

"Surely she's not surprised. People died. Her son stands accused. The families are bound to be very upset."

"But it's her *son*. He didn't do this. Nicola's pretty upset, too, and nobody seems to care about that very much." Marcia stopped to breathe and stared pointedly at Jess. "We know what that's like."

Jess nodded. "Tell me what I need to know about Alex Cole."

"He's been like a son to me. Especially since…" her voice trailed off, and she cleared her throat. Jess knew what she meant. Since her daughter went missing. "I watched Alex grow up. Elementary to high school. Even when he went off to college, he used to come back all the time. He has always been close to his parents."

"Brothers and sisters?"

Marcia shook her head. "Only child. And his father died three years ago. Young. Heart attack."

Jess grimaced. "So it's just him and his mom now?"

"And this is killing her, Jess. She *knows* Alex didn't do this." Marcia nodded, glassy tears pooling in her eyes. "We both do. He couldn't have blown up that plant. He would never do something like that. And he's no terrorist, either. No matter what people say."

"There's a lot of evidence against him, Marcia," Jess gentled her tone to confirm what Marcia had to know already.

Marcia's eyes blazed, and she stuck her chin forward. "No way. Not Alex. He's being set up, or these cops are incompetent. They've got the wrong guy. And the sooner they figure that out, the better."

Jess understood Marcia's loyalty. She nodded with sympathy. "Unfortunately, we will need more than your strong convictions, or his mother's, to get the charges dropped."

She didn't say that the frame around Alex Cole was so tight, they'd need nothing less than the actual terrorists confessing on the record in an airtight smackdown to get Alex out of trouble here.

"He's a kind soul, Jess. Completely non-violent. He doesn't even eat meat because he can't bear the slaughter of animals." Marcia wiped her nose and shook her head vigorously as if the intensity of her denial would make all the difference.

Jess put a comforting hand on Marcia's arm because nothing she could say would make any difference.

Marcia bowed her head and blinked away more glassy tears. "He became a scientist because he liked research, to conduct controlled experiments. He bought a big place outside of town to give him enough room for his work."

"Did his work, these experiments, involve explosives?"

"Not at all." Marcia shook her head, fast. "He liked to make things. Mostly computer-controlled things."

"The FBI believes he had a lab where he made the explosives used in the bomb. Alex's lab has been searched." Jess patted her arm. "They found a lot of things that could easily be lethal in the right combinations."

"He's as normal as any kid, Jess. Nice girlfriend, good to his mother..." She seemed to run out of steam, bewildered, confused, and clearly frightened to death.

The evidence against Alex Cole, what Jess was aware of, was solid. And there was a lot of it. Overwhelming, really. Pressing Marcia with those facts wouldn't help much.

"Meet with Alex. Talk to him. Judge for yourself." Marcia put her hands together and stared at them. "Remember when they found those Boston Marathon bombers? I could just see them as killers. When you find out who did this, it'll be the same way. Alex isn't like those guys. When you meet him, you'll know what I mean."

"I'll try. That's why I came here. But law enforcement agencies are experts these days. They know what they're doing. They have vast resources." Jess paused a moment for breath.

"Jess... I trust you. Meet Alex first. You'll see." Marcia looked up, her eyes pleading as loudly as her words. "Please?"

Jess patted Marcia's shoulder awkwardly. "Of course, I'll talk to him today. Maybe he'll help me figure out what's going on. But first, I've got an appointment with Ethan Remington."

"He's had it in for Alex right from the start." Marcia's lip curled, and her whole demeanor changed. She'd caught a glimpse of something across the street from the corner of her eye. "I've got to go. Be careful, Jess. I don't know what's going on here, but someone is trying awfully hard to pin this thing on Alex Cole. Whoever is doing this is dangerous. Watch your back."

Marcia jumped up and dashed around the corner. Jess cocked her head and watched as two men emerged from the drugstore across the street and hoofed quickly in the same direction.

Jess hurried to the corner to warn Marcia, but she was already gone. And when Jess turned back toward the two men, they had already slipped into a black SUV parked at the corner.

She fished out her phone and snapped a quick photo of the license plate and the back of the SUV as it pulled away from the curb. She dialed Marcia, but her voicemail picked up.

Jess gnawed on the inside of her lip.

CHAPTER FIVE

Tuesday, August 16
10: 30 a.m. West Africa Time Zone (WAT)
Off the coast of Angola, Africa

ISABELLA BOBBED ON THE swell. The yacht was half of a mile from the shore, and the seabed had yet to rise up enough to turn the gentle, near perfect sine waves into crashing foamy breakers.

Rafa Lopez stood on the third floor, the upper deck. The boat was long and low. Toward the front was the smaller of two sundecks. The upper edge of the wall around the sides of the yacht, technically the gunwale, rose toward the bow, all but shielding the sunbathers from the public eye.

At the stern was the bigger sundeck. Even with its array of soft furnishings and sun-loungers, fifty people could be comfortably accommodated. Two crew members were busy setting up a buffet alongside a bar lined with silver champagne buckets that glittered in the sun.

To the west, hidden in the glare of the morning sun, a boat

approached. Even though an impressive speedboat itself, it was an inconsequential dot to the *Isabella* and the vastness of the ocean. The people inside, doubly so.

Alongside the yacht, steps had been lowered to the waterline. Lopez took the two flights of stairs down to the main deck and waited by the steps.

The speedboat came alongside, the pilot pulsing the engine to keep the two craft stationary relative to each other.

A crew member helped two guests from the speedboat onto the *Isabella's* steps. The first guest was tall, her regal bearing accentuated by the vivid patterns that shimmered on her long silk dress.

Thick black hair spiraled upward around her head and was held in place with multicolored wooden pins. Dark sunglasses hid her eyes.

Lopez held his hand out. "Welcome aboard Mrs. Neto."

She took his hand, and stepped onto the boat. "Thank you, Mr. Lopez." She smiled. "But let's not be so formal, I am Ana."

Lopez returned her smile. "And I am Rafa."

The man behind her stepped onto the deck, a big grin on his face. "And if you forget my name, perhaps I shall have to throw you in prison."

They all laughed. Lopez slapped him on the shoulder. "Forget you, General? I don't think so."

Lopez led the party to the rear deck. The crew raised the steps and secured the speedboat to the rear of the *Isabella*.

The buffet was prepared, and drinks were already in glasses on the bar, ice glinting in the sun.

"It is good to have the chance to entertain you both."

The general gestured to the *Isabella*. "When you said you had a boat, I didn't think you meant a beautiful yacht like this."

Lopez waved the compliment away. "A fortunate purchase during a downturn in the market." He bowed his head forward and whispered the truth conspiratorially, "It was a steal."

The general laughed. "With you, Rafa, I don't doubt it."

A deckhand in a crisp white uniform handed each person a glass.

Lopez gestured to a sun lounger. "Ana," He swept his arm around in a great arc, "relax, enjoy the view while I show your husband my latest acquisition."

She frowned. "Can't I—"

"You want to see the engine room?"

She waved at the sea. "I'll sit here and enjoy the view."

She leaned back in the lounger and raised her glass. "Bye, bye."

Lopez bowed his head and swept General Neto along the walkway around the side of the yacht.

"We aren't required to view the engine room, are we?"

Lopez raised an eyebrow. "Unless you have an interest?"

Neto laughed.

"Then let us enjoy the foredeck for a few minutes."

The foredeck was a quarter the size of the aft deck, but it too was laden with refreshments. Three large sofas were arranged around a massive television screen. Vanna Sánchez stood quietly in the back of the room.

Neto picked up a glass of clear liquid on ice. "Vodka?"

"The best, of course."

Neto took a sip and nodded his approval. "What do you have on your mind, my friend?"

Lopez picked up a full glass and tilted it in a mock toast. "I need your help again."

Neto offered a flat smile. "I warned you last time that things would not be so easy in the future."

"I understand. But still, I find myself asking."

Neto shifted his weight. "What this time?"

"Like last time."

Neto stepped sideways, shaking his head. "That won't be possible."

Lopez arched his eyebrows and did not reply.

"Things have changed," Neto said.

"Things always change."

Neto grunted. "This change came with more oversight."

"For you? One of the country's most powerful generals?"

"For everyone in government. You read the papers, I know this is not a surprise to you."

Lopez shrugged. "There was oversight before."

"Not like this."

"What is so different now?"

"They are cracking down. The UN has been pushing its pet phrase: waste, fraud, and abuse."

"Pah. The American agenda."

"It's our government's agenda now."

Lopez gestured to Neto, "With us, the government does not lose money. I will be paying. Handsomely. And to you in particular."

"There are new requirements. Throughout the services. Believe me, my friend, nothing is easy anymore." Neto had drained his glass, and Vanna Sánchez replaced it with a full one without comment.

Lopez sighed. "These have been tumultuous times. You have done well."

"I try." He bowed his head.

"Reorganizations. Shifting loyalties. Changing priorities." Lopez shrugged. "I understand."

"There is always a need for a military, no matter who is in power or what is happening in the world." Neto nodded.

Lopez raised his glass. "And we are lucky to have men like you."

Neto glanced toward the aft deck. "I think we should rejoin my wife."

"In a moment." Lopez picked up a remote control. "I have something to show you."

Neto shrugged. He drained his glass again. Vanna Sánchez dealt with the problem instantly.

The television screen burst to life. A grainy picture appeared with the sound muted. A luxury hotel suite. A naked couple frolicked in the hot tub.

Neto stared.

Lopez glanced toward Vanna. Her cobalt eyes watched everything simultaneously. She nodded. The video was ready. Lopez turned up the volume. Two voices could be heard. Deep, masculine murmurs followed by feminine giggling.

The girl emerged from the tub, naked, moving toward the bed. The man levered himself out of the water. He was also naked. Heavier, and slower, but his wife would recognize Neto instantly.

He wrapped his arms around the girl, and they rolled onto the bed.

Lopez froze the video while Neto's face looked directly into the hidden camera.

Neto's mouth clamped shut. His eyebrows drew into a deep frown.

Lopez nodded to the image. "She was pretty. Very pretty. So young. She looked older, perhaps, but she was not even sixteen. Any man would have been tempted, don't you think?"

The general didn't make eye contact, but beads of sweat glistened on his forehead.

Lopez saw Vanna's smirk from the corner of his eye.

"There is a paper trail to consider, General. The hotel's records." Lopez felt the warmth of Vanna's satisfaction behind him. "Not booked in your name of course, but it is your handwriting on the room service receipts and in the spa, among other things."

Neto slumped into his seat.

"Your credit card, too." Lopez smiled. "That is, one of the credit cards you use for such activities."

Neto's anger burned as cold as the vodka he tossed down his throat. "You set me up."

Lopez shrugged and waved for another refill of Neto's vodka. "What we must decide, is what you do now."

"You are a treacherous—"

"But let me show you the end before we decide." Lopez pushed the remote to the last few seconds of the recording. This time, he did not glance toward Vanna to witness her satisfaction.

The girl was alone in the room. Still naked. Splayed on her back across the bed. Mouth open in a silent scream. A man's necktie knotted tightly around her neck. Dead eyes stared at the ceiling, unseeing, from her grotesquely mottled face.

Neto's eyes bulged. His nostrils flared. "What did you do?!"

"General, you're confused. It was not me in the room with young Sophia." Lopez shrugged. The statement was true enough. "We all make mistakes."

Neto glowered. "But you know I did not do this. Sophia was alive when I left her. I swear!"

"Suicide. Such a dreadful end to your distinguished career." Lopez offered a sympathetic smile that didn't reach his icy stare as he shook his head slowly. "Everyone will feel sorry for your wife, of course. Do not worry. She is beautiful. She'll find another husband quickly enough."

Neto sighed, his head hung down. "I cannot provide an aircraft like last time. I cannot maneuver the bureaucracy as I could just months ago. Everything has changed." He looked at Lopez. "You must believe me."

"Oh, I do believe you."

Neto frowned. "What, then?"

"I don't need a single aircraft. I require five pilots."

Neto inched back, shaking his head. "Impossible."

"Your best."

A long pause. Neto swirled the ice around his empty glass.

"Don't worry," Lopez said. "There will be no side effects this time."

"Side effects?" Neto's eyes widened. "*Side effects*? People *died*. Hundreds of people, Lopez."

Lopez pressed play, and the video started again. Neto in the hot tub. Neto on the bed with the girl. Neto placing his necktie around her beautiful throat. Neto closed his eyes and whispered. "Please."

Lopez stopped the video. "Experienced pilots. Transports. Antonov 12s."

Neto frowned. "We don't have Antonov 12s."

"Your pilots will travel with my men. Experienced men." Lopez cocked his head. "Some may have worked for your government before."

Neto did not reply.

Lopez grunted. "You will be well rewarded. As always."

Neto glanced at the television where the sex continued, and back at Lopez.

Lopez shrugged. "Our business is done, general. We have had our differences, resolved them, and now we can move on."

Neto lowered his gaze.

Lopez slid a square of paper across the table. "The airbase. I am sure you're familiar with it."

Neto picked up the paper, frown lines on his forehead deepened and his eyebrows pressed hard over his broad nose. "You expect me to sacrifice my men to the forces of another country?"

"It's your choice, General." Lopez shrugged. He pressed the volume. The video's sound resumed. "We can find another supplier after you're dead if you'd prefer."

CHAPTER SIX

Tuesday, August 16
12:25 p.m. CDT
Chatham, Iowa

JESS HAD RUSHED TO her meeting only to be stashed in a conference room at the Chatham Police Department for twenty minutes waiting for the FBI Special Agent in Charge of the bombing case.

Ethan Remington finally arrived, without apology or explanation. Strike one. Basic courtesy was the price of admission to her cooperation and respect. She was predisposed to trust this guy because Henry Morris seemed to like him. But Remington was off to a bad start.

He was taller and tighter than he'd looked on television. His charcoal black suit stretched across broad shoulders like a second skin, leaving no doubt that regular workouts had winnowed all visible fat from his body.

His nose was twisted like it had been punched more than once over the years. Brown eyes darker than hers peered impassively across the table.

"I'm talking to you as a favor for Morris," Remington said as if he had a few trust issues of his own. Which was probably normal for a skeptical FBI Agent.

"I understand." She'd have argued about the public's right to know, and the value of basic justice, but her instincts said he didn't give a crap about the first and felt he was on the right track for the second. Besides, she needed a favor. Antagonizing him immediately wasn't the way to get one.

He cocked his head. "We've done plenty of press briefings already. You're late getting into this."

Jess nodded. "*Taboo* doesn't just cover crimes, though. We're looking for—"

"I know what you do. We don't need your help with this case." His tone implied the day would never come when he'd need help from her or anyone else.

Which got her back up. "I'm here because someone I trust thinks you have the wrong suspect in custody. She says Alex Cole is not your guy."

"That sounds to me like you're trying to butt into my case."

"Agent Remington, you like Henry Morris, right? Respect his judgment? We've worked together before. Which is why he recommended me. Shouldn't that be enough?"

He narrowed his eyes to study her briefly and, after a moment, nodded. "Look, Ms. Kimball, we've got more leads than we know what to do with and a ton of follow-up to do. It requires patience and legwork, but that's what we do. We'll tie up all the details. It takes time. And we'll let you, and everybody else, know what we find out."

"You've already arrested Alex Cole, though." Jess nodded. "Tell me why you did that, at least."

"I've already released the details supporting the arrest warrant, which is also a matter of public record." When she didn't reply, Remington shrugged and ran down the summary. "His phone was used to detonate the bomb. We found bomb-making supplies on his property. He owns several weapons, various types, all lethal. He even had a homemade rail gun. You know what that is?"

Jess gritted her teeth and exercised patience of her own instead of smacking him down with exactly how much she already knew about his case, and how much worse the actual facts were than what he'd covered so far.

She knew, for example, that the FBI had separated mangled equipment from the remains of the bomb. The explosion had vaporized most of the bomb's elements. After an extensive search on Saturday afternoon, they found thin wires connected to a circuit card.

The card's components were destroyed. Only the remaining solder allowed engineers working overtime to guess the card's origin.

But the significant evidence didn't come from the card itself.

At the other end of the thin wires were the melted remains of a tiny loudspeaker.

An industry search had revealed the circuit card and speaker were used in several types of cell phones.

Sifting through the rubble, crime scene techs finally found a portion of the plastic casing of a SIM card on Sunday.

With careful image enhancement, long strings of numbers on the casing were visible enough to decipher.

Cell phone records had narrowed the list of matching phones down to seven in the Chatham area.

By Monday morning, they'd discovered that only one of

those phone numbers had received a call at the exact instant of the explosion.

That phone belonged to Alex Cole.

Monday afternoon, Alex Cole was arrested.

She said none of this. Not yet.

Patiently, she displayed understanding. "You're saying Cole owned an electromagnetic gun."

Remington's eyebrows shot up. As she'd suspected, he thought she was unprepared or unsophisticated, or worse. Her best cases often developed because her opponents underestimated her preparation and tenacity. She hid her smile behind a quick cough.

He nodded. "Those things can fire projectiles like nails at speeds of thousands of miles an hour. Nails make nasty, lethal weapons when fired at those speeds. They'll rip up a human body in ways that can never be repaired. There's no reasonable recreational use for a rail gun."

"I see. But no one used a rail gun connected with this explosion." She cocked her head. "Why did Alex Cole bomb the Kelso Products factory?"

"Who knows? Right now, he's not talking." Remington shrugged. "Could be lots of reasons. Wasn't happy with his employer. Or his colleagues. Jealousy. Maybe one of the victims stole his research or his girlfriend. Hell, maybe he was hungry, and someone swiped his lunch out of the company refrigerator in the break room."

"All possibilities," Jess nodded agreeably to hide her irritation. "But what evidence do you have? For any single motive?"

"We're six days into the investigation. We've got some 'plain as the nose on your face' evidence. Alex Cole is our best suspect, and he stays behind bars unless a fancy lawyer gets him out." Remington's expression made clear what he thought of fancy lawyers. "Like I said, plenty of legwork left to do. We'll get the rest of it."

What an ass. Jess squared her shoulders and questioned the facts head on, speaking in the most reasonable tone she could manage. "What explosive did he use?"

"I can't tell you that."

"Type of detonator?"

"Can't tell you."

"Size of the bomb?"

"Again, I can't tell you. It was smaller than you might think, though, given the extent of the damage."

"Suitcase size, or handbag?"

He glanced at Jess's fifteen-inch nylon tote bag resting on the floor. "Handbag."

"He'd need access to a powerful explosive to do so much damage with a small bomb, then."

Remington raised his eyebrows to indicate the answer was obvious.

"But you're saying this was not a fertilizer bomb, which just about everybody around here has access to, with all these farms."

"Definitely not a fertilizer bomb." Remington shook his head. "This was a professional job. Made from the sort of chemicals you don't just throw together and hope for the best. Chemicals Alex Cole has in his workshop."

Jess nodded. "Where was the bomb planted?"

"We covered this in the press briefing already," Remington practically snarled as if she was deliberately wasting his time. "The factory produces one main product, which is a powder. The powder is stored in several large tanks. The bomb was in one of the tanks. The powder and oxygen mix increased the intensity of the blast, spreading the fire. Pipes conducted the explosion to a second tank. Some of the labs were damaged."

"Which labs?"

He frowned. "Three and four. Four took the brunt of it. Damage there was much worse."

"How was the bomb planted?"

"We're still gathering evidence, but we believe strongly that Alex Cole put it there."

"Surveillance cameras don't show him or anyone else placing this handbag-sized explosive in or near the tank?"

"Nothing more than the footage you've already seen plastered everywhere online." Remington shook his head. "The company doesn't believe in spying on its workers."

"Very noble of them in this day and age," Jess smirked.

He grimaced. "Not really. The union threatened court action."

She nodded. Security cameras inside workplaces were a touchy subject for a lot of people. "No incidental video? Nearby stores? Gas stations?"

Remington shook his head. "It's a big factory on a large tract of land. There's nothing near enough to the explosion site."

"Security guards?"

"Several, but no one saw anyone unusual near the tanks."

"Visitor logs?"

"Still checking."

Jess cocked her head. "Alex Cole was home sick on the day of the explosion. He wasn't at the plant at all that day."

"So I've heard. How convenient." Remington's turn to smirk.

"Does he have any corroboration? Doctor visit? Over the counter medications? Anything?"

"Again, he's not talking. But we've found nothing like that." Remington shook his head. "He called in sick in the morning, but that's the only evidence we've got that he was actually home sick that day. People call off work for all sorts of reasons. When the company doesn't give them a list of available play dates, they say they're sick. Nothing unusual about that. Happens millions of times in America every day."

"Cole called in using a cell phone?"

"Home phone. Landline." He held his palm facing out to curb any protest. "Seven-forty-three in the morning. Five hours before the bomb went off. Proves nothing. He had plenty of time to spare between the phone call and the explosion."

Perhaps not, but at least he'd been home at seven-forty-three. It was a place to start. "If the detonate command came from a cell phone, there must have been a phone in with the bomb to serve as a remote trigger, right?"

Remington nodded. "Burner phone. Purchased with cash a month earlier from a supermarket chain here in Chatham. Never used until that day. Standard procedure, as anybody who's ever watched a crime show on television would know. Extremely common."

Which it was. So common and so easy that some DIYers even used old cell phones to set off fireworks. All it takes is a phone, five bucks worth of parts, and a few minutes to watch any of the tutorials online, followed by a bit of tinkering. Put the phone in with the explosive and then place a call to that phone. The incoming call sets off an electrical current on the modified cell phone and, well, just about anybody can get a very big bang.

Jess chewed the inside of her bottom lip. "No ownership records on the phone?"

"Nothing."

"And the cell phone used as the remote trigger for the bomb? Who owned that one?"

Remington grinned like the Cheshire Cat. "Alex Cole. Hadn't been used for thirty-two days. Prior to that, a few calls with friends and some with his mother."

Jess did not reply.

"Now you know everything we've released." Remington glanced at his watch and stood up to signal her time had expired. "We may release more details in a few days, depending on how the rest of the investigation goes."

Jess glanced at the clock behind him. He'd promised her thirty minutes. She hadn't used them all yet. She remained seated. "Do you think a guy smart enough to get a Ph.D. would be dumb enough to use his own phone to set off a bomb?"

Remington frowned. "It's a head-scratcher, sure. But at the moment we're going with the evidence. Which is that Alex Cole detonated that bomb and killed three people. There's three more in the hospital that might not live, so the death count could go higher. If you've got anything proving otherwise, now's the time to tell me."

Jess shook her head. "Not yet. I just got here. But when I find the proof, I promise you'll be among the first to know."

Remington offered a flat smile. "Cole is downstairs. He says he wants to talk to you. No surprise."

Jess wasn't surprised, either. Partly because Marcia McAllister had probably pleaded with him to see Jess. And partly because, unlike the calls from distraught families of crime victims, which she never ignored, she received hundreds more calls from inmates than she answered. The system had many resources to help the accused. Her mission was to help the victims that the system too often failed.

Right at the moment, it was unclear on which side of the line Alex Cole rested. It was only her commitment to Marcia that motivated Jess. Otherwise, the evidence would have persuaded her to agree with Remington.

CHAPTER SEVEN

Tuesday, August 16
12:35 p.m. CDT
Chatham, Iowa

PERHAPS NAMES WERE DESTINY after all because Alex Cole's hair was coal-black and curly. Big eyes, rimmed with blue-black lashes, moved lazily. He was reed thin. In the videos she'd watched, he'd seemed six feet tall. Perhaps he was. At the moment, she couldn't tell because he was seated on the other side of the thick safety glass that kept him separated from her.

The speaker on her side of the partition reproduced his voice clearly. She assumed he could hear hers perfectly, too. She tried to get comfortable in the molded plastic seat.

"I was sick that day. Really sick." His voice was medium range, cadence neither fast nor slow. If he was nervous or distraught, neither was reflected in his words. "Bad seafood. My mother's friend did the cooking."

"A useful alibi."

"Remington says that, too. But it's true." He shrugged. "I was sick. I stayed home from work. Last I heard, that's not a crime."

Jess nodded. Cole's demeanor was quiet. Calm. Almost as if he considered his situation as an interesting puzzle to be solved. Jess had met many engineers and lawyers and other analytical types who approached life the same way. Most of them weren't accused of murder, though. Defendants were usually more animated, in her experience.

Cole shrugged. "If I'd known I'd need an alibi, I'd have come up with a better story, don't you think?"

Possibly. Some defendants did have better excuses. Many didn't. "You worked in one of the destroyed labs?"

He shook his head. "Lab One. We do the fundamental stuff."

"Where is Lab One?"

"At the other end of the plant from the explosion. The bomb was in Lab Four."

She cocked her head. "So if you'd been at work, you wouldn't have been caught in the blast."

"Not even if I'd been chained to my desk." He shrugged, as if being charged with murder was exceptionally curious, under the circumstances. "Remington says either I planted the bomb knowing I'd be safe, or I stayed away, just in case my calculations on the explosion were wrong."

"Lab Three was also damaged."

"Four took the worst of it, though. Good thing really."

She frowned. "Why do you say that?"

"Four is used mostly for storing samples. Not as many people work there. Means fewer people were hurt by the blast." Cole shook his head. "Remington says I knew that which is why I put the bomb over in Four."

Jess nodded. "The FBI found the chemicals for the explosive in your workshop."

He raised his eyebrows "Which chemicals were those?"

"They didn't tell me."

"It's possible they'd have found small amounts of whatever they were looking for." He shook his head. "I did a lot of experiments in my workshop, but I didn't have significant quantities of any chemicals."

"They said they found gallons."

He shrugged. "Not me. Not mine."

"They said they found other weapons in your workshop, too."

He smiled. "My attempts at building a rail gun? I did that just for fun. To see if I could do it. The one I built is not much of a *weapon*. It's bolted to the floor, for one thing."

"It works, though, doesn't it?"

"Of course," he pushed his chin out, somewhat offended. "It's a small-scale thing. Not that complicated. Just a linear magnet moving a piece of metal. I didn't try to build one of those fire-breathing things you can find on the internet. Mine shot nails across the room. That's it. Nobody's claiming I used it for anything else, I hope."

"Not as far as I know." Jess shook her head. "How many cell phones do you own?"

"You mean did I own the one used to detonate the bomb? Remington says the remote signal was sent by a call from my cell phone. He's probably tracked that down, so it's likely true. But my cell phone had disappeared. I hadn't used it in a while."

"There was a second cell phone on the bomb."

He nodded. "The detonator, Remington says. A disposable cell phone."

"Was that one yours?"

"I'm a single guy who lives alone. I have one cell phone and one landline." His tone became curious. "How many do you have?"

"Just one. I'm not home enough to justify the cost of a landline." Jess smiled. "Have you found your cell phone?"

"Before they arrested me yesterday, you mean?" He squeezed his lips together and shook his head. "I've been thinking about it. I don't remember leaving it anywhere. The most likely place is my workshop, but I looked in there and didn't find it. I suppose it could have been stolen, but that doesn't seem likely, does it?"

"Doesn't it?"

"Well, I haven't had a break-in or anything like that. My closest neighbor is a mile away. The only people around my place are those who come to see me. Chatham is not exactly New York City, Ms. Kimball. We don't have home invasions here." He smiled genuinely as if he weren't wearing chains and sitting in jail, accused of crimes that carried the death penalty.

"Did you talk to anyone the morning of the explosion? Tell anyone you were sick?"

"I made two calls that morning. My boss, and my mom. Both before eight o'clock." He smiled somewhat sheepishly. "After that, I surfed the internet on my home computer. I'm sure the mighty FBI can confirm that for you. A big desktop setup with lots of screens and peripherals attached to it. The system isn't mobile at all, so I had to be sitting there to use it."

"What time were you using the computer?"

"Ten to eleven, maybe. I wasn't watching the clock."

"I'll ask Remington about it. Did you do anything traceable after that? Preferably before the explosion? Something that puts you somewhere away from the Kelso Products plant?"

"Unfortunately not." He lifted his shackled hands and ran

one unsteady palm over his face. The first indication of a crack in his calm that she'd seen. "My stomach bug went downhill for a couple of hours. Got sick again. By the time I was feeling better, the whole thing at Kelso already happened."

Jess frowned as she watched Cole through the glass. Their conversation was being monitored and recorded. Remington was probably watching and listening remotely. She wanted to find an angle Remington hadn't already explored. But she was six days behind him, and he was too good at his job.

But she was good at hers, too. There was more to this situation than she'd learned so far. A lot more.

CHAPTER EIGHT

"TALKING ABOUT MY CELL phone, maybe you're right, though. Maybe someone did steal it." Cole sat back in his chair, his head cocked as if something new had occurred to him.

Jess widened her eyes. "What do you mean?"

"The last maybe eight months or so at the plant has been, I don't know, maybe weird is the best way to put it."

"Weird in what way?"

"Nothing as major as this bomb. But there's been some petty theft. A couple of laptop computers. One time my log book disappeared right off my desk. No one admitted borrowing it, and I don't know why they would want to." He shrugged. "Everything in my notebook was already recorded in our databases, and the whole team had access to those. But stuff like that soured the atmosphere among our team. As I said, it was weird. Like sabotage or something, but not that serious. Just little things, annoying but no more than that."

Jess nodded. "Six months ago, the local newspaper reported Kelso's network server room was ransacked, but nothing was stolen."

"That was a big thing," Cole nodded. "Wanton destruction. Our security staff never caught the vandals."

"Who do you think did that?"

"The official word we got was kids." He shrugged. "Thing is, kids wouldn't have had physical access. People who live here joke that Kelso Products is more secure than the Pentagon."

"Kelso makes insecticides, right? Why would they be so paranoid about security?"

"Like any plant, I guess. Doesn't want the liability." He shook his head. "People can get hurt around the machinery and equipment. It's not safe unless you're wearing proper equipment and you know where you're going."

Jess leaned forward. "Industrial espionage seems more likely, then? Was it an insider, looking to make a few bucks selling Kelso's trade secrets?"

He shrugged, and his face scrunched into a mask of perplexed confusion. "Doesn't matter who it was. But once he gained physical access, it would have been a lot easier to hack into our networks and find whatever he was looking for. Much easier than hacking remotely, for sure."

Jess arched her eyebrows. "Really? I thought just about anything could be hacked from halfway around the world these days."

"Television. It'll be the death of us all." He grinned and shook his head. "Maybe that's true for some systems. But I worked in IT at Kelso both before and during college. Believe me, at Kelso, physical access is everything."

Jess chewed her lower lip on the other side for a while as she considered what she knew, and what she needed to know. She was running long on her interview time. She figured Remington would let her keep going as long as she seemed to be making progress.

"How did you feel when your log book was taken?"

"How did I *feel*?" His expression suggested the concept was entirely foreign to him. Which it probably was. He didn't seem like a man in touch with his feelings much. "How would you *feel*? My notebook wasn't important in the big scheme of things. I didn't even remember it until now. I guess losing it was just annoying, you know? I had to start a new one."

"Were you angry?"

"Yes, I was ticked off at the time. For like a day. As I said, it was annoying." He leaned forward and spoke earnestly. "But not angry enough to blow the place up months later. That's irrational. Makes no sense at all, does it?"

"Your notebook never turned up?"

He shook his head.

"Any idea who took it?"

He shuffled in his seat and appeared to give the question serious thought. "At the time, I thought it was Marco Benito. Italian guy. Older than me. Acted all cool and everything. Worked at the company for about three months. Did nothing but cause trouble. I was pretty sure he took it just to, you know, get under my skin."

"You didn't get along with this guy?"

"He was an idiot. A real jerk."

"Where is he now?"

"He went back to Italy I think. I don't know. I was just glad he left." He shook his head. "Like I said. The notebook wasn't important. It doesn't matter if he took it, now that he's gone."

Jess could feel Remington getting antsy somewhere. He'd kick her out soon. She searched for another topic. "Marcia tells me you have a girlfriend."

Cole frowned. "A while ago. We were just friends."

"Were?"

He shrugged. "Well, we're still friends."

"You got along well together?"

"She's smart. We had a lot in common. We're both biochem Ph.D.s and worked on mosquito control methods. She'd call in the middle of the night to talk about the statistical correlation of our lab results. Odd stuff to most people, but..." His voice trailed off, which seemed like a metaphor for what happened with the relationship.

"It's good when you have things in common with other people, isn't it?" Jess paused. "The work sounds interesting. Was it?"

"Yeah. I mean, people say that killing mosquitoes is a public service in itself. But control mosquitoes and you begin to control malaria, West Nile, encephalitis, Ebola, and a whole host of other things. It was work we were doing at Kelso a while back." He stared at Jess, and his lifeless dark eyes sparkled for the first time. "Do you know a million people die from mosquito-borne diseases every year? We were doing good work. Worthy work. The sort of stuff that could change millions of lives for the better."

Jess nodded. It was one of those statistics that was just too large to forget, or to fully absorb.

"Debbie was really passionate about saving lives. Like every day we didn't get closer to controlling mosquitoes really bothered her."

"Debbie?"

He blinked as if he'd forgotten Jess was sitting there. "Yeah. Debbie."

"Debbie...?"

He shifted in his seat. "Elden."

"You spent a lot of time together?"

"We did." He laughed. "She was the one who challenged me to make the rail gun. Brought a vase as my first target."

"Did it break?"

His eyes glowed with enthusiasm. "Shattered to smithereens."

"Really?"

His demeanor changed. "She wasn't that impressed, though. She'd seen better rail guns on the internet, she said."

"Did she ever build anything in your lab?"

He shook his head. "She tried to make some of the Kelso mosquito control products using common stuff. She had this idea that third world countries could make their own and do it cheaper." He leaned forward and winked. "Don't tell that to anyone at Kelso."

"None of her efforts panned out, I take it?"

"Unfortunately."

Jess nodded. "Where does Debbie live?"

He shrugged. "She's not around anymore."

Jess widened her eyes. "Did she leave her job at Kelso Products?"

"She was pretty mad when we lost our funding back in the spring." He nodded as if Elden's decision to quit her job made perfect sense. "Went to work somewhere else. Foreign conglomerate, I guess."

"Do you know where she's working now?"

"Not in Chatham." He shook his head.

"You don't keep in touch?"

He shrugged.

She softened her voice. "You miss her, don't you?"

"I'd do anything for her. Anything within reason." He rolled his eyes. "But I didn't blow up Kelso. That would be stupid. And it wouldn't bring her back, would it?"

Jess heard the doorknob twist the lock open behind her. "Well, thanks for speaking to me, Alex."

"You're lucky." He looked at her and grinned. "I didn't have anything else on my calendar for today."

She smiled. Not many men accused of multiple murder and terrorism kept a sense of humor. Whether that made him innocent, guilty, or plainly crazy, she wasn't sure.

"Just one last thing. You said, 'It was what we were doing here a while ago.' Kelso isn't working on mosquito control anymore?"

"Yes and no." He shrugged. "We were looking at biological control methods back then. Poisons, you know? But that's expensive and difficult, so when we ran into money problems, the work got shelved. We went back to plain old chemical methods. I'd like to start up the bio work again, though. I really think we were close to a breakthrough. Before this bombing thing happened, I thought we might start the research up again." He shook his head, sadly. "Now, I don't know."

CHAPTER NINE

JESS LEFT THE CHATHAM Police Department building with her phone in her hand. When she reached the rental, she started the engine and spent a few minutes online.

She surfed the Kelso Products website. The organizational chart wasn't as extensive as she'd expected. There were the usual collection of titles and portraits arranged in a pyramid to demonstrate the hierarchy.

Curiously, the head of security's position was occupied by nothing but an empty blue box. No picture and no text. Had he been fired because of the bombing? She shook her head. Getting rid of the guy was not the way to deflect criticism of Kelso's security team.

The VP of Security position was one of several that reported directly to the woman at the top of the pecking order, CEO Claire Winter.

Jess had seen Winter on screen in news video over the past few days. She looked good enough in person, but her official portrait was stunning.

Winter was fifty-one, according to the biographic snippet, but she looked younger. Dark blonde hair was combed straight back and fell to her shoulders, artfully streaked with platinum to camouflage the gray and accentuate vibrant blue eyes. Despite deeply tanned skin and perfectly arched eyebrows, her forehead was as smooth as any twenty-year-old's. Bright white teeth sparkled against impossibly full lips.

Jess wondered how many stylists had to prepare her before the elite photographer used his skill behind the camera, finishing the portrait with his airbrush. Together, they'd created Winter's perfect style. Which was equal parts devil-may-care wealth, formal boardroom boss, and arm candy for men twenty years older than her.

Winter's jaw jutted forward a fraction. She was in control, no question about it. She used the restrained smile to disarm, and it worked, most likely.

Minuscule text under Winter's picture directed inquiries to Kelso's press office. Jess automatically dialed four of the digits before she disconnected. The call would be a waste of time.

Scheduling an interview with Claire Winter was notoriously difficult, even under normal circumstances. Like many skillful CEOs, Winter avoided the press except when she found extensive coverage useful to further her own agenda.

A cold call from a magazine, even a national glossy with a sterling reputation like *Taboo*, wouldn't get past the answering service.

If there was one person she could trust to do the impossible, it was her assistant Mandy Donovan. She pressed the speed dial and listened for the call to connect.

"Hey, Jess," Mandy's can-do attitude was another plus. "What's up?"

Jess smiled. Right to the point. She liked that about Mandy, too. "I need to talk to Claire Winter, CEO of Kelso Products."

"You're covering the explosion at the Kelso plant in Chatham, Iowa, right?" Mandy paused. "And you're willing to be, shall we say, not negative about the company?"

"Yeah, sure. Why not?" Jess ran her fingers through her blonde curls. She could lead with some fluff if that's what it took to get the interview.

"You might try to be a bit more enthusiastic about it." Mandy's trilling laugh could be heard through the connection as clearly as if she was walking alongside Jess. "You're willing to take any day and time I can get?"

"Sooner is better."

"Understood. Anything else?"

"That's all for now."

"Call you back soon." Mandy hung up.

While Jess waited for Mandy's return call, her thoughts circled back to Alex Cole. Could Marcia McAllister be wrong about him?

He was a loner. He had the ability to create a bomb. And he might have felt snubbed by the potential girlfriend. But did he perpetrate this extreme violence?

And what about Elden? He seemed sorry that his relationship, whatever it was, with Elden had ended. But had they really lost touch? The internet made such a thing almost impossible these days for young techy types like Cole and Elden.

Jess used her phone to search the internet for Debora Elden.

Several social media accounts popped up after a fraction of a second. A slew of Eldens with various permutations of Debora's first name.

She filtered through Debs, Debbies, and Deborah's seeking references to Iowa, Chatham, and Kelso Products.

Fairly quickly, she'd culled a list of five possibles.

Three hadn't been used for several years.

The last two fell quiet a few months ago.

The pictures showed a cute-as-anything fresh-faced girl about Alex Cole's age, maybe a bit younger, with brown hair tinged an unnatural shade of red. Wide smile, perfect teeth, and dimples in her cheeks that conveyed an impish good humor. Her body suggested a woman much more athletically inclined than Alex Cole's introverted existence.

Elden had opened her social media accounts while she attended The University of Illinois. Like many young people do, she'd posted way too many status updates, substituting social media for daily human contact, perhaps.

Jess flipped through candid photos of various athletic pursuits from hiking to kayaking. Easy to see why Alex Cole found her attractive. She seemed happy and full of life.

Jess thumbed through another eight pages of search results before she found a link connected to "Debs" that looked like it might be Elden.

A picture of a university building was front and center.

When she zoomed in, she could read a sign above the door that identified it as dedicated to "Biochemistry and Molecular Biophysics."

Jess clicked on the photo.

A website for something called "Local World Action" opened.

Images of activist groups blocking wild game hunting, protest marches with placards, and a convoy of trucks distributing food and medicine in an unidentified war-torn country cycled through.

A whaling ship appeared. Underneath were the words *good riddance*. Jess's skin tingled. The ship had been in the news a few years earlier. It was rammed by a dinghy packed with explosives.

Jess searched the page for a way to look deeper into the website but didn't find one.

Ready to give up and call Mandy back, a moment of indecision allowed her finger to hover over the phone's off button. The website's background picture changed to a protest march.

She enlarged the photo. A few hundred people walked along the National Mall in DC. The Washington monument stood tall and proud in the distance as the march headed toward the Capitol building.

Marchers held hand-lettered signs protesting cuts in government funding for a clean water program in Africa. It wasn't the signs that caught her attention.

She enlarged the right-hand edge of the picture.

A fresh young face atop an athletically toned body.

A woman holding a Local World Action placard high overhead with both hands.

Unmistakably, Debora Elden.

CHAPTER TEN

Tuesday, August 16
10:00 p.m. Central Africa Time Zone (CAT)
Zambia, Africa

The Zambian dry forest stretched for miles in all directions. Its tall tree canopy and low levels of undergrowth allowed good visibility in the moonlight.

A mixed blessing, Tebogo knew. The environment was "see and be seen." He preferred clandestine conditions, like the dead of cloudy nights, when night-vision gear separated the professionals from the amateurs.

Tebogo was a mercenary. When money called, he answered. The boss was someone called Lopez. A name so common it had to be fake, but in this business, who cared? Money was the only thing Tebogo wanted from this Lopez and all the others like him.

The Europeans paid better than the Russians, worse than the Americans. This particular European was a regular source of income. Tebogo liked that. His life was measured one contract at a time.

The operation was stupid, though. For two days, he and his brother in arms, Kago, had done nothing but zigzag their way across a hundred-mile square of western Zambia in an old yellow pickup truck. Toyota HiLux. Tebogo drove while Kago navigated a long list of GPS coordinates. At each stop, they installed a small mosquito monitoring station.

They had both been thoroughly briefed on the procedure. Find the precise GPS location. Set the timers. Take photographs. And most important, no one must know. Absolutely no one.

The monitoring stations had two parts.

The first was a trap to collect mosquitoes. Two simple chambers. Tebogo set the timers to trigger two days apart. In a week, they would return for the traps.

The second instrument was a curious cylinder, maybe nine-by-thirteen-by-three. About the size to hold a gallon of gas. With a series of probes on the top.

The probes looked as though they might sample the air, but Tebogo wasn't sure. He'd been told to set the timer to activate midway between the two mosquito collections.

Mosquito sampling wasn't illegal. Lots of companies did it. Which made him a little curious because he never got paid for work without danger. But then he remembered the money, and his curiosity was silenced.

He guided the HiLux around a tree stump in the middle of the rough track.

"Stop," Kago said.

Tebogo eased the Toyota to a halt. "Are we there?"

Kago shook his head and pointed through the windshield. A plume of dust in the distance from a vehicle traveling fast enough to leave a trail. A rookie mistake Tebogo was careful to avoid.

Kago pointed to a small patch of undergrowth. Tebogo engaged first gear and crawled off the track to put the bushes between them and the speeding vehicle.

He stepped out and used his binoculars. "Land Rover Defender. Unmarked."

The speeding vehicle slowed and turned in his direction.

"We should go," Kago said.

Tebogo shook his head. "Thirty miles to the next village, and we'd be in the only pickup in town."

Tebogo grabbed the camera from between the front seats. "Tell them we're taking pictures for a tourist website."

Kago grunted. "Or we could just shoot them."

Tebogo waved the camera. "Pictures."

They walked away from the truck and began snapping pictures in the moonlight.

The Land Rover Defender bounced over the rough ground, traveling in a straight line until it stopped beside the HiLux. Two men climbed out.

The first man was tall and thin. He wore thick glasses with black plastic rims. The second man was shorter. His biceps bulged from his short-sleeved shirt.

Both men had pistols on their belts. The small badges embroidered on their shirts identified them as Luiwa Plain National Park wardens.

Tebogo knew the type. They walked with an exaggerated authority, but their uncertain footsteps told him they were more comfortable in their vehicle.

Tebogo smiled and greeted them in Zambian. "Bwanji!"

The men nodded and shook hands in the traditional style, pressing thumbs.

The tall man spoke. "I'm Chola, and this is Ephraim."

Tebogo tapped his chest, and nodded to the warden badges. "You're a bit far from home."

"Been for supplies." Chola shrugged. "Saw you and got curious."

Tebogo held up the camera. "Pictures. Advertising. Tourists."

Chola eyeballed him. "Hunters?"

Tebogo shook his head. "Photo safaris."

Chola grunted. "There's nothing much to see here."

"The website wants pictures. The real Africa they call it. Not just the glossy stuff."

Chola gestured to the HiLux. "What's in the truck?"

"Camera gear. Stuff."

"You hunting?"

Tebogo shook his head. "More money in pictures."

Chola stared a moment as if the idea were preposterous. "Okay."

The wardens detoured around the HiLux on the way back to the Land Rover.

Tebogo knelt, steadying himself to take a picture.

Kago tapped him on the shoulder to get his attention.

Chola leaned into the rear of the Toyota. He flipped the tarpaulin back.

Kago grunted.

"It's nothing. We'll explain it away," Tebogo said.

"My AK-47 is there."

"Why not inside!" Tebogo hissed.

The wardens exchanged a comment, and Chola flipped the tarp back into place. He smiled and waved. The pair walked to their Land Rover.

Kago stepped forward. Tebogo grabbed his arm.

The wardens turned. Four pairs of eyes made contact. Instantly, both sides knew what had happened. The wardens had seen the equipment.

They had seen the gun, too. Not a hunting rifle. A soldier's weapon. In this case, a soldier of fortune.

Both wardens dived into the Land Rover. Its engine roared.

Tebogo and Kago ran for the HiLux. The Defender raced away, bouncing wildly over the rough ground.

Tebogo rammed the Toyota into gear and banged in the clutch. The truck bounded forward. It lurched erratically, the HiLux being built more for paved surfaces than off-road.

Kago wrestled a Daewoo K7 submachine gun from under his seat. It was a mid-length weapon with an integral suppressor and a thirty-round magazine. The suppressor did little to hide the sound of the gun being discharged, but its design threw the noise in all directions, making it difficult for an opponent to identify the shooter's location.

He set the gun for three-round bursts and loosed a couple of blasts. The shots went wide. The Land Rover accelerated.

Tebogo mashed the accelerator into the floor. "Wait till we're closer."

CHAPTER ELEVEN

Tuesday, August 16
3:00 p.m. CDT
Chatham, Iowa

AFTER JESS WAS ON the road, Mandy called back and rushed
through her news.

"Claire Winter is finally giving a press conference at the
plant in fifteen minutes. It's her first public statement since the
explosion, probably because the FBI asked her not to speak
before now. Can you make it?"

"On my way." Jess glanced around for traffic cops and
pressed the accelerator. The plant was ten minutes away. "Let
them know I'm coming. If I need a badge, ask them to have it
ready."

"Way ahead of you."

"Excellent. You're a genius."

"I'll remind you of that at my next salary review."

Jess grinned. "I'm sure you will."

Mandy laughed. "Gotta go."

Jess increased her speed and made it to the Kelso Products parking lot in double quick time. The police cruiser was still stationed at the driveway, but it was unoccupied, and no officer was checking IDs.

Large sections of the lot were deserted, but a knot of cars surrounded the silver and glass front entrance. Rentals, she figured. Belonged to the temporary press contingent.

Jess parked in the first open spot and raced to the building.

She dashed into the revolving door at the entrance. The glass had been replaced after the explosion, but the mechanism needed adjustment or something. She put her whole body into the effort, but the door was heavy and slow and seemed to barely move.

An attractive, well-dressed woman was seated behind a large counter checking press credentials. Three armed security guards patrolled the foyer.

One of the guards stepped in front of her as the door finally rotated into the small room.

"Press?" he said.

Jess held out her credentials. "Jessica Kimball. *Taboo Magazine.*"

"I have her badge, Charlie," the woman called out.

Charlie collected the badge and handed it to Jess. "Wear this at all times. The badge allows you to attend the press conference. *Only.* Stay with the group. Got it?"

Jess nodded.

"You're late." Charlie ordered, "Follow me."

Without waiting for her reply, he waved a white and red proximity card in front of a card reader. The security device clicked, and he stepped through the door into the main building at a fast clip.

Jess glanced around briefly as she hurried to follow.

The decor beyond the security point was far from high-end. The wallpaper was brown tinged with age, and the carpet was so faded it could have been in place for at least a couple of decades.

Charlie continued his brisk pace and stopped abruptly at a double door. "The meeting started a couple of minutes ago."

He peered in through a porthole above her eye level. He pushed the door open for her. "Follow the crowd back when it's over. We keep track of all the badges. Don't wander off."

"Okay." Jess walked into a large room. At the far end was a temporary stage with a raised podium. To the left of the stage was a door.

Reporters mingled, speaking softly among themselves. Camera crews were lined up along the walls with long lenses that seemed out of place indoors.

Rows of folding chairs faced the stage. The front row was already filled with reporters, mostly men, mostly dressed in dark jackets that would film well for television, paired with light colored chinos that would never be revealed on screen.

A few women were sprinkled here and there dressed in stylish suits in similarly muted colors. A woman beckoned Jess to sit in an empty seat beside her.

She extended her hand. "Sally Meecham. Human Resources. Call me Sally. Everyone does."

"Jess Kimball, *Taboo Magazine*."

Sally nodded. "I talked to your assistant. Mandy. She's delightful."

Jess smiled. "Everybody says that."

A hush fell over the room when the door at the far end of the stage opened. A woman entered first.

"Claire Winter, our CEO," Sally whispered.

Jess nodded. She recognized Winter from her photographs.

She was every bit as perfect as her pictures.

Jess didn't recognize the man trailing her. "Who's that with her?"

"Her assistant."

Winter stepped behind the podium. "Thank you for coming." Winter's smile was flat.

Video was rolling, and a few still cameras clicked furiously. She waited for the clicking to fade before she spoke again.

"At the request of the FBI, we've waited until now to talk to you directly, although we wanted to speak to you long ago. Like everyone in the country, all of us here at Kelso Products are devastated by the horrific events that have taken place. I want to express my profound sadness and the condolences of everyone at Kelso Products to all those who have lost loved ones, friends, and colleagues. Please know that my grief and heart are with you."

Sally Meecham sniffed and wiped her nose with a tissue.

Winter shifted her weight. She took a deep breath. "I am saddened to tell you that as a result of injuries sustained in the explosion, we lost a fourth member of the Kelso Products family this morning. At the request of their families, we are not identifying the victims on camera today. We ask for your discretion in honoring their wishes as well."

Sally moaned softly.

Winter closed her eyes briefly and took another deep breath. She turned away from the reporters to wipe tears from her eyes. She pushed the tissue back into her pocket.

She looked out at the audience again and cleared her throat. "There are no words that will alleviate the pain our community continues to suffer. Kelso Products will use our full resources to provide whatever assistance we can to support the victims of this tragedy. We will release details of our plans as appropriate once we have them in place."

She cleared her throat again and sipped from a paper cup on the podium. "You've no doubt heard that the authorities have acted swiftly and made an arrest of the man they believe is responsible."

She took a deep breath to steady the quiver in her voice. "We are all trying to make sense of the events that unfolded here. I ask you to join me in offering support to the Kelso Products employees and their families who have been so devastated by these horrific events."

She paused and bowed her head as if to pray. When she looked up again, her eyes were glassy with unshed tears. "Thank you."

Silence descended on the room for a moment then several hands rose seeking permission to ask questions.

Winter dealt simple answers, deferring to the FBI until the room grew quiet again.

Jess stood when Winter's eyes fell on her row. "Jess Kimball. *Taboo Magazine*."

"Yes?" Winter said.

"Are you confident the authorities have arrested the right man?"

"I'm not authorized to discuss the FBI's actions, but they have assured me they have the right person in custody. I have no reason to doubt that," she said, evasively.

Jess said, "And do you think he acted alone?"

Winter frowned. "The police and FBI have told me that is the case."

"What motive did he have to harm the good people at Kelso Products, Ms. Winter?" Jess asked.

Winter's eyes widened, and her mouth formed a little "O," as if she was astonished at the question. She shook her head. "You'll need to ask him."

"I already have. Thank you." Jess sat down. She'd cover the rest of her queries privately.

Several more questions were asked before the conference came to an end.

As the reporters filed out, Jess dodged through the flow and reached Claire Winter on her way off the stage.

Jess held out her card. "Can we talk for a moment?"

Winter frowned at the card. "Are you planning an article on us for *Taboo Magazine*? Kelso Products is a little bit outside your readership, isn't it?"

"Our readership is always interested in the truth, Ms. Winter."

"Yes, of course." Winter nodded her head. "I know your magazine and your work."

"Do you know Alex Cole?"

"Not well. We have fewer than a thousand employees here, Ms. Kimball. I know all of them at least a bit. When he was identified as a suspect, I learned more about him." She shrugged. "He works in our research department. A hard worker, his supervisors tell me."

Jess cocked her head. "He's exceptionally well-educated, and practically the poster child for a geek researcher who minds his own business and never causes trouble."

"Where are you going with this?" Winter frowned.

"Doesn't it seem strange that a man as smart as Alex Cole would be dumb enough to use his own phone to detonate the bomb?"

Winter shrugged. "The whole situation is strange to me, Ms. Kimball. It's astonishing that Cole or any other Kelso employee would detonate a bomb in the first place, actually. I can't quite wrap my head around it, even now."

"Alex Cole told me that an Italian researcher caused a lot of trouble here a while back. Marco Benito?"

Winter waved the comment away. "He came with good credentials, but he didn't fit in at Kelso."

"In what way?"

"This is Iowa, Ms. Kimball. We work hard. We have a can-do culture here. Everyone helps each other out. We always have. Since the company was founded by the Kelso family decades ago. Benito didn't understand us. He didn't fit in. He left of his own free will, quite a while ago."

"Were you aware of any antagonism between Benito and Alex Cole?"

She shrugged. "Like I said, I don't know every employee on a personal basis. Do you think this is significant as to why Alex Cole planted the bomb?"

"*If* he planted the bomb, you mean? I don't know yet. Possibly."

"Then you should share your evidence with the police. And the FBI. We all want the truth. Now if you'll excuse me." Winter turned to leave.

"What about Debora Elden?" Jess said, walking along toward the exit. "Do you know her?"

Winter held her mouth open a fraction before speaking. "Should I?"

"She worked here until a few months ago. Another researcher. On a project you shut down."

"Kelso has been having financial problems. We've had to make cuts in several areas. That's no secret." Winter shrugged.

"Debora Elden and Alex Cole were dating at one time."

"Well, if you think this Elden girl is significant, bring her to the FBI's attention, too." Winter walked out of the room, closing the door behind her.

CHAPTER TWELVE

Tuesday, August 16
10:15 p.m. Central Africa Time
Zambia, Africa

EPHRAIM CROUCHED LOW IN the Defender's seat. "Automatic fire," he said.

Chola ignored him as he struggled with the radio crudely bolted to the top of the dash in the bouncing vehicle. "We're out of radio contact range. Keep going."

Ephraim veered around an outcrop of rock, not lifting his foot from the accelerator. "Tell them they're mercenaries with some weird equipment. Tell them. Tell them."

Chola let go of the microphone. "It's hopeless. We're miles out of range." He pulled a Ruger Hawkeye rifle from clip behind his seat. "Six shots against automatics."

As if to hammer home his point, the glass in the rear of the Defender exploded.

The Land Rover bucked as they flew over a tiny dry stream.

Chola pointed the Hawkeye in the HiLux's direction. There

was no hope of aiming as they sped over the rough ground. He fired five shots, frantically cycling each spent round out of the chamber and loading the next.

The HiLux swerved and hung back a moment.

Chola grabbed a box of ammunition from behind his seat and reloaded. "Just keep moving and hope I get lucky."

The HiLux arced left, taking advantage of a clear patch to make up ground.

Automatic fire tore through the Land Rover's hood. Large chunks of metal spiraled into the air. Chola hunkered down.

The Land Rover's engine slowed. Chola snapped his head up, ready to shout for more speed when he saw Ephraim. Blood spread across his shirt, and his head lolled backward. He was dead.

The HiLux veered toward the slowing Land Rover.

Chola grabbed the steering wheel, and rammed his elbow down on Ephraim's leg, flooring the accelerator.

The Land Rover responded, gaining speed as its engine churned louder.

The HiLux was ahead and to the left of him. Chola arrowed the Defender toward the Toyota.

He hit the Toyota's side at fifty miles an hour. A screeching tear of the metal.

The Defender's steering wheel twisted out of his hands. The HiLux bounced and rolled up onto two wheels. He watched, praying it would roll over.

The Land Rover glanced off, its weight keeping it down, and momentum carrying it on. The HiLux crashed down on all four wheels. Chola cursed. His best hope had been to wreck their vehicle.

He twisted his head to look at the Land Rover's path

ahead and screamed. A valley's edge was a hundred feet away.

He twisted the steering wheel. The Land Rover leaned hard on its tires. The vehicle turned a fraction too late.

The edge was abrupt. The valley was wide and tree covered. The drop was less than a hundred feet. The slope was soft sandy soil. But none of that made a difference.

The Land Rover lurched over the edge, and both left side wheels dropped like stones.

Chola grabbed his seat.

The Land Rover rolled sideways, pitching Chola onto the roof.

The engine screamed.

He crashed onto the roof as the Rover turned upside down and continued to roll.

The remaining windows smashed, raining broken glass into the passenger compartment.

He screwed his eyes shut as he was alternately pounded between the floor and the roof.

The slope leveled out.

The Defender came to a stop, rocking on its roof.

Chola lay on a carpet of glass.

The engine sputtered and died.

Ephraim's bloody body lay in the rear of the Rover, one arm twisted unnaturally behind his head.

Chola looked away and swore.

The driver's side of the vehicle had borne the brunt of the impacts. The roof had caved in, blocking the windshield and driver's window. Chola's glasses were caught in a string basket hanging from the back of the driver's seat. He brushed off shards of glass and put them on.

With a deep breath, he crawled past the still body of his friend, and out the back of the Defender.

His balance swam. He sagged down on his haunches and looked up at the valley edge.

He saw nothing moving along the ridgeline above him.

But the mercenaries would not leave without checking to be sure Chola and Ephraim were dead.

Blood ran down his left arm. He wiped it on his shirt. He hated to leave his friend, but he had to move.

He'd seen several thickets of trees with sprawling undergrowth. The valley floor had access to localized water. He looked at the rear of the Rover. It was the easy way to see inside the vehicle. Logically, the mercenaries would stand there.

He scrabbled inside and found his Hawkeye rifle and the remains of a box of ammunition. Using the side of the Land Rover, he levered himself to his feet.

His head spun. He took a deep breath and moved toward the nearest crop of trees. His legs grew steadier with use, and he jogged the last hundred feet. He dived into the bush and checked the valley ridge. Everything was still.

The trees in the center of the crop were taller with more limbs and foliage. He weaved his way through the weeds, and climbed the first twenty feet up a tree until he found a clear sightline through the foliage to the rear of the Land Rover.

He chambered the first round in his Hawkeye and reloaded the magazine's empty slot. The gun had been tossed around inside the Defender as it rolled. Any damage to the Hawkeye would be revealed when he tried to fire. He wiped his brow and shoved the thought to the back of his mind.

An engine revved in the distance.

The HiLux was descending the valley side at an angle and a steady speed. The driver was no idiot. Keeping a good distance, the HiLux circled the remains of the Land Rover. Satisfied there was no danger, it closed in, coming to a stop as Chola had predicted, at the rear.

He nestled the Hawkeye in the crook of his shoulder, his face down against the side of the gun, and settled his aim on the driver.

He'd never shot a human being before, but this wasn't the time to be philosophical.

He breathed out, steadying his aim, and squeezed the trigger.

The Hawkeye boomed.

The recoil hammered his shoulder.

His glasses bounced.

Hot air washed over his cheek and arm.

Cracks radiated out from an inch-sized hole in the middle of the windshield.

The dry earth around the vehicle seemed to leap into life with the shockwave.

Chola kept his eyes on the truck as he cycled the spent cartridge out and a new cartridge in.

The HiLux's engine roared.

He'd missed.

The driver was still alive.

Chola fired again.

He saw the passenger's head whip backward.

The HiLux wheeled around, throwing up a storm of dust.

Chola fired his last four shots in quick succession, flipped the rifle over, and reloaded, wedging the rounds into the magazine like his life depended on speed.

The HiLux circled the trees.

The passenger might be down, but the driver had identified Chola's location.

He shinnied down the tree.

When the mercenary grew tired of searching, he'd hose down the trees with bullets, starting at the top.

The HiLux halted next to a set of trees that formed a natural shield.

Chola moved sideways, keeping the HiLux in view, his gun up, waiting for movement.

He inched around a treeless area. The opening had a view of the sky and three-foot-high undergrowth.

The HiLux was behind. If the driver entered the woods, he would likely reach the edge of the open area, even if he didn't cross it.

Chola knelt, his gun held at eye-level. Mouth open, breathing steadily, fighting the urge to run.

All he needed was a sign.

A full minute passed. His knees were tightening in his crouch. He adjusted his stance.

Across the opening, the undergrowth rustled.

He whisked his gun around and fired into the vegetation.

He loosed all six rounds spacing them a couple of feet apart.

The leaves and branches danced as the hot metal speared through their tranquil world.

Movement stopped.

No scream.

No cry for help or mercy.

Chola swore to himself and rolled his rifle over to reload. The dappled light of the woods threw his gun into darkness. He turned.

A thick black gun barrel pressed into his face.

He caught a glimpse of the trigger, and a roaring filled his ears.

But only for a second.

TEBOGO LOWERED HIS GUN. The headless body slumped to the ground.

He turned to one side and spat.

It was a cold victory.

The wardens were dead, but Kago was too.

He spat again.

If only the damn wardens hadn't looked under the tarp.

He walked away.

There was no point in hiding the body. His effort would be wasted. He didn't have time to dig a proper grave, and a shallow grave would be found by animals overnight.

He'd have to depend on Africa's greatest strength, its size. They were far from the main routes. The chances of someone finding the body were slim.

He walked back to the rolled Land Rover.

A radio was screwed to the dashboard. It buzzed and clicked, but no one responded. With luck, no message went out from here.

He pulled Kago's dead body from the HiLux, stripped him of any identifying items, and dropped his body in the undergrowth.

With a log and some exertion, he levered the Land Rover upright. Using the gentle incline of the valley floor, he rolled the wrecked vehicle into the bushes.

He found a wad of newspaper and swept the glass from the HiLux.

The truck started immediately.

He took one last look in the direction of Kago's resting place and started up the valley wall.

Out of the valley, he balanced the GPS on the dashboard and set off for the next location.

Two more monitoring stations to deploy. He would complete the task and collect his money.

Only one good thing came from the encounter. They were mercenaries. One job, one price.

If only one of them came back, so be it.

Kago's share of the Spaniard's money now belonged to Tebogo.

CHAPTER THIRTEEN

Tuesday, August 16
4:00 p.m. CDT
Chatham, Iowa

SALLY MEACHAM HAD WAITED for Jess as if her job were to make sure every last member of the press followed orders to leave the building after the press conference. They were the only two remaining in the conference room. "We'd better go."

"Yes, of course." Jess followed her out into the corridor and walked with her toward the exit.

"I've been an admirer of your work for a long time, Jess. You're doing a lot of good in the world." She paused. "And I'm very sorry about your son. I hope you'll find him soon."

"Thank you." Jess nodded. She used her celebrity to keep Peter's case in the public eye. The best chance she had of finding him now was a tip from an observant reader, like Sally Meacham. She was grateful for each and every one of them.

"I heard you asking Ms. Winter about Debora Elden. I remember her. Pretty smile. Hard worker," Sally said. "She left

Kelso Products about three months ago. We were sorry to see her go."

Jess raised her eyebrows. "Why did she quit?"

"We stopped funding the research she was working on. We've been struggling, financially, as you probably know. It was a costly project we simply couldn't afford to continue. We'd have been happy to reassign her to a different project, but she wasn't interested." Sally walked slowly as if she was in no real hurry to rush Jess out the door. "Some of the scientists are really dedicated like that. The research is more important than specific jobs to them. Or personal lives. Or anything else. Debbie Elden was one of those. She was exceptionally passionate about her work."

"Where did she go?"

Sally seemed to think about the question. "I'm not sure if she told us. Abroad somewhere, I think."

"Do you know Alex Cole?"

"Not really." Sally shook her head. "He kept to himself mostly. I guess that should have been a warning sign, but honestly, a lot of the scientists we've had here are like that, too."

"Don't worry." Jess smiled. "If being introverted and solitary was a marker for terrorism, half the people in the country would be locked up."

Sally grimaced and waved her badge in front of the card reader beside the door to the lobby. The lock clicked open.

"What about Marco Benito?" Jess asked. "Did you know him, too?"

"Horrible man." Sally shuddered. "We had a lot of complaints. Some personal, some work-related."

"Such as?"

"I can't be more specific." Sally pursed her lips. "Let's just say he had no respect for his coworkers."

Jess smiled and nodded. "Really?"

Sally shifted her weight. "With the men, he interfered with their work, and with the women it was…well, more personal."

"Was there anyone in particular he harassed?"

She shook her head. "He bothered just about everyone he came into contact with, one way or another."

"I don't suppose you know where Benito lived back then, or even better, now?"

"I don't. And I couldn't tell you if I did. Unless you have a court order, that is." Sally stopped by the revolving door, her hand out. "Funny you should ask about Debbie Elden, though. When I conducted her exit interview, I cleared her access cards, computer accounts, all that stuff. It's routine, you know?"

Jess frowned. "Of course. Like locking the doors between tenants in an apartment. Makes total sense."

Sally nodded. "Right. But the really bizarre thing is that earlier in the day, a couple of hours before the explosion, one of the guys in our IT department discovered her account was active on our servers. Like it had not been deactivated or something."

Jess widened her eyes. "What does the FBI say about that?"

Sally shook her head. "In the confusion, until you mentioned her, I'd forgotten all about it. I'm on my way to call Agent Remington about the Elden girl now. This is definitely odd."

"Thank you, Sally. Alex Cole's getting a raw deal here. I'm not sure what's going on, exactly. But he didn't do this. And whoever did this is still out there." Jess handed her a business card. "Here's my cell phone number. If you learn anything that might be helpful, please call me."

Sally took the card and read it before she slipped it into her pocket.

CHAPTER FOURTEEN

Tuesday, August 16
5:15 p.m. CDT
Chatham, Iowa

JESS'S HOTEL ROOM HAD two queen beds. She put her overnight bag on the one farthest from the door. She freshened up in the bathroom before setting up her laptop on the room's small desk. In a moment she was connected to a private wireless network through her portable hotspot and accessed *Taboo Magazine's* private, massive databases.

Taboo had been in business a long time and had accumulated a great deal of data, particularly on people who had been or might one day be newsworthy.

Taboo also had connections with many newspaper, magazine, and media organizations around the world.

Educational records, passports, driver's licenses. You name it, Jess could access it through Taboo's search engines, given enough time and a few key pieces of information with which to start.

She began with Marco Benito's name. Several hits came back, but none were scientists.

Five matches in *The Journal of the American Biochemical Society* were summaries of published research papers, all with long and complicated arcane titles.

She couldn't access the content without subscribing to the *Journal*, but she wouldn't have been able to decipher them, anyway.

Marco Benito's biography listed his employment at a university in Turin, Italy.

A bespectacled, gray-haired gentleman probably between sixty and seventy smiled in his photograph.

Benito looked nothing like the man Alex Cole described as "acting all cool and everything." How could this possibly be the same guy?

She spent a few more minutes searching for another, younger, hipper, Italian research scientist named Marco Benito before she gave up. She had a better option and now was the time to use it.

She snagged her phone and selected the name at the top of her list of favorite numbers. She smiled as she listened to his phone ring twice before he answered.

"How's Iowa?" Henry Morris said.

"Interesting."

"How long are you staying? A storm is heading your way."

"Huh?"

"On the radar. There's a storm coming down from the Dakotas," Henry explained patiently. "Nasty weather. Tornados are predicted. You'll want to get out of there while you still can."

"Yeah. Okay. Thanks." Jess barely heard his warnings or her responses. She was focused on something else. "I met Alex Cole today. Talked to him for a while. He's pretty calm, which could be an indicator of some sort, I guess. But he doesn't seem to appreciate the extent of the trouble he's in."

"I looked at some of his statements. He seems level-headed to me. There's a psychological evaluation in the files by some head doctor who hasn't met him personally. I haven't had time to read it, and—"

"You can't tell me what's in it anyway," she said. "Yeah, I know."

"Remington's team has found a lot of records, though. Over several years, Cole's purchased all sorts of chemicals, equipment, computers." Henry paused. "But here's the thing. No proof that he bought the TAPT components used in the Kelso bomb. At least, not yet."

Jess's eyebrows shot up, and her mouth dropped open. "But the chemicals were found at his property. Remington released that to the press as one of the justifications for arresting Cole. It's listed in the arrest warrant."

"Right. The chemicals were there. But no proof that *Cole* bought them," Henry explained. "He might have paid cash. Or he could have stolen them, I guess. Lots of possibilities. Just no purchase records. So far."

"Presumably, Remington's team is looking into that, right?"

"A case like this? They're not going to leave a single loose end."

"Which brings me to why I called."

"And here I thought you wanted to hear my dulcet tones."

"Nah." She grinned. "Your dulcet tones are just a bonus."

"You're such a sweet talker." He laughed and sipped something. Maybe coffee. He was still at work so it wouldn't be alcohol. "What do you want?"

"A couple of things. First one's easy. Someone was watching Marcia McAllister today. I've got a photo of the license plate. I figured it was Remington's team."

"Sounds like a reasonable assumption."

"But I ran it through our databases and came up empty. If I send you the photo, can you run it for me?"

"Yep," Henry said. "What else?"

"Alex Cole mentioned an Italian guy named Marco Benito. Called him *cool*. But the HR director told me he'd been a big problem. She said he didn't fit in. Caused some trouble, and quit just ahead of the boot on his ass, from what I gathered."

"Okay."

"The picture I found in the *Journal of the American Biochemical Society* doesn't look like the sort of person Cole would describe as *cool*." She blew out a long stream of air. "Not even close."

"Why is this relevant?" He sipped again, which made her want something stronger than coffee, but she needed clear thinking as much as he did.

"I'm not sure how it's relevant. I'm trying to figure that out." She paused, cocked her head, and closed her eyes to think. "Cole said several weird things had been happening at Kelso Products over the past several months. He said stuff was stolen. Someone broke into the main computer room. And this Italian, Benito, was causing a lot of trouble before he left."

"The investigative file backs that up. Several unsolved break-ins at the Kelso plant are noted. A rash of them four to six months ago. Nothing about any Italian suspects, though."

Jess nodded. "Here's another odd thing. Cole was dating a coworker. Debora Elden. She left the company voluntarily, but

Kelso's IT personnel recently discovered her account is still live on their servers."

"That's pretty lax security," Morris said. "But what does it prove?"

"I'm not sure it proves anything. The CEO, Claire Winter, claimed she didn't know Elden at all, and then called her a girl."

"You said her name was Debora. Girl is a fair description."

"Actually, you're right. She's fresh-faced and looks a lot younger than she is. Girl is a perfect description," Jess paused. "But who calls a grown woman a 'girl' like that? Especially if the woman is unknown? That's strange, don't you think?"

"Perhaps."

"Not only that, Debora Elden seems to have some kind of activist background."

"That is the sort of thing that usually raises a red flag," Henry said, slowly. "Might be nothing, but it's certainly worth following up."

"It certainly is. Her face appears on a website for a group called Local World Action. One of the pictures shows that whaling boat that got rammed by a dinghy full of explosives."

Henry whistled. "I remember when that happened, but wasn't it in the Far East?"

"It was, but still."

"Is Elden in the same picture?"

"No."

"Any solid connection?"

She gave an exasperated sigh. "No."

"I'll look into it." Henry paused. "Anyway, how do you know about Debora Elden when Remington's file doesn't mention her at all?"

"Cole didn't volunteer the information to me. I got it from

my friend Marcia McAllister and then pressed Cole about her. Not likely he's going to volunteer the name of anyone he's dated to some hulking FBI agent who wants to send him to death row. I wish I'd known about Elden's access card when I was talking to Cole, but he probably wouldn't tell me anything useful." Jess swiped both hands through her blonde curls. "But don't worry, G-man. I'm holding nothing back. Remington knows everything I know. I'm one thousand percent sure he was observing my interview with Cole. Probably recorded the whole thing, if you want to see the brilliant journalist at work."

Morris grunted. "Sounds like you've got no hard evidence yet. I'm beginning to suspect that's why you called."

"You're exactly right. I can look into Cole, Elden, and Winter. But I need help with Marco Benito. Any chance you can check his visa records for me?"

Morris didn't respond immediately, but Jess heard the clacking of his keyboard. "If he's Italian and working at a US manufacturing facility, he must have applied for and received a visa. I may be able to get a photograph. But it'll take some digging."

"That would really help. An address or other contact information would be helpful, too."

"I'll get you what I can."

"I knew there was a good reason to call you." She grinned and put the humor into her voice. "I mean, in addition to hearing your dulcet tones."

"Yeah, yeah. Just try and keep out of trouble, Lois Lane."

"You too," she said. "I don't want to have to come back there and save your ass again."

They both laughed and talked about personal things for a few minutes before Jess ended the call.

She stared unseeing through the window. She'd never thought about it before, but dulcet did describe his voice. Sweet and soothing. Henry could be all of that.

When he wanted to be.

She dragged herself back to the real world and returned to her computer.

The next search was a lot simpler. Finding Debora Elden in *Taboo's* databases took fewer than four seconds. The entry listed an apartment address and two phone numbers.

She leaned closer to her computer screen. Despite Cole's claim that he didn't know where Elden lived now, her address was listed and it wasn't far from the hotel.

Jess tried both phone numbers. The first was disconnected and the second kicked over to voicemail. Debora Elden had an upbeat sounding voice, not artificially high-pitched, but energetic.

Jess hung up without leaving a message.

The *Taboo* database identified the number as a landline located in Elden's apartment.

"Why leave the country and keep an apartment with a phone line in Chatham, Iowa?" Jess said aloud to the empty room. "What are you hiding, Elden?"

When no one answered her questions, she ordered room service, including a nice bottle of red wine, and kept working. She had a very long list of questions and a short list of answers.

When her eyes were too scratchy to stare at the screen, she showered and rolled into bed. Early day tomorrow. She had a plan.

CHAPTER FIFTEEN

Wednesday, August 17
6:30 a.m. CDT
Chatham, Iowa

JESS WAS DRESSED BY six-thirty the next morning. She grabbed a coffee and bagel as she passed through the hotel lobby on the way to her car.

The air was crisp with a tinge of humidity that made the morning feel cooler than it was.

She had memorized the route to Debora Elden's apartment the night before. It was hard to reconcile the local address with Cole and Sally's belief that she had left the country. But if Elden was in Chatham, an early morning visit was the best chance to catch her.

She munched on the bagel and sipped her coffee as she stopped at the traffic lights. The entire trip didn't take long.

Debora Elden's apartment complex looked only a few years old. Colonial style buildings with straight lines and dark roof tiles were stacked for three floors. Apartments on the two top floors had small balconies.

Jess parked as close to Elden's building as she could get. She hustled up the steps to the third floor. On each floor, two apartment entry doors were on either side of a narrow corridor between them.

A man wearing dark clothes and a cap pulled down over his eyes knelt in the corridor in front of an access panel near Elden's front door.

He looked up at Jess. "Got to turn off the water in the whole building for some maintenance."

He waved a large screwdriver. "Damn panel won't open."

Jess saw tools spilling out of a well-worn canvas tool bag near his feet.

The access door finally sprung open. He grunted, twisted a tap inside the wall, and stood up. He waved to Jess. "You can go ahead."

Jess nodded. "I'm looking for three-fourteen."

The man jerked a thumb at the door behind him. "You won't find anyone home. Don't know why she bothers paying the rent on the place."

Jess gave him a card. "Jess Kimball. *Taboo Magazine*."

His frown deepened. "I'm Dan."

Jess flashed her friendliest smile. She pointed to the door to 314. "Do you know her?"

He shrugged. "Only seen her a couple of times. Pretty, though."

"I thought she'd be home. I'm a little worried about her." Jess frowned. "I could call 911, but I hate to waste their time if she's just on vacation or something. Does she live here alone?"

"Never seen anyone else here, so I guess." Dan looked at Jess as if he was sizing her up and approved. "I need to check she hasn't got water leaking into her place anyway. Want to come in, make sure she's not sick or something? Just in case?"

He pulled a big ring of keys from his pocket and turned

toward Elden's apartment. "Step this way."

The door to apartment 314 opened onto the living and kitchen area. A couple of plates were stacked on the draining rack. The microwave door hung open.

The apartment smelled stale.

The walls and carpet were probably a color called something like oatmeal. The wood trim was painted a matching shade of bland.

The living room furniture consisted of a dark wood table and a checkered light green sofa. A small, flat-screen television was perched on a cardboard box sporting a photo of the china on the kitchen drying rack. Behind the television were a game console and a bundle of wires.

While Dan checked the rooms for water leaks, Jess moved into the kitchen.

The cabinets held several cans of soup and a couple of boxes of cereal. One box had gone out of date last month. She shook it. The box was half full. The fridge contained nothing but three bottles of water and a jar of pickles. The trash can was empty.

She took a few pictures with her phone and moved into the bedroom.

The double bed rested in a frame with no headboard and was neatly made. One bedside table had one lamp perched on it. A small closet without a door housed a selection of four white T-shirts and two pairs of jeans as well as two pant suits, one black, and one navy.

The bedside table had three drawers. Jess checked each one quickly. A jumble of chargers and batteries in the bottom. Underwear in the middle drawer. Sleepwear in the top.

Jess dialed Elden's phone number. She heard no ringing in the apartment. The call clicked over to voicemail, the same as the night before.

The bathroom had a selection of eco-friendly shampoo and hand lotions in sizes that suggested Elden had collected them in hotels. A bone-dry toothbrush rested on a clean yellow washcloth on the counter.

Hanging on a hook on the back of the door was a white cotton bathrobe, and slung over the top of the robe was a Kelso Products lanyard with a clip at the bottom and no keycard attached. It looked like the ones Jess had noticed several Kelso employees wearing yesterday.

Jess took pictures of the lanyard, bathroom, and bedroom, and returned to the living room.

The game console had two controllers. Jess turned them over. Both had wires that were twisted and knotted. It was the first sign that someone other than Debora Elden might have been here at some point. Alex Cole?

A sheet of paper under the game console revealed a list of words in tiny handwriting. Usernames and passwords for streaming services, probably.

One of the usernames was in small characters that Jess recognized as kanji, a Japanese style of Chinese. Henry's "Far East" comment about the whaling ship popped into her head.

Dan came out of the kitchen. "Looks like her pipes are good. And she's not here like we thought."

Jess snapped a picture of the paper and tucked it back under the console.

"I feel better that we checked, though." She took one last glance around the room.

"Me, too," he said.

"I guess I'll just keep calling until she answers her phone."

Dan closed the front door.

CHAPTER SIXTEEN

Wednesday, August 17
7:40 a.m. CDT
Chatham, Iowa

JESS SAT IN HER car and called her assistant, a notoriously early riser. Mandy had probably completed a five-mile run, eaten a full breakfast, and looked like a million bucks already.

She answered almost before the phone rang. "Morning, Jess."

"Hi, Mandy. I need more help."

"That's my job. What can I do?"

Jess smiled. Mandy was always ready for anything. "Our databases have two phone numbers for Debora Elden here in Chatham. Neither one is a cell number. Both landlines. One number is disconnected, and the other keeps switching over to voicemail. There's an address for the working line, but no phone at that address."

"So it's forwarded somewhere. You want me to find out where the call goes?"

"Please. And anything else you can get about the number."

"I might be able to find an address and when it was redirected, but that'll be it unless you want me to ask one of our lawyers to get a court order."

"Skip the court order for now, but put somebody on call in case we need it." Jess chewed the inside of her lip. "And I need a full profile on Claire Winter, CEO of Kelso Products. Dig up what you can on her past and contacts."

"Will do. When do you need all this?"

"Guess."

"Last week." Mandy offered a good-natured sigh. "Well, I'd better get to work."

"You're the best." Jess hung up to answer an incoming call without checking the caller ID.

"Hi, Jess. It's Sally Meacham." The greeting was tentative, hesitant.

"Hi, Sally. What can I do for you?"

Sally paused. "I'm not exactly sure. You said to call if I noticed anything. And, I think, maybe this might qualify?"

Jess nodded slowly. Sally seemed like a woman who needed coaxing. "Okay. Tell me, and we'll figure it out together."

"It's what you said about Alex Cole. Got me thinking. If he's not the one who bombed the plant, then we're still in trouble here. More people could be hurt?"

"Unfortunately, I'm afraid that's true.'

"Agent Remington thinks Alex Cole is the right guy. But what if he's not?"

"Um hmm," Jess made reassuring noises, afraid to say the wrong words until she knew where the conversation was going.

"And Debbie Elden? I've tried to call her, and she never answers." Sally's voice quivered. "I'm really worried about her. She's a nice girl."

Jess had no reassurances to offer on that score. "What do you think we should do?"

Sally took a deep breath, and her words rushed out. "Turns out that Debbie Elden's access card is missing. We keep strict controls on those cards, Jess. I'm sure I collected it from her when she resigned. I'd lose my job if I didn't follow the procedures. I'm sure I did it here. Absolutely sure." Her tone was something approaching panic at this point. "But it's not in the locked drawer in my desk now."

Jess didn't know what to say, so she didn't reply.

"Could this be my fault? Do you think whoever planted that bomb stole Debbie Elden's card from my office?" Sally choked back a sob. "All those people are dead because of me?"

At that point, Sally broke down completely.

The clock on the dashboard read seven-forty. Jess started the engine and drove through morning rush hour to Kelso Products while she waited for a chance to say something. But that never happened. Sally disconnected the call, and when Jess tried to call back, Sally didn't pick up.

Cars and trucks flowed into the parking lots. Like workers everywhere, Kelso employees had their routines down cold. Vehicles barely slowed for four-way stops, and there was no quarter given for indecisive newcomers.

Jess followed a woman driving an old Chevrolet truck sporting a bright blue paint job. The truck turned several times and finally parked on the far edge of one of several lots surrounding the Kelso plant. She jumped out of her truck the moment the engine stopped.

Jess parked two spaces away. The flow of people seemed unrelenting as they converged on three tall turnstiles set into an eight-foot-high barbed wire fence.

The turnstiles resembled a medieval torture device.

The clock on her dashboard showed 7:56 a.m. People were rushing to clock in on time, she guessed.

After five minutes, the clock flipped over to 8:01 a.m. and the flow of workers through the turnstiles slowed. A few stragglers ran across the parking lot, and fewer slackers sauntered.

The horizontal metal bars of the turnstile were six-inches apart. Two sets were combined into a single unit. One fixed set of horizontal bars was welded to the entranceway. The other set was divided into thirds. Interleaved like lacing fingers, it rested inside the fixed set and moved like a revolving door.

Each turnstile rotated in thirds. The first rotation locked the person inside the turnstile like a prison. The key card reader came next. Anyone foolish enough to enter the turnstile without a card would be trapped inside and held there until security hauled them away.

The key card was used to release the turnstile's locking mechanism. After the card reader clicked, the revolving turnstile dumped the employee into the Kelso Products facility. Then the turnstile completed the full rotation empty to wait for the next employee.

Jess tried Sally's number again.

She answered this time. Her voice sounded congested and teary, still. "I'm sorry, Jess. I can't...I don't..."

"Sally, I'm in the employee parking lot outside the turnstiles. Can you duplicate Elden's keycard? It needs to be exactly like hers. And meet me here with the duplicate? I have an idea."

"Oh, Jess, I can't do that. I mean, I can duplicate the card. But I can't see the screen that tells what access Elden had to various areas of the plant. Only the Vice President of Security can see that. I can't bring the card to you, though. I just can't."

"Okay. Then how about I come by the main entrance, and you come out and give me the keycard to try?"

"But—"

Jess took a deep breath. "Look, Sally, I don't think this is your fault. And I'm trying to help you here. But I can't do it unless you give me that access card."

"Well—"

"I'm already on my way. See you in less than two minutes. Just come outside and give me the card. You can go right back inside. I'll return it to you when I'm done. I promise." Sally didn't agree or disagree, so Jess said, "You don't want to feel guilty about this forever, do you?"

She hiccoughed on the other end of the line. She finally whispered, "Okay."

CHAPTER SEVENTEEN

THE HANDOFF WENT AS smoothly as planned. Jess was gone from the employee entrance for less than two full minutes.

When she returned to the turnstiles, Jess watched a few employees run through the process with practiced ease in short order. When it was her turn, she pulled the card from her pocket, nervously stepped into the turnstile, and rotated through the first click.

She waved the keycard in front of the gray box-shaped card reader. The box beeped once, and the turnstile emitted a loud click. She pushed the bars and followed them through as they rotated into the plant.

The reader beeped again behind her. A man barged through and ran toward one of the big buildings.

The roads around the plant were almost deserted. If she stood around, she'd be an obvious target for a visit from security.

She followed the man at a brisk pace.

The man waved his card in front of another gray box to open a side door and disappeared inside.

Jess reached the door a few moments later. She waved her

card by the card reader. It emitted a grating double buzz. She tried to turn the knob, but the door remained locked.

A second man jogged up, pushed in front of Jess, and waved his card at the reader. The door beeped and clicked open.

He waved his card at Jess, pointing to a blue band around it. "Production, see?"

He grabbed Jess's card and held it up. "Red's research. Won't let you in here."

He shrugged. "Sorry, lady."

He turned and jogged into the building.

Before the door closed behind him, Jess glimpsed large tanks connected by a mass of pipework. Heat and humidity oozed out. The air had a chemical tang that irritated her nose and made her sneeze.

Jess stepped away from the door. The turnstile entrance was quieter now. The area around the building was deserted. Everyone who had entered earlier was now inside, somewhere.

She turned the card over in her hand. Keycards only granted access to specific areas, and employees helped to enforce the rules.

Which meant Kelso Products did take security seriously enough.

It also meant that Elden's card was only good for limited access.

Why did someone want it?

And what did they use it for?

Jess looked around until she saw a sign pointing toward "Research Labs." She walked briskly in that direction.

The grounds were vast fields. Enormous buildings were plopped here and there as if a giant hand had placed them on a game board from above. Between the buildings, deserted gravel paths wandered like wide gray ribbons.

Jess glanced over her shoulder. No one followed, but she felt exposed. Agent Remington had said there were no cameras monitoring workers inside the facility, but any curious person could look out of a window anytime.

At an angle to her left were several single-story buildings leading toward the explosion site.

All were brick, painted white. Pipes stuck up from their roofs. Enormous air-conditioning units from which condensing water vapor rose were placed along one exterior wall. Concrete separated the buildings.

The building closest to her was labeled "Lab 1." Alex Cole's workplace.

Large windows overlooked the concrete, but they were covered by closed Venetian blinds.

A single-story building in the front was labeled "Research and Development." Beneath it, in large letters, was the phrase "AUTHORIZED personnel only."

She saw through the large, uncovered windows into an unoccupied open area beyond double glass doors.

Jess took a deep breath and walked toward the entrance. She saw no card reader in place here, and when she was close enough to engage a sensor, the doors parted automatically.

She paused at the threshold. Three interior doors led from the foyer. Each had a gray card reader box. Elden's duplicate card might not work, or worse, it could notify security immediately. Jess could be trapped inside by those automatic doors.

She took a deep breath and stepped inside. The glass doors hissed shut behind her. The three interior doors were solid wood panels. No signs identified the areas beyond each entrance. But she didn't plan to go deeper into the building. She wanted to know whether the card would allow her to breach security.

If Jess could steal a card and get inside the building, another unauthorized person could have done so, too. Which meant that someone unknown, someone other than Alex Cole, could have set up the bomb.

Jess began with the first door on the left. She waved the card in front of the gray box. It emitted the same grating double buzz that denied entry to the production building.

She waited a moment. She heard no bells or sirens.

She took another breath and waved the card before the second reader. The same rejection buzz sounded loud enough to wake the dead.

She stepped straight to the last door with the card held out, and passed it across the sensor. The gray box offered a nerve-soothing single beep. The door's lock clicked. The door popped open a fraction.

She grabbed the knob and pulled the door open a few inches.

A brightly lit, blue-carpeted corridor lay beyond.

Several solid doors adjacent to large glass observation windows on the right-hand side led to lab rooms, she guessed. The first door was only three feet from where she stood. Its window was another two feet beyond the door.

Her heart thumped hard against her ribs. She'd proved what she came to do. Alex Cole wasn't the only person who could have set that bomb. Others, known or unknown, had as much or more opportunity to do so.

Debora Elden, for one. Her lanyard was hanging in her bathroom. She could easily have the card in her pocket. She'd have had access to this area even though she'd resigned and left the country three months earlier. She maintained an apartment here with an active telephone number. She could have been in town last Thursday.

Jess didn't need to go any farther. She could turn back now.

She took a deep breath and stepped through onto the blue carpet. The door locked behind her.

Beside the first inside lab door, just below eye-level, a clipboard hung on a big hook and a pen dangled on a cord next to it. Several sheets of paper were held under the clip that looked like sign-in sheets with columns for the date, names, arrival, and departure times.

The top sheet was completed about halfway down the grid and dated four months ago. The list of names was handwritten, presumably by their owners as they entered and left this lab room.

Jess read the list quickly. Elden's signature appeared several lines down on the top sheet.

She flipped through the sheets beneath, which were stacked in reverse chronological order. Multiple entries every day for several weeks. Each day's sign-in sheet had Elden's name on it, right up until the last day. Which was two weeks before Elden left Kelso.

After the last day, three more dates were listed on the top sheet, but no signatures, just a small check mark by the date. The handwriting was small, too. Like Elden's signature, possibly. An expert would need to say for sure.

The door into the lab had its own card reader. Jess was too deep inside the plant to risk trying the door. The obnoxiously loud rejection buzzer would surely bring investigators running. But she wanted to know what was going on in that lab room.

The observation window was her best option.

She strode past the window like a woman who had every right to be there. Her head angled toward the glass, and her eyes strained to see who was working on what inside that room.

There was no one in the lab at all. Totally unoccupied. Not even a four-legged lab rat.

She stepped back and peered through the window. The room was completely metallic. The walls, ceiling, and floor were solid sheets of shiny silver metal, like highly polished stainless steel. The corners appeared welded to eliminate seams. There were two tables and several chairs, all metal. A rack against one wall was loaded with scrub suits and full-face masks. Several red and blue gas cylinders were hung on the wall.

In the corner was an open shower with a large loop of chain. A red plaque hung from the lowest point of the loop. It bore one word in black lettering on a yellow background. *Drench.*

At the far side of the room was a metal door with a gray card reader, requiring a card to exit. This reader was encased in a glass bowl sealed against the metal wall. Beside the door was a long set of instructions painted on the metal wall. The door was stenciled with the words, *Entering BSL-3. Follow all instructions. No exceptions.*

CHAPTER EIGHTEEN

Wednesday, August 17
8:30 a.m. CDT
Chatham, Iowa

JESS SHOVED THE KEYCARD into her pocket. She didn't know what lay beyond the steel door, but she wouldn't go inside that room on a bet. She pulled her phone from her pocket and snapped a few quick photos. First chance she got, she'd send them into the cloud.

She left the same way she entered. The door didn't require the card reader. It opened with the handle from the inside. When she approached the automatic double entry doors on the other side of the foyer, they opened to let her out and closed behind her. She retraced her same path around the production building to the turnstiles and out to her car.

In mere moments she was leaving the parking lot. She called Sally Meacham to return the card, but Sally didn't answer. Jess stuffed the card in her pocket where she imagined it burning a hole straight through to her skin.

A couple of miles down the road she stopped at a supermarket's parking lot.

Jess made a quick search of *Taboo*'s databases on her phone. BSL-3 meant Bio Safety Level 3. It was a standard used by the US Centers for Disease Control and Prevention for the handling of potentially lethal poisons that are transmitted just by breathing.

Another search showed there were more than a thousand such labs in the US, and they were strictly controlled.

Her phone rang. Henry Morris. She answered immediately. "Hey, Henry."

"How's the reporting?"

She exhaled. "Tell me what you found first."

"Okay." He stretched the word out to emphasize he knew Jess was holding back on him. "First, the vehicle following Marcia McAllister was a team from Remington's office. No big mystery there. Second, Marco Benito did apply for a visa. The text of the application was from the actual Marco Benito's résumé, but the picture isn't him. The photo matches an Interpol mug sheet for an Italian thug. His real name, which he hasn't used in years, is Franco Olivetti. He holds a degree in biology, which is probably how he managed to pass himself off as the real Benito for a while. He's also under suspicion of several violent crimes in four European countries, according to Interpol records."

"So, what was he doing at Kelso Products?"

"Hard to tell, and we can't ask him. He got into a fight one night with a British soldier in Johannesburg."

"What do you mean?"

"The soldier was on vacation, apparently. According to the official reports, Olivetti mugged the soldier outside a restaurant.

A knife fight. They killed each other."

Jess whistled. "Why would a guy like that be working at Kelso Products?"

"My guess is industrial espionage. He has a long record of burglaries and assaults. I can't see him going to the trouble of getting a visa under a false name and trying to pass himself off as a scientist for any other reason. Can you?"

Jess felt like she was drowning in tension. "I just found out that Alex Cole's girlfriend, the one who allegedly quit her job and left the country..."

"Yeah, Debora Elden."

"Well, her keycard that allows her into Kelso Products research labs is missing."

"How do you know that?"

"I'll tell you later. But, she also still has a little-used apartment in Chatham and a phone number that has been diverted somewhere else."

"Give me the number and I'll trace it."

Jess repeated the number from memory.

"You realize I'm passing this on to Remington?"

"You bet. He needs to know. His team has the clout to get better answers from Winter, and whoever else knows more than they've been telling."

"Maybe. But I have one other piece of news. Three months ago Alex Cole drove to Detroit. Apart from a burger in Delray, he didn't use a credit card for the whole trip. No gas stations, nothing. Must have paid cash everywhere."

"And?"

"He visited a small engineering company there. They make specialist robotics equipment. Small-scale. Cole bought a bunch of stuff with cash."

Jess leaned back in the driver's seat and closed her eyes. "Incriminating stuff?"

"No."

Jess's ability to breathe returned.

"But the owner remembers a discussion about the manufacture of TAPT. That's acetone peroxide. They spent some time discussing the dangers of handling it. The owner remembers the conversation clearly. He notified the police when he saw Cole's picture and heard about the arrest on the news." Morris paused. He lowered his voice as if he were delivering a fatal blow and he knew it. "So, the chemicals were found on his property, which is possession. And now we have someone who corroborates his interest in that type of explosive."

"It's looking worse and worse for Alex, isn't it?"

"It is. Even if he didn't act alone. It's still not good."

There was a long silence while Henry waited for her to absorb everything, she guessed.

"Am I wasting my time?" she finally said.

"Hard to say. You know I'd never bet against the FBI, but you have uncovered, shall we say, *irregularities*."

"You think what I've found has nothing to do with the bomb," she said.

He sighed. "Are you out of options yet?"

"No."

"Then I'll give you the advice a retiring agent once gave me. When evidence goes against your gut, work it a little longer."

She nodded. "Can I get one more favor? Can you find Debora Elden?"

He paused for a few extra beats before he said, "I can find her air travel easily enough. I'll email you the results."

"Thanks, Henry. I appreciate the help. If it turns out that

Alex Cole did this, Marcia McAllister will be devastated. I don't know how much more that poor woman can take." Jess ran her hand through her hair. "First her daughter, missing more than two years. And now her best friend's son? A terrorist? I'm really worried about her, Henry."

"I don't have any doubts about what you're doing there, Jess. Stick with it. Sometimes, even the smallest irregularity can unravel the whole thing."

She smiled. "Thanks, Henry."

She hung up.

She'd told him the truth. She hadn't hit a brick wall, but promising leads were thin on the ground.

Cole might be the one. It was possible. She didn't want to believe it, and he didn't really seem like the type to her. But the evidence was piled high against him and getting worse.

She still couldn't fathom why he would plant that bomb. What was his motive? Human behavior wasn't always predictable, and people didn't always do the smart thing. But in the absence of a mental illness, surely Alex Cole needed a reason to destroy those people with a bomb like that, didn't he?

Then there was Elden.

She had access to a research lab that was highly controlled.

She conducted experiments at Cole's place, hoping to enable third world countries to make Kelso's products cheaper and easier.

She belonged to a group that approved the bombing of a whaling boat in the Far East, and Japanese kanji characters were written down with a list of usernames and passwords in her apartment.

The FBI's evidence had piled up against Cole, but Elden's activities seemed far more suspect to Jess.

And she'd promised Marcia McAllister. Jess couldn't bear to disappoint Marcia again. Not while Marcia's daughter was still missing.

Somehow, helping Alex Cole felt like helping herself, too. Or maybe Jess was trying to create good karma for the times when her son, Peter, needed it.

Whatever the reasons, Henry was right. She couldn't give up. Not yet.

She'd work the evidence a little longer. Maybe she'd get lucky.

CHAPTER NINETEEN

Wednesday, August 17
9:30 a.m. CDT
Chatham, Iowa

JESS FETCHED HER LAPTOP from the trunk of her car, connected it to her phone, and brought up the Local World Action website.

The background pictures cycled through the same series of images she'd seen before. She waited until the picture with Elden appeared, and took a screenshot.

After all the images cycled, the login prompt popped up again. This was the end of the road unless she could log in.

She found the photo she took in Elden's apartment of the usernames and passwords Elden kept under the gaming console. She used every name on the list, entering each one meticulously. She had to try several more than once because the writing did not distinguish certain letters well enough. She skipped the Japanese writing as she had no way to enter the kanji characters on her keyboard.

After ten minutes she'd worked through the entire list. None of the combinations logged her into the site.

Nice try, but no cigar. Now what?

Jess shuffled the laptop into the passenger seat to answer Mandy's call. "I could use a little good news. What have you got?"

"You were right. Debora Elden redirected her landline to her cell phone, and her cell is registered at her apartment in Chatham. But that's the end of the road. I can't get any further." Mandy was a bigger bulldog than Jess on this kind of thing, so Jess waited for the rest. "I talked to the lawyer. He says we could get more with a court order, but it will take a couple of weeks. I told him to get on it, but I guess that's too long."

"Thanks for the hard work." Jess grimaced, even though this was the answer she'd expected. "What about Winter?"

"Totally different story. Way too much information out there on that woman." Mandy's tone implied she was rolling her eyes. "Winter has a strong reputation as a kick-ass CEO. She turns troubled companies around, and she's done it more than a few times. If I had to guess, I'd say she's a stress junkie."

"Yeah, I can see that. She was cool, calm, and collected when I met her, even though she was under fire from all sides."

"A board member at one of her previous companies said that she has 'a knack for spotting talent.'" Mandy was reading off a screen or notes. "She doesn't suffer fools. Lots of disgruntled employees at all levels are more than happy to complain about her. But she does the job. She gets a company turned around in three or four years then moves on. She has three big successes to her credit in the past decade. Names you'd recognize."

Jess nodded. "How long has Winter been the CEO at Kelso Products?"

"Two years."

"So she came in when they were in trouble. She cuts costs and trims down. That's when they stop the research that sends Debora Elden packing." Jess was thinking out loud. Mandy waited for a question. "Is the company turning around? Making money?"

"Seems like making pest control products is a tough business these days. Kelso was publicly traded when she joined, but she took the company private and found funding to make that happen. Otherwise, a few analysts speculated Kelso would have been bankrupt by now." Mandy paused. "But here's something. She's from right there in Chatham. Originally, I mean. Born and raised."

"She might stick around longer than three years, then?"

"Seems like it. If this bombing thing doesn't put Kelso under, she could."

Jess's phone beeped. "Good work. If you have the time, keep looking. I've got to go. I have another call coming in."

Jess swiped to the new call. "Henry?"

"I've got some details on Elden's number."

"Mandy just told me. Redirected to her cell phone."

"Did she tell you the location of that cell phone?"

Jess grinned. Henry and Mandy were involved in a kind of friendly rivalry where Jess was concerned. It had been a long time since she'd had that in her life. She liked it. They were both sweet to care about her so much. "Show me your stuff, G-man."

"Elden's phone was pinging off cell towers in Spain last night. Specifically, in the area code assigned to Zorita. I can't get any more accurate than that."

"Zorita? Where is that?"

"Southeast of Madrid, toward the coast."

"Wonder what she's doing there?"

"Hard to say. But the phone has been there three months." He paused to be sure she was still listening. "And get this, Zorita is the headquarters for Grupo Lopez, Europe's largest manufacturer of pesticides."

"And Kelso Products' biggest competitor." Jess cocked her head. "Sally Meacham said Elden had taken a job overseas. Grupo Lopez makes sense."

"There's no doubt about the location. She's had calls from her parents, and a couple from numbers at Kelso Products, all redirected from her landline. There's a bunch of calls from Alex Cole's land line and his cell phone to her cell phone, but they stopped a while ago."

"Any outgoing calls we might trace?"

"Nothing much. One to her parents on her father's birthday. I'll send you the list."

"Thanks."

"Also, Remington's team is following up with Winter about the keycard situation." He sighed. "To them, it's a loose end to tie up. They remain convinced that Cole's the right guy."

After he hung up, she received his email on her laptop.

Elden's phone had been active for four years. The source and destination for each call during that time were identified.

Elden's calling behavior changed after she resigned from Kelso Products and moved with her phone to Spain.

Since then, her calls had been limited. Alex Cole, a couple of Kelso Products numbers, and her parents.

Jess closed her eyes and replayed her interview with Alex Cole. He'd denied knowing Elden's present location. She shook her head. That had to be a lie. Which meant he was hiding something. But what? Maybe she'd stolen Kelso secrets and handed them over to the competition?

There was no point in asking Cole about Elden again. What she needed was independent verification.

She looked at the list of calls once more.

Elden's parents lived in New Mexico. Jess could be there in a few hours if there were a good reason to do a live interview.

She dialed the number. The phone rang several times before a breathless man answered.

"Hello?" he said, his voice deep and smooth.

"Hi. I'm Jessica Kimball with *Taboo Magazine*. Is this Mr. Elden?"

"I'm sorry, dear, but we're not interested in a subscription."

"I understand. I'm trying to get in touch with Debora, now that she's moved."

"Moved?"

"I thought she moved? A new job?"

"No. I think you have the wrong person."

"Debora Elden?"

"That's our daughter, but she hasn't moved."

"She still lives in Chatham, Iowa? I thought she moved?"

"My wife and I moved a couple of years ago. Didn't want to, but the winters, you know?"

"So, Debora hasn't moved? She still works at Kelso Products?"

He chuckled. "That's right."

"She's okay after the explosion, I hope?"

"We spent the day worrying when we saw the news, but she called. She's fine."

"Is that the last time you've heard from her? Last week?"

"She calls when she can. We don't want to pressure her. She has a lot going on. Her own life to live."

"Of course. I'm glad she's safe."

"What did you say your name was?"

"Jessica Kimball."

"I'll let her know you called."

"Thank you." Jess hung up.

Debora Elden called her parents from Spain, but she hadn't told them she'd moved, or taken a new job outside the country.

Jess added this one to her list of Elden's questionable activities as she ran through them in her head.

Elden was hiding her location.

She tried to undercut Kelso's business while she worked for the company.

She had access to a lab containing potentially dangerous poisons.

She was featured on a website that supported and perhaps perpetrated a bombing attack against a foreign ship.

Alex Cole, the man accused of the bombing attack on Kelso Products, was protecting her.

She texted her list and plans to Morris first, and then called Mandy.

"I need you to book me a plane ticket."

"Back to Denver?"

Jess shook her head. "Zorita. Spain."

CHAPTER TWENTY

Thursday, August 18
5:00 p.m. Central European Time Zone (CET)
Zorita, Spain

ZORITA WAS A MEDIUM-SIZED city close to the east coast. There had been a settlement on that spot for well over a thousand years, undoubtedly because two rivers joined at that point. There were rail links, and the city was well served by freeways, called autopistas.

Jess caught a flight to Chicago and then Swiss Air to Zürich. More than eight hours in the air. She wrote up her notes from the past two days. After that, she studied maps of Spain and reviewed the research she'd downloaded before takeoff.

The geography held her interest with beautiful images until she dismissed it all to study the list of industries in the area.

Two auto parts makers employed the majority of factory workers in Zorita, but Grupo Lopez employed more than two thousand locals.

Grupo Lopez had holdings all over Europe. An evaluation

she'd found from a financial specialist rated the company's research and development far above its manufacturing capability.

Although Grupo Lopez was larger than Kelso Products, both companies were in trouble. The herbicides and pesticides market was locked in a race to the bottom, with each company undercutting the other to trade market share for profit.

Jess closed her eyes to think.

Henry's speculation about the Italian thug, Marco Benito's role in industrial espionage seemed more reasonable.

Grupo Lopez was the most likely benefactor.

Which could mean the bombing at Kelso Products was not the product of ideological terrorism but plain, mundane corporate greed.

It could also mean Debora Elden was either involved or in danger.

What about Alex Cole? He definitely knew more than he'd shared with Jess. But was he involved in criminal activities or simply clueless? Or something in between?

Her flight landed in Zürich on time. Unlike the Swiss railways that usually ran a perfect schedule, her connecting flight to Valencia was an hour late. The plane was full and so cramped that she'd been forced to gate check her carry-on.

She waited an eternity for her bag to be returned at her final destination. By the time she reached the rental counter, it was 3:30 p.m. local time and the time zone change added another seven hours to her body clock.

The roads to Zorita were smooth, she could drive comfortably on the right side of the road. The scenery was photo-worthy, but Jess kept her foot down on the Mini Cooper's accelerator. She arrived at the outskirts of Zorita at five o'clock. A loop road led her around to the north, and finally, an autopista brought her to Grupo Lopez's front entrance.

The town of Zorita had grown around the plant. What must have at one time been open space was now a bustling community.

The plant reminded her of the Kelso Products facility. A collection of large, aging buildings surrounded by somewhat smaller parking lots. A six-foot chain-link fence with barbed wire at the top surrounded the buildings. The entrances were manned by security guards instead of turnstiles and high-tech card readers.

Jess drove the Mini Cooper around the plant's perimeter drive. The parking lot signs pointed out the locations of various departments. Most were a mystery to Jess. The only departmental name she recognized was *relaciones públicas,* or "public relations."

She had to park a good distance away from the main entrance. She walked fast and arrived after a few minutes.

The management offices were a modern wall of steel and glass, dramatically different from the manufacturing buildings. A large sign written in Spanish at the top of the building repeated the message in English. The words declared this Grupo Lopez's main worldwide chemical production facility.

Two revolving doors were set into the glass. A waist-high metal rail formed a thirty-foot arc around the doors. A bored looking security guard waited behind the metal rail.

Jess pulled out her press card and approached the guard.

"Buenos días," he said, with no hint of warmth.

"Mi nombre es Jessica Kimball. Me gustaría hablar con—"

"Inglés?" he asked.

"Americano."

He grunted. "You are here for work?"

Jess held out her card. "I'm with *Taboo Magazine*. I'd like to see one of your employees."

The guard took her card and frowned.

"An interview," she said.

"Ah." The guard lifted a section of the metal rail. He gestured to the appropriate door and returned her card. "Ask for personnel."

Jess entered a wide, two-story reception area. Large abstract paintings that Jess guessed were intended to portray some aspect of chemistry hung on the walls. A mass of tiny LED lights was suspended from the ceiling casting a warm glow over everything.

White painted chairs were grouped around white coffee tables. Behind them was a white reception counter, arched in the same manner as the metal rail outside.

Two women sat behind the counter. One offered a welcoming smile.

Jess offered her card. The woman studied it carefully before speaking.

"My name is Sofia. How can I help you?"

"I'd like to speak to Debora Elden. She's an American."

"Does she work here?"

"Yes." Jess infused her tone with false confidence.

The woman nodded, making notes on a pad with a pen. "And may I tell her the reason for your visit?"

"It's personal," Jess said.

"Our employees must conduct personal business on personal time." Sofia pursed her lips and returned the card.

Jess nodded. "I understand. But it's not that sort of personal. It's also not a secret. Her ex-boyfriend has been implicated in a crime."

Sofia frowned. "Then I am afraid that is a matter for the police."

"He has been wrongly accused. Ms. Elden may be the only one who can help him."

"Even so, Grupo Lopez does not get involved in police business unless they approach us directly." Sofia shook her head. Her tone was stern. "It's our policy."

"The crime was committed in America. The American police won't interview her here."

Sofia kept her lips tightly together.

"Please. I've traveled a long way," Jess heard herself pleading and cringed. She cleared her throat. "Please just check with your personnel department before you turn me away. This is very important. A matter of life and death."

Something Jess said caused Sofia's expression to soften. "They will say the same thing, I am sure, but I will check."

She donned a headset and conducted a rapid-fire discussion on the phone. Jess's rusty Spanish couldn't keep up, but she caught her own and Elden's name several times.

Sofia finished the call and offered an apologetic smile. "It is as I thought. We cannot reveal personal details of our employees. However, if you would like to leave a business card, they will pass it to Miss Elden."

Jess smiled. She'd accomplished something. The first solid thing she'd found since she started her investigation. She'd confirmed that Elden worked here. Which was more information than she had an hour ago. And more than anyone else knew. Including Agent Remington.

She dug out a second business card. On the backside, she wrote "Alex Cole has been arrested. I suspect he may be innocent. Please contact me." She signed it with a flourish.

Sofia took the card and read the annotation. "I will pass it on." She smiled. "Perhaps she will contact you."

Jess nodded. *Perhaps I'll sit outside and wait.*

"Thank you," she said before she left the building and returned to her car.

CHAPTER TWENTY-ONE

Thursday, August 18
5:15 p.m. Central European Time Zone (CET)
Zorita, Spain

RAFA LOPEZ WAS THE great-grandson of the man who had started a small chemical company in the hills to the south of Zorita. Today, Rafa ruled the conglomerate Grupo Lopez had become with an uncompromising hand.

His father's decision to take the company public ten years earlier had been a mistake. Lucrative at the time. But still, a mistake.

His father was dead now. But his decision to steal Rafa's birthright lived on.

Instead of being the sole owner, Rafa was merely the CEO. He deserved total control. Every day, the company was a battleground. Every day he had to fight his opponents before they had the chance to oust him.

He was close. So close. Grupo Lopez would soon be his. As it should have been all along.

He was not born to serve. He was born to own.

A mere hundred million more and he would be his own master. He needed a groundbreaking product. And he was almost there.

Around the dark wood table in the executive boardroom sat six successful men. They wore expensive suits with bright white shirts and dark blue silk ties. A corner of Rafa's mind seriously wondered if they had coordinated their attire when they dressed this morning.

Rafa shook a sheet of paper. "I cannot accept this. Will not accept it."

"We believe it is the lowest risk."

"I don't pay you to analyze risks. I pay you to achieve the best outcome for my business."

Oleastro, the lawyer sitting closest, pointed at the paper in Rafa's hand. "That is the best outcome."

Fire raged in Rafa's bloodstream. He shook the paper like he meant to rip it to pieces. "*Best outcome?*" Rising, still shaking the paper, he shouted, "This is the *best outcome?*"

Oleastro said, "Yes."

Rafa threw the paper at him. "Twenty-five million in compensation? That's the *best outcome?*"

Oleastro eased himself backward. "There are worse scenarios. The Africans found Grupo Lopez paperwork in the area of the sepsis outbreak. They are blackmailing you. Privately, for the moment."

"Are you deaf?" He leaned toward Oleastro and shouted. "Didn't you hear what I pay you for?"

"Our competitors are facing similar threats."

"Do I care about my competitors?" he bellowed.

Oleastro shifted in his seat. "We know a man has been

watching this plant. He could cause enough trouble without even having conclusive proof."

"What man?"

"Tall. Muscular. Professional."

"Name?"

"We have not been able to identify him."

"So, you expect me to run from ghosts?" Rafa walked around the table. "I was very clear when this business started. I. Will. Not. Accept. Liability. Under no circumstances. Never."

The six craned their necks to follow his movements. As if they were paying attention, though he noticed they avoided eye contact.

He pointed to the paper that had landed on the table. They seemed grateful to look at the crumpled sheet instead of their ranting client.

"We know their case is weak," Rafa said. "They have what? A few old people and a couple of drug users?"

"Two hundred people," Oleastro said. "So far."

Rafa glowered. "One, ten, twenty? What does it matter?"

He slammed both palms on the table and leaned down to stare at each of them individually. "We *will not* be held accountable for claims from such people. This is Spain! Not," he lowered his voice to hiss, "the U-S-A."

The room remained silent. The lawyers had lowered their eyes. And so they should have. Grupo Lopez paid their firm millions every year.

They had grown soft.

He pointed at the paper. "Which of you wrote that?"

They shuffled in their seats.

"I wrote it, and I stand by it," Oleastro said. "It's the wisest thing to do, under the circumstances."

Lopez nodded. "You are done. I never want to see you here again. I will not pay you to work on any case involving Grupo Lopez. And if your firm disregards my instructions again, we will change firms."

Oleastro opened his mouth. Rafa cut him off. "Is that clear?"

Oleastro sagged back into his seat and nodded. His firm worked only for Grupo Lopez. Removal from Grupo Lopez files meant he was finished in Zorita. No firm would hire him. His career was over. His wife and children would be devastated.

Rafa knew all this and didn't care. He looked at each of the remaining lawyers, one at a time. They shifted their weight and fidgeted in their seats.

The last lawyer at the end of the table made eye contact.

Rafa nodded to him. "What would you do?"

"We must undermine the families. Perhaps different private investigators from Madrid that are more...effective. Use intermediaries to avoid repercussions."

Rafa nodded.

"We can have a new recommendation within a week," the lawyer said.

"One week. Do it." Rafa left the room.

The boardroom connected directly to Rafa's office by a private corridor. At his desk, he punched a button. A big screen displayed a view of the conference room. The lawyers were filing out. Five of them waved their hands and talked rapidly.

Oleastro dropped his arms to his sides. Head down, he followed the others through the door and closed it behind him for the last time.

His lesson had produced the desired effect.

The man who stupidly allowed Grupo Lopez paperwork to be found near the sepsis outbreak had been punished. The side effects were unfortunate, but he refused to allow a few miserable lives to stand in the way.

Rafa punched the monitor off.

A manila folder lay on his desk. It bore a circular black seal. He slid his finger under the seal, prying open the folder. The seal snapped in two, revealing the white letters "Advertencia" on the black background.

He pulled two dozen papers from the folder and spread them on his desk. There were tables and colored graphs. A pie chart on the third page was an almost solid circle of green. He ignored a small sliver of red. What was a 5 percent problem against 95 percent success? The numbers were good enough for another large-scale test.

After the graphs was a one-page report from Zambia. The monitoring stations that would prove his success were ready, which was good.

But two dead wardens were a problem the authorities would not ignore.

He slammed his closed fist on the desk. "Idiots!"

The intercom on his desk emitted a single discreet buzz. He might have ignored it, but he hadn't hired his assistant on looks alone. Vanna Sánchez was as fearless and capable in a dark alley as she was organizing executives. He pressed to answer.

"Yes?"

"Personnel called. A reporter has been asking after one of the employees in the south lab, Debora Elden."

He leaned closer to the intercom. "Why do they want to talk to Miss Elden?"

"Her ex-boyfriend is in some trouble with the police in America."

"Has anyone checked that story?"

"The ex-boyfriend is Alex Cole, arrested for the bombing at Kelso Products."

"Damn. Why didn't I know about that connection?"

"It's not in her file."

He scowled. "Then I'll need a review of her background and activities immediately."

"Yes, Sir."

"And who was the reporter?"

"Jessica Kimball. *Taboo Magazine.*"

Lopez leaned back in his chair. He knitted his fingers together and rested his chin on top. "*Taboo* is very influential."

His assistant had known him long enough not to reply.

"Where is Elden?" he said.

"She will be going home soon. I'll make arrangements to keep her away from Kimball."

"Have security keep tabs on her."

"Yes, sir. She's also known to have a current relationship with a lab tech here, Felipe Cantor."

"Oh, for Christ's sake." He ran a hand through his hair and blew out a long stream of frustration. "Have security remind Cantor that we do not permit talking to the media. And make sure he understands the consequences."

"I could deal with him."

"Not yet."

He ran a quick internet search for *Taboo Magazine* while Sánchez waited. Jessica Kimball's picture appeared on the front page of the site. Her expression was determined, but she could not be a serious threat. Not to him.

"Is Kimball still in Zorita?"

"Security has confirmed she is registered at the Hotel Alfonso."

He looked at her picture again. She was definitely attractive, in a wholesome way that he didn't normally desire. He made up his mind. "Make dinner reservations. I will speak to her myself."

"Shall I put Kale on her, to be certain?"

He cocked his head for a moment before he shrugged. "Yes. Do that."

"One more thing," Sánchez said. "Tebogo reports the Antonovs are in place in Zambia. Pilot training is completed. The mission is on schedule."

Lopez smiled. Finally, some good news.

CHAPTER TWENTY-TWO

Thursday, August 18
6:00 p.m. CET
Zorita, Spain

A SLOW TRICKLE OF workers sauntered from the buildings and weaved their way out of packed parking areas as Jess walked toward her car.

Farther along the side of the plant was a larger pedestrian exit. A cement sidewalk crossed the parking lots leading to the street where bus stops lined the road.

Jess parked near a sign declaring *Investigación y desarrollo* and directed her attention through the pedestrian gate. If Elden was working inside today, she'd probably be in there, the Research and Development area.

She leaned against the Mini Cooper and checked to be sure her phone had connected to the local Spanish networks.

Minutes passed. Jess shifted her weight from foot to foot. Diesel buses came and went.

A loud horn sounded three blasts. Jess looked up. The sight

behind the pedestrian gate changed in an instant.

Several streams of people advanced toward the gate. Men and women, walkers and joggers, all intent on a common destination. The inevitable happened. The streams converged at the exit, twisting and jostling to merge.

She watched the exit, although actually locating Debora Elden in the throng was a long shot. Jess would recognize Elden's face, but would she see it clearly among the crowd of more than two thousand people streaming from the plant at quitting time?

The guard lifted the barrier across the exit and the workers streamed out. Some went toward the parking lots and others headed to the bus stops. The joggers continued to jog. Walkers broke into a run waving to catch buses down the street.

Jess could see the faces of people only on her side of the throng. She threaded her way into the crowd, working to a street lamp anchored in the middle of the flow.

The concrete pillar was an immovable object. People diverted around it, creating twice as many faces she could observe. Elden could have used another exit in a different area of the plant, but this was the best Jess could do for now.

She studied the mob. Most wore light clothing in muted colors. Here and there, one carried a briefcase, but almost everyone grasped a bag. Tiny backpacks were popular with girls. The women carried handbags with long straps and the men clutched tailored pouches, some with short hand straps.

After a while, the river of workers became a trickle.

Rush hour was over.

Jess spied an attractive woman, partly obscured by a tall, thin man with short, dark hair and designer stubble. Her hair was cropped short, but it was thick and red-brown, and her face glowed like a younger girl. Debora Elden. No doubt.

Jess left the protection of the lamppost, and moved to intercept.

The man with designer stubble gesticulated with his hands in the Latin way. Elden carried an overstuffed green canvas satchel with both hands. They broke into a jog toward the last red bus, diesel engine chugging lazily.

Jess rushed after them, but they boarded the bus just as the driver closed the doors. The bus set off.

Jess ran toward the bus. The driver stopped two feet from the curb, opened the door, and waved her on.

She stepped onto the bus and held out her credit card.

The driver shook his head and scowled. He tapped a sign that showed an icon of a credit card with a superimposed red circle with a slash across it. No credit cards. Cash only.

Jess looked at the passengers. Elden and her companion were seated toward the back. Impatient travelers stared at her.

The driver said something she didn't catch.

"I need a ride," she said, holding her card out again. "I don't have any cash."

The driver shook his head and flicked his hand toward the door.

"But—"

He glared.

She stepped off.

The doors closed, and the engine revved. She jogged away from the black cloud of diesel fumes as the bus pulled into traffic.

The Mini Cooper was only a hundred yards ahead. She'd catch up easily.

CHAPTER TWENTY-THREE

Thursday, August 18
6:10 p.m. CET
Zorita, Spain

JESS GLANCED BEHIND HER to check the bus's progress as she dodged between the cars on the way to her Mini. She hopped in, started up, raced out, and looped around the periphery of the parking lot.

The bus reached a junction at the end of the street, and disappeared from view.

She stomped on the gas and the Mini Cooper responded, leaping forward with a chirp from its tires. She weaved around a moped and squeezed through the traffic lights as they turned amber.

The Mini clung to the road like a go-cart, staying flat as she twisted the wheel ninety degrees.

Several cars and a delivery truck were between her and the bus. A block later, two cars in front of her turned off, leaving only a Nissan and the delivery truck between her and the bus.

The delivery truck slowed. Its hazard lights flashed.

The oncoming lane was empty.

Jess eased out into the center of the road.

The Nissan did the same.

The truck slowed further.

The gap between her and the bus widened.

Jess downshifted. The Mini's engine responded with a whining noise.

The Nissan's turn signal flashed to indicate he was heading around the truck.

Jess kept close behind.

The truck braked to a stop.

Jess pressed on the accelerator, expecting to pass.

The Nissan slowed and turned left.

Jess stomped on the brakes.

The Mini's tires squealed.

The hood dipped as the car's mass angled forward.

The Nissan flashed in front of her. A woman glared from the driver's side window.

Jess held a white-knuckled grip on the wheel too hard to wave an apology.

A car behind her honked long and loud and passed her on the inside, weaving back out to clear the parked delivery truck.

The next driver was more polite. A silver Ford slowed to a halt and flashed its lights to let her go first.

Jess rammed her car into first, veered around the truck, and raced back onto the correct side of the road.

She caught a glimpse of red as the bus turned right. The car in front of her this time was quick. She reached the turn in a few moments.

A one-way sign indicated she was heading in the correct direction.

She turned without looking closely.

Her first reaction was to brake and her second was to curse her luck.

This wasn't a street, it was a bus station.

It opened out into three lanes. An arrow pointed cars to the right-hand lane. Buses were parked along three islands. Pedestrians milled from bus to bus. None of the buses were moving, which gave her no clue which bus Elden had boarded.

All the buses looked identical.

In her haste to run to her car, she'd neglected to read the bus number. She couldn't remember the advertising on its side. All the ads were similar.

She had no choice but to check each bus, one at a time.

She slowed the Mini alongside a line of vehicles and dove into a small space perfect for the diminutive car.

Two buses pulled away. She ran across the road watching the right-side windows as the buses passed, hoping to find Elden still sitting where Jess had seen her.

Elden wasn't there.

It wasn't a far trip from the plant. Maybe she could have changed buses and moved to the opposite side.

Jess darted through the crowds lining up along the first island, checking the buses on either side. No Elden.

As she crossed to the second island, she caught a flash of neon green. She stared. Elden's canvas satchel?

Jess ran alongside the bus.

Yes! She fist-pumped the air.

Elden was there. Still seated beside Designer Stubble, her green bag wedged against the window.

Jess memorized the vehicle's numberplate, and dashed to her Mini. She squeezed out of the tight space and edged down to the end of the island.

The flow of traffic was one-way. The bus would have to pass her.

A driver honked his horn because her car was poking out into the travel lane. Jess ignored him to focus on Elden's bus as it passed by. She pulled out after it.

This time, no vehicles blocked her view of the bus. She breathed easy. The bus stopped occasionally. When it did, Jess moved close to the curb, leaning over to watch the passengers disembark.

After fifteen minutes, they were approaching the busy center of Zorita.

The bus slowed by a line of shops. Jess leaned over, watching the passengers.

Elden disembarked with the same man, and they walked north along the sidewalk. Her neon green bag was unmistakable.

The bus pulled away. Jess scanned for a parking space. The curb along the shops was painted yellow, which she assumed meant no parking. The yellow line disappeared around the corner, but the street was packed with parked cars.

She raced around the block without any luck, and emerged onto the main road again.

Elden had the green satchel folded up under her arm. She and Designer Stubble exited a dry cleaner. They continued north, away from Jess.

Jess rolled past the walking couple. She turned at the corner and halfway down the side street she found a car pulling out. She waited on the side of the road with her signal flashing to claim the spot.

In her rear-view mirror, she saw Elden and the man cross the side street.

Jess twisted the steering wheel hard, dived into the parking spot, and ran after the couple.

She spotted them two blocks away. She followed briskly.

Catching up with Elden in the street might not be the best idea. Ordinary people didn't appreciate being interviewed in public places.

She slowed her pace when she was a block behind Elden, walking purposefully. They were headed home after a day's work, not idling time away on a stroll.

They went into a supermarket. Jess lingered at the front of the store until Elden was in line at the checkout.

Jess stepped outside. The light was fading. Cars streamed by. She recognized the silver Ford that had let her into the flow of traffic earlier. A minute passed.

The supermarket windows were wide and tall, brightly backlit. Jess glanced inside again. An old lady was at the register where Elden had been standing. Elden and the man were no longer in line.

Jess went inside and walked along the row of cashiers. She hurried to the rear of the store. *Dammit!* They must have exited through the back door.

Jess darted outside. She had driven this street looking for a parking space. The sidewalks were as busy here as they were out front.

She peered in both directions. A flash of green to the north might be Elden's satchel. Otherwise, the couple had simply disappeared.

Jess headed north at a brisk pace.

She dodged left and right, looking two moves ahead to avoid being caught behind slower pedestrian traffic.

Up ahead, she spotted Elden turning into an alley. Jess stepped out into the road and hustled around the traffic. When she reached the alley, she ran to the far end just as Elden climbed toward an upstairs apartment.

Jess approached the building. A locked door with an intercom and a single button. She pressed the button and heard a buzz somewhere inside, but no one answered. The building contained several apartments, so she waited on the sidewalk.

Thirty minutes later, no one had entered or exited. She rang the buzzer again, but got no response. Again.

Her adrenaline had waned and she realized how exhausted she was. She needed food and sleep.

She shrugged, and walked back to her Mini.

Finding Elden had been a stroke of luck. Tomorrow Jess would be ready.

CHAPTER TWENTY-FOUR

Thursday, August 18
6:45 p.m. CET
Zorita, Spain

JESS QUICKLY CALCULATED THE time back in Denver, which was eight hours earlier. Henry should be in his office. She pushed his number on her speed dial. She waited through a long delay and several clicks before his phone rang. He answered almost immediately.

"How was the flight?"

"Exactly as expected. Which is all we can hope for these days, right?"

He laughed. "And Europe?"

"I can't speak for all of it, but the part I'm in is pretty nice. I found Elden."

"Already?"

"She works at Grupo Lopez."

"What did she say?"

"Nothing. I saw her leaving work, but lost her in the crowds. I'll try again tomorrow."

"I have a little more info for you. Elden traveled from Zorita to Chatham three times in the last three months. Always on a weekend."

"Interesting."

"And it could still be perfectly innocent."

"Apart from the fact she hasn't told her family and friends that she's moved abroad and doesn't tell them when she's coming in and out, either."

"Also, Remington's team questioned Winter. She's a pretty tough cookie, apparently. She denied all but the vaguest knowledge of Debora Elden, and swore Elden does not have access to Kelso Products labs."

"I used her card to get to the door of a BSL level 3 lab."

"I didn't pass that information along." He cleared his throat. "Anyway, Winter seemed agitated when she was told Elden's cell phone had been located in Zorita."

"But was she surprised?" Jess asked.

"Dunno. She admitted that Grupo Lopez is a competitor. She speculated they're working on something new."

"How does she know that?"

"Apparently, the company that supplies Kelso Products with equipment for their labs also supplies Grupo Lopez."

"Ah. What kind of new product?"

"Winter didn't know, but apparently they ordered some expensive stuff from the equipment supplier. The sort of things used in a top-end biological lab."

"Are you going to follow up?"

"Me? No. It's not my case. Remington's team asked the Spanish police to question Elden, and they might do it. But since

Elden was in Spain at the time of the explosion, Remington isn't too concerned with her."

"Great." Jess ran a hand through her hair and closed her eyes.

"Sorry. But Remington thinks the link between Elden and Grupo Lopez is not relevant."

"Any links from Alex Cole to Grupo Lopez?"

"Don't know, and Remington isn't going to spend any resources on that. He says it's unlikely that a foreign competitor set off the bomb."

She sighed. "Well I'm not leaving here before I've talked to Elden."

"Just don't get too attached to Elden as a suspect, Jess." He'd lowered his voice to the tone he used when they were alone.

"You mean I should accept that Alex Cole actually is a bomber."

"It's looking that way."

"A bomber with no motive."

"No *known* motive." He paused. "Yet."

Jess sighed. Henry could be right. She could have wasted two days and a good deal of the magazine's money and might never have anything publishable here.

"Maybe," she replied. "But that answer still doesn't feel right to me."

CHAPTER TWENTY-FIVE

Thursday, August 18
6:45 p.m. CET
Zorita, Spain

HADLOW WATCHED THE BLONDE woman return to her rented Mini Cooper. She talked on her phone for several minutes.

He stepped back into a shadowed doorway out of sight. Four years as a commando and seven years in the British SAS before he'd moved to MI-6 had trained him well.

He was too tall and fit to remain invisible in a crowd. He wore clothes meant to conceal and avoided situations where he was likely to be spotted or identified.

A sepsis outbreak in Africa three months ago rang alarm bells everywhere. Two hundred people died. The cause of the outbreak remained unknown, but MI-6, the CIA, and other agencies were convinced the outbreak was caused by a new bio-weapon.

A terrorist was killing people with poison. Had to be. Nothing else made sense.

Hadlow and other agents were dispatched to chemical plants across the globe. He'd drawn the short straw. Monitoring scientists at pesticide manufacturer Grupo Lopez had been nothing but a snooze fest.

Until the blonde turned up.

She'd followed Felipe Cantor and the Elden girl from Grupo Lopez, but lost them in the crowds. She'd almost lost them at the bus station, but persevered. She was an amateur. But he gave her kudos for sheer dogged effort.

Who was she and why was she following Cantor and Elden?

She finished her call, started her car, and pulled out.

Hadlow hustled to his silver Ford, and followed a half dozen cars behind her toward the center of Zorita.

She stopped at the Hotel Alfonso. Not the best hotel in Zorita, but by far the oldest. A sprawling place with towers and domes and balconies. The entrance was shielded from sun and rain alike by a portico shaped like a tent with a gracefully curved roof.

She pulled up in front. A young valet rushed to open her door and fetch her luggage.

Hadlow swung his Ford into the first space he found, and jogged into the lobby.

The woman was checking in.

He sat in a giant red velvet armchair and consulted his phone, surreptitiously taking pictures.

Another porter escorted her to the elevators.

Hadlow remained seated. In the close confines of the Alfonso, she was easily monitored.

Three minutes later, the porter returned. Hadlow followed him outside to the valet stand. Twenty euros later, Hadlow knew the woman's name and room number.

He returned to his car, pulled out his phone, and dialed his boss.

"Yes?" Nash's thick accent came from the north of England.

"We've got company. An American. Jessica Kimball. Five-four, curly blonde, light but athletic. Arrived today. Probably flew in on a commercial airline."

"Anything more specific?"

"She tailed Elden and Cantor."

"Make contact?"

"No. And she's not a professional, unless US standards are slipping."

"They don't have agents in Zorita."

"Well, it would be nice to have a little help here. I've only got two hands," Hadlow replied.

"We've been over this. I've got no one I can send to Spain. We're all stretched thin as it is. Anything else?"

"I'll send her picture momentarily. She made a long phone call twenty minutes ago on a mobile." Hadlow paused, but Nash said nothing more. "I've got her room number. I'll check it when she goes out. Meantime, you'll need to earn some of that fat salary you rake in."

"Keep the lip to yourself. You're there to do what you signed up for. Remember that." Nash was old school. Do the job. Keep your opinions to yourself. Those were the tenets he lived by. He expected his subordinates to comply as well.

Hadlow ground his teeth. "I need to know whether her arrival is important and exactly who I'm dealing with. Because if it comes down to it, I'm the one who has to do the dealing."

Hadlow hung up immediately. He had no time or patience for Nash's inevitable tongue-lashing. He'd endured the shouted lectures from his superiors once. Long ago. When he was a soldier and had no choice.

But not now. MI-6 wanted results. As long as he delivered results, Nash's preferences were irrelevant.

Besides that, Nash wasn't sending reinforcements no matter what Hadlow wanted. He was wasting his breath even bringing the matter up.

Hadlow was on his own.

CHAPTER TWENTY-SIX

Thursday, August 18
7:15 p.m. CET
Zorita, Spain

THE ALFONSO'S STYLISH CONTINENTAL vibe was accomplished by pastels mixed with strong colors and heavy gilt on everything. The bed was firm and the bathroom gleamed white and gold and silver.

Jess's phone rang. The display said the number was unknown, which meant nothing because she was outside the US. "This is Jess Kimball."

"Vanna Sánchez from Grupo Lopez." She spoke with a distinct Spanish accent, but her command of English was excellent. "I understand you were at our offices this afternoon."

"Right," Her attention perked up and her desire for a nap disappeared.

"Rafa Lopez, our CEO, would like to have dinner with you this evening."

Jess frowned. "Actually, I was hoping to meet with Debora Elden."

"We will pass your message along, of course. In the meantime, Mr. Lopez is familiar with your magazine, and would consider it an honor to host you at dinner this evening."

Jess raised her eyebrows. The request seemed odd, to say the least. CEOs rarely sought her out unless they wanted favorable coverage in *Taboo Magazine*. She wasn't working on anything related to Grupo Lopez and didn't plan to. Unless the Alex Cole story led straight back to Grupo Lopez. In which case her story wouldn't be favorable at all.

"It's dinner, Ms. Kimball. Surely, you'll need to eat," Vanna coaxed, but the underlying message came across. An invitation from Rafa Lopez was not to be refused. "I assure you the meal will be excellent."

"I'm sure it will." Jess frowned. Vanna Sánchez wasn't the only one with an iron will. "Tell Mr. Lopez to bring Ms. Elden along and I'll be more than happy to join them."

"Shall we say eight-thirty? I will arrange a car to collect you at the Alfonso." Vanna Sánchez hung up before Jess could say anything else.

How did Vanna Sánchez know Jess had checked into the Alfonso?

Jess stared at her phone. *Taboo Magazine* was international. Requests for features were fairly common. But escalating from an impromptu visit with a receptionist all the way to a command performance with the CEO the same day was unprecedented in her experience.

She glanced at the clock. Not much time to grab a shower before the car arrived.

The water was hot and invigorating, but the bathroom's

ventilation did little to dissipate the moisture. She dried off in the bedroom, then tamed her curly hair at the dressing table.

She hadn't packed for dinner with a CEO, but she felt good in an ivory silk dress and heels. She clipped a gold chain around her ankle and stared at herself in the mirror. Fashion had never concerned her. She was here for business and she looked like it. Which was exactly what she wanted to convey to Rafa Lopez.

At eight-thirty, the phone by the bed rang. A young man said her car had arrived. She checked her voice recorder, unplugged her cell phone from its charger, and dropped both into her purse.

A tall man with muddy brown eyes wearing a loose jacket followed her down the corridor to the elevator. They stood in silence until the doors opened. He gestured for her to enter first.

She stood in the back corner of the descending elevator. When the doors opened, he gestured forward and she moved to exit. He started walking too soon and bumped into her. He flashed a sheepish grin and when she nodded forgiveness, he hurried off in the opposite direction across the lobby.

A black Mercedes-Maybach idled under the awning at the front entrance. The chrome trim was a smoky gray and the windows were darker black than legally allowed back home.

A chauffeur stood at attention by the rear passenger door until Jess approached. "Miss Kimball?"

She nodded.

He opened the door. A woman was seated inside.

Jess stopped.

"I am Vanna Sánchez, Ms. Kimball. Please join me."

The vehicle was huge. Jess stepped inside and walked across the vast interior to reach the rear seat, which was smooth and supple. The air was rich with aromas of highly polished wood and soft leather. Discreet lights glowed under the seats and the headliner displayed random pinpricks of light like twinkling stars in the distance. Smoked glass separated the passenger seats from the driver's.

The chauffeur closed the door with a soft thump.

Sánchez offered an ethereal smile, but not a friendly one. Deep blue eyes set in flawless skin and full lips tapered to sharp points on either side of her mouth gave her a distinctive beauty. Her silk jumpsuit was padded with incredibly square shoulders. Her upright posture seemed to float above the seat.

Jess held out her hand. "Jessica Kimball."

The woman gripped Jess's fingertips with her own and squeezed for a fraction of a second.

Jess leaned back into the luxurious seat, and fastened her seatbelt.

The woman pressed a button on a console between the seats. "Drive on," she instructed.

The Maybach moved away silently.

Vanna Sánchez said nothing more.

Jess stared through the darkened window. Only faint shapes and bright lights were visible. Soon, Zorita's city lights were left behind. Her heart rate picked up a fraction.

"Where are we going?" she asked.

Vanna glanced sideways. "Rafa's villa."

Jess wasn't immediately concerned about her safety, but she didn't appreciate being hijacked. She found her phone and sent a message. "I'll just let my editor know where he can find me."

Vanna smirked.

A few minutes later, the driver slowed and turned into a long driveway between the trees lining the road.

A gate crossed the driveway at a stone pillbox security building that looked at least a hundred years old. A guard approached the Mercedes with a flashlight, which he pointed through the dark glass. The light focused first on the driver, then Jess, and finally, very briefly, Vanna.

The driver released the trunk. The guard finished his inspection and closed the lid with a barely perceptible thump.

The gate opened, and the chauffeur drove through.

On the other side of the gate and the line of trees, an expansive lawn ran up to an enormous four-story house lit by hundreds of lights.

The walls were a honey-hued wash of old rocks and artisan mortar. The roof's traditional Spanish barrel tiles joined at complex angles and shapes where several sections of the house came together.

The road ran up to the front door in a sweeping arc. The area around the front door was festooned with plants, and the plants were festooned with lights. The front door, at least ten feet tall, arched at the top and was made from aged wood. Hidden lights gave a glow to the outside edges as if entering the house would transport the visitor to another world.

Windows punctuated the stone at artistically irregular intervals, which gave the giant structure a comforting feel. As if the place was a home created by love, instead of a large crew and serious construction equipment.

Despite Vanna's cold reception, arriving at Rafa Lopez's villa was magical.

The Mercedes-Maybach rolled to a stop with the rear door in a direct line with the entrance to the villa.

Jess moved for the door handle. Vanna placed her hand on Jess's arm to stop her.

The chauffeur walked around the car, and opened the door.

Vanna released her. "Make the most of your evening."

"You're not joining us?"

"We have a busy day tomorrow." She offered a faint smile. "Please don't keep him up too late."

Jess stepped out into the evening and watched as the Mercedes drove away.

The villa's entrance opened and a butler in a jet-black suit stepped out. "This way Miss Kimball. Señor Lopez is waiting."

CHAPTER TWENTY-SEVEN

Thursday, August 18
8:50 p.m. CET
Zorita, Spain

HADLOW SLOWED HIS SILVER Ford and cruised past the driveway. The big Maybach had stopped at a security post in front of a wrought iron gate. A guard was checking the vehicle.

Hadlow rolled on, keeping his foot frozen on the accelerator, not raising or lowering the tone of the engine. He'd been worryingly close to the Maybach at times, but the chauffer hadn't seemed to notice.

He took a left turn at the first opportunity, following the edge of Lopez's giant estate until he found a suitable place to pull off the road. He lowered the windows and turned off the engine.

The night was still. He listened, occasionally angling his head to better hear or locate a sound. He checked the rearview mirror constantly, as he had done throughout the evening.

After a minute he was satisfied he was alone. He stepped out of the car holding a small black box.

Inside the box were several circuit cards, with wires trailing between them. A large battery took up half the space. Two tiny, dim LEDs were illuminated. The red light confirmed the box was powered on, the green light confirmed the device was recording. He placed the box in the crook of a tree limb.

Kimball would remain at Lopez's mansion for several hours. The rural countryside provided little cover for covert observation. The recorder would suffice. He'd collect the results later.

Hadlow drove away from Lopez's estate. Two miles later, his cell phone rang. "How can I help you, Nash?"

"Anything?" Nash asked.

"The reporter is still alive, if that's what you mean."

"Very glad to hear it. It's always inconvenient to have to tell our friends at Langley that we watched one of their citizens die."

Nash meant it as a joke. Black humor. A pen-pusher's failed attempt to bond with a man in the field. Hadlow clenched his teeth and waited.

Nash coughed to cover his embarrassment and restarted the stalled conversation. "Is she with Lopez?"

"Just arrived, and the recorder is running."

"The device?"

He smiled to himself. "In her bag since our elevator ride."

"I'll be waiting for the upload," Nash said, his tone suggesting he was unimpressed with Hadlow's spycraft.

"It'll be a few hours." Hadlow hung up.

He took a meandering route back to his hotel, looping around a series of city blocks, and parked a five-minute walk away.

CHAPTER TWENTY-EIGHT

Thursday, August 18
9:00 p.m. CET
Zorita, Spain

JESS'S SHOES CLICKED AS she followed the butler across the marble floor. An ornate staircase led up to a grand balcony. Two sets of double doors on either side of the foyer, and a corridor to the right of the stairs led deeper into the house.

The doors and the stairs were the same dark wood. The warm patina glowed after years of polishing.

The butler opened the first set of doors on the right. He stepped inside the room, and held the door for Jess.

She walked into a ballroom with a parquet floor and life-size pictures hanging on the walls. Gilt everywhere. Georgian Regency period furnishings dotted the expanse, grouped in small clusters. Each table held a flickering candle.

Rafa Lopez stood near a fireplace on the west wall. He was not quite six feet tall. Salt and pepper hair marked him as being firmly into his fifties, but his brilliant blue eyes flashed like those of a much younger man. His suit was tailored for a perfect fit to his lean, athletic body.

He looked more like an aging soccer star than a mogul.

He walked toward Jess. "Welcome, welcome, welcome."

He shook her hand firmly and gestured to the room with a sweep of his arm. "My home is yours."

"It's a wonderful house," Jess replied. "You must be very proud of it."

He smiled widely, white teeth and blue eyes sparkling against his handsomely tanned skin. "I cannot deny that my home gives me great pleasure. Please, come in. Let us talk."

He led Jess to a pair of red velvet armchairs beside a gold and black Louis XVI occasional table. Two glasses and a bottle of red wine waited on a silver tray on the table. The wine had been uncorked. He held out the bottle for Jess to read the label.

"From the vineyard of Alvaro Palacios' L'Ermita. To the north of here. A beautiful area. Vines from the start of the last century." He pointed to the label, "*Velles Vinyes*. Old-vines. The very heart and soul of my country."

"Thank you," Jess said.

He poured two generous portions.

Jess held the glass in her hands and swirled the wine. The rich berry aroma with hints of spice reached her nose.

Lopez took a sip, holding his mouth closed as the aftertaste worked its way over his palate.

Jess was no expert in wine tasting, but she followed his lead. The flavor was intense and fruity. The spice and the alcohol warmed her throat.

"Raspberry," Lopez said. "Really there are no raspberries in it, but it is the dominant impression. Most excellent."

He placed his glass on the table. "Tell me, you have traveled alone, but do you have a family?"

Jess shook her head. "It's complicated."

He laughed. "That is why we call them families."

"I lost my son when he was just a baby."

Lopez's face fell. "I am most sorry. Accident? Illness?"

"Abducted."

Air hissed between his teeth. "Terrible. Only animals steal babies."

"I'm still looking for him."

He nodded. "Of course, of course. The police? They have no…"

"They have done what they can, but now I rely on private investigators."

"I cannot imagine." He tutted.

Jess sipped her wine. "Where is Debora Elden? I was told she'd be joining us."

His eyebrows shot up. "Really?"

Jess didn't believe he was the least surprised. "That's why I accepted your invitation."

"I'm sorry for the confusion." He shrugged. "She works for Grupo Lopez, but I am not personally acquainted with her."

Warmth flooded her cheeks, but she tamped her annoyance. "What work does Ms. Elden do at Grupo Lopez?"

He cocked his head as if he was merely curious. "What is your interest in Miss Elden?"

"Her ex-boyfriend is accused of a bombing attack. She knows him better than I do. I want to talk to her about him."

"That is a serious situation." Lopez's eyes widened, again throwing off a disingenuous vibe.

Jess was fairly certain that he knew the answers to every

question he'd asked so far. "Several people died, and many more were injured."

"In the USA?"

"Yes."

He raised his eyebrows. "The explosion at Kelso Products that's been on our news?"

"Yes."

"This is most concerning. You think Miss Elden was connected with this?"

"The authorities say it doesn't seem likely." Jess shook her head. "I think she may be able to help me with our reporting on the incident."

"Forgive me, when you say *our*?"

"*Taboo Magazine*."

"But this is a criminal investigation, surely?"

"Of course."

"The authorities have not approached us about Miss Elden."

"They are pursuing other lines of inquiry."

He considered this for a moment. "Then they do not believe Miss Elden is involved?"

"I'm sure you understand that the authorities do not confide in me. I can't say what they believe or don't believe."

"So the American slang for your visit is a 'fishing trip,' isn't it?"

"My magazine wouldn't send me here on a mere fishing expedition, Mr. Lopez."

"Call me Rafa. Please. Everyone does." He sipped his wine.

"What does Debora Elden do at Grupo Lopez?" Jess asked again.

"She works in our research department. We are known for our innovation. We employ many researchers."

"What sort of research is Miss Elden conducting?"

"I am not sure of her specialization." He offered a lopsided grin. "If I had known you were so interested, I would have more complete answers for you."

With significant effort, Jess kept a smile in place. She had approached Grupo Lopez about one thing, and that was Debora Elden. So, when the CEO asked to meet with her, she had expected him to have something to say on the subject.

"I can come to your office tomorrow," she said, as pleasantly as she could manage.

"You are very persistent, but yes, come tomorrow afternoon." He smiled. "For now, please enjoy your wine."

She sipped obligingly before she returned to her agenda. "What does Grupo Lopez produce in Zorita?"

He stood, and topped off both glasses. "Shall we take a walk? I believe the air will have cooled by now."

She followed him through a door into another large room. He flipped a switch, and the far wall of French doors began to fold like a concertina until the entire space opened to the garden.

A flagstone patio ran the width of this section of the house. Statues and plants, artfully lighted, dotted across the flagstones.

In the middle of the patio was a tall table and two bar stools. Tiny candles floated in a crystal bowl. The air was cooling and fresh after the day's heat. She put her glass on the table and wondered when they would eat so that she could leave.

The garden sloped gently down from the house. A large fountain gushed water into a reflecting pool.

"This is beautiful," Jess said.

He smiled toward the view. "It gives me great pleasure, but..."

Jess waited.

He turned to her. "This house, this garden, you, me? We all are objects in time. We come and go. When I bought this house, it was almost a ruin." He waved a hand at the garden, "What is now lush and green was overrun with weeds. I have changed everything here. Perhaps, in time to come, the next owners will change these things, too."

Jess nodded. "Beauty is in the eye of the beholder."

"But more than that. Possessions are trinkets in the universe. People live and die. Too soon, we will be forgotten." He clinched his fist and snapped his fingers open. "Poof. We're gone."

He looked straight into Jess's eyes. "There is only one thing that stands the test of time. Only one thing that cannot be erased... Ideas and the benefits to mankind that we make from them."

"I guess." She narrowed her eyes, wondering what he wanted her to take away from here tonight. She recognized Rafa Lopez as another in a long line of CEOs seeking positive publicity from *Taboo Magazine*.

"The inventor of the wheel is lost before the age of communication, but his invention? No one knows who invented money, but have you used money today?"

"Those ideas probably didn't emanate from a single person."

He laughed. "Exactly! But Aristotle's logic? Or Euclid's geometry? Newton's physics or Darwin's natural selection? Einstein's special theory of relativity?"

"Marx and Engels," she said, nodding. "Of course, these were great men throughout time."

He held out his hands, his palms toward her in agreement. "Yes! You see? Ideas and the men who generate them are never forgotten. They become immortal."

She nodded. "Yes."

Rafa smiled more broadly, as if she were a particularly apt pupil of whom he, the great professor, especially approved. "But do you know what you need to spark a great idea?"

Jess shrugged.

"*A great problem.* Not trivial. Big, sweeping, intractable. Something that has defeated great minds for centuries. So large it paralyzes the mind." He stopped to breathe, his arms stretched wide like DaVinci's Vitruvian Man. "That is what you need for a revolutionary idea. With the right problem, comes the opportunity for immortality that few will ever reach."

"Like Aristotle and Euclid." She paused and smiled. "Or Henry Ford."

Rafa laughed for a while, as if mentioning Ford in the same breath as Aristotle and Euclid was hilarious. But she had the feeling he was more interested in collecting billions for a product like Ford, than any grand idea simply to serve humanity.

When he stopped laughing, Jess asked, "Is that what you're doing at your plant in Zorita? Working on a great idea for an intractable problem?"

CHAPTER TWENTY-NINE

THE SILENCE LASTED A long time before he lifted his gaze. "The air is good, no?"

It took her a moment to change gears. "It is refreshing after the day's heat."

"Do you notice the insects?"

She looked and listened. "Now that you ask, no. I don't."

"Do you know why?"

She cocked her head. "A Grupo Lopez product?"

Lopez walked a circle in front of the table. "In the past, evenings in this area were miserable. Multitudes of flying insects made life too difficult."

"It's the same in most areas."

"But it doesn't have to be." He stretched his arms wide. "Now we are able to enjoy the evening."

"Because you've used a special pesticide here to kill them all?" Jess frowned and curled her lip.

Rafa's eyebrows shot up. "You say that as if taking control of our environment is a bad thing."

Jess nodded. "How does that old song go? Give me spots on my grapes, and leave me the bird food?"

"But why not do both? Treat the problems and keep all the good things as well?"

"How do you propose to do that?"

He walked to the edge of the patio. "DDT went too far, but it was a crude start. A first jab at what we really needed."

"And what's that, exactly?"

"Look at us. Here. Now." He gestured beyond the patio. "People like us want freedom from insects to provide a certain lifestyle. For many, the issue is not luxury but survival."

Jess frowned.

"Mosquitoes are a plague across the face of the earth. In your own country the numbers are growing. The USA conducts large-scale control programs. There is even suspicion that as the DDT is finally disappearing from your ecosystem, mosquitoes are coming back in greater numbers and even stronger."

"I've heard that said, but I'm not sure about the science."

He laughed. "Many countries cannot afford the control programs that are used in America. They need a better solution."

"A solution that you and Grupo Lopez have created?"

"Unfortunately not." He shook his head. "But this is a truly great problem, don't you think?"

"But it is the great problem you're researching at your plant here in Zorita, isn't it?"

He turned to face her, nostrils flared. "How many people do you think die from malaria every year?"

It was a terrible statistic. She knew it well because Alex Cole had mentioned it two days ago. Softly, she said, "A million people die from malaria."

"A million. Yes. Each and every year. A million people.

Dead. Gone. A most horrible way to die, too. Severe shaking. Chills. High fever. Profuse sweating. Vomiting. Diarrhea. Abdominal pain." Lopez stepped toward Jess, both hands clenched. "And those who survive?"

Jess nodded. "Yes."

"My mother had malaria. I watched her life-long miserable existence with recurrences of the original infection that couldn't be eradicated." He sat on his stool and took a drink of wine.

"I'm sorry," she said.

"Thank you. She's been gone a long time. I don't speak of her often." He nodded and squared his shoulders and the anger was back. "But what do we do? The great nations of this earth? The big industries? The millionaires and billionaires? What do our politicians say about this terrible mosquito-borne disease?"

"I don't know."

"Nothing." He shook his head. "They say nothing."

"There is research being done—"

"No. There is not." He shook his head more violently. "Experiments on single samples, maybe two. Useless. This is a big problem. It needs big thinking. Big experiments."

"Forgive me, but you can't be the only person to realize this."

He laughed. "True, true. But your CDC is barely funded for the effort, and I know of three of our competitors who have given up their research because it is expensive and...difficult." He emphasized the word with scorn.

"Like who?"

He waved her question away. "Every year lost is another million people dead. Governments, agencies, even non-governmental agencies drag their feet. And do you know why?"

She remained silent, certain he was about to enlighten her.

When he did, the scorn was palpable. "Because they are timorous, afraid of their own shadows, too scared to take necessary chances."

"So that's what you're doing. Taking chances." She cocked her head. "What kind of chances?"

"We are researching. We are spending our own money." He stabbed his thumb in his chest. "My money." He stood up, his arms in the air, including his entire estate in the gesture. "I would risk it all to solve this problem."

"And we will all be grateful if you figure this out."

"I'm not seeking gratitude." He shook his head. "I do it because the human race needs me to do it. So that no mothers, fathers, or children will die. It is a fight and a quest, and when the battle is won, I shall be remembered as the one who answered the call."

Jess nodded. An egomaniac. Like so many others who chased money, power, and immortality. "It sounds like a major effort."

He sighed and sat back down. "It is."

Jess waited for him to elaborate. When he didn't, she asked, "Is Debora Elden working on this research?"

"As I said," he smiled and shook his head, "I am not familiar with her or her work."

"But you will find out and tell me tomorrow when I come back to Grupo Lopez."

He stared at his garden. "Why are you so interested in Miss Elden's work? How is her work related to Alex Cole and this bomb?"

"I need a complete profile of his background. She's an important part of that background."

He shrugged. "I will see what I can do."

"Thank you." She sensed that was as far as he would go. Whether he would follow through on that vague promise was unlikely. "Do you know Marco Benito?"

He shook his head. "I can't say that I do."

The butler appeared and discreetly cleared his throat.

Rafa said, "I believe dinner is ready."

"Good because I'm starving." Jess finished her wine. "And afterward, I'll need to get back to my hotel. I have a lot of work left to do tonight. Shall I call a car?"

Rafa frowned. "That will not be necessary. You are my guest. I will take care of you."

His tone caused an involuntary shudder to travel down her body.

CHAPTER THIRTY

Thursday, August 18
11:55 p.m. CET
Zorita, Spain

RAFA LOPEZ SAT IN his library, cradling a snifter of brandy. Kimball had left thirty minutes ago. She was not what he'd expected. Her interest in Debora Elden was tedious. Elden was a minion. A nobody. Kimball should have focused on him and his work instead. Rafa had no further use for her.

Perhaps it was just as well. He was close to achieving the goal many believed impossible. He would become a legend. More importantly, the value of his stock would rise, and he would buy out his creditors. He would own Grupo Lopez once more.

Kimball's excuses for pursuing Elden were pathetic. Which meant she had secret reasons for her actions. Rafa could not allow Kimball to continue. He was too close to his goal now.

Vanna stood quietly at his side as he sifted through the papers she had prepared. The evidence was damning. He studied it carefully before reaching his final decision.

He said, "To be clear, Debora Elden has returned to the US three times since she started work for us."

Vanna peered down her aristocratic nose. "According to the terms of her contract, she was required to alert us to any foreign travel. She did not."

"I want to know everything she's been doing." He tilted his head to glance up at her. "Everything."

"I will handle that immediately."

Rafa noted Vanna's choice of words. Not arrange or organize, but handle. Vanna was excellent at her job. She understood him almost telepathically. She'd never disappointed him. Not once.

He pointed to a chart showing Elden's travel itineraries. "The destination is listed as Chicago."

"We do not have direct access to passenger history on American domestic flights. In the morning we will acquire the information from our contacts."

"Chicago is the most likely route to Chatham."

"We can't rule out other options," Vanna said, as if he needed to be reminded.

He nodded, although he already knew he was right. "We knew it was a risk taking her on, but her experience was vital."

"Are you finished with her, then?" Vanna asked.

"We must plan for contingencies." He pursed his lips. It was too bad, really. Elden was such a vibrant girl.

"Kale watches her as we speak."

"Good." he replied. "She's leaving for the south lab tomorrow. This trial is also vital. Keep her under observation at all times. Until we know the results of the trial, we must be prepared."

"By keeping her alive? Or shall I deal with her as I handled General Neto's hot tub date?"

"Alive. For the short term." He nodded slowly. "Later, the choice is yours."

She smiled and a light danced in her eyes. "And Kimball?"

He handed the sheaf of papers to Vanna. "A reputable contact in the US media would have served us well. But…"

Vanna nodded. Once. But she didn't suppress the warm smile that stole across her face. "I fear Ms. Kimball will have an unfortunate accident tomorrow."

CHAPTER THIRTY-ONE

Friday, August 19
6:00 a.m. CET
Zorita, Spain

THE HOTEL'S BED WAS sublime. The mattress was just the right combination of support and suppleness, and the duvet was light and sensuous to the touch. Jess slept well and awakened early.

The room's floor to ceiling drapes covered French doors that opened onto a balcony looking out over the front of the hotel.

There was a sophisticated coffee machine at the wet bar in the corner. She studied the pictograph instructions before opening a small bag of beans, dropping them into the automatic grinder, and pressing the espresso button.

The machine gurgled as it heated the water and ground the beans, followed by thirty seconds of hissing as it forced the water through the coffee. Heavy black liquid ran from a tube to a colorful espresso cup and saucer. The amazing aroma of perfectly brewed coffee filled the room.

She waited until the last drop had dripped from the tube then carried the espresso outside to sit at a small wooden table on the balcony.

She savored the taste and warmth in her throat as she drank.

From below the horizon, the first rays of the sun were reaching Spain. A warm honeyed light picked out wisps of cloud in a sky made deep blue by the blackness of night.

It was almost six a.m. and the city was coming to life. The traffic was building. White panel vans buzzed through the streets, taking workers to job sites. A few cars were filled with office workers, keen to get a head start on the day.

She cradled the tiny cup's handle between her thumb and forefinger as she savored her espresso. The caffeine tingled her senses and chased off her jet lag.

She finished the last of the amazing brew and placed the cup back in the saucer with a chink.

The sun's light grew stronger by the minute. Drawing herself away from it was harder than prying her body from the luxurious bed, but she had work to do.

The shower was a large glass walk-in affair. Three jets of soft water produced an endless stream of soap bubbles, providing a good excuse to stand under the jets a while longer to rinse.

She toweled off, leaving her natural curls to air-dry while she dressed and applied light makeup.

Five minutes later, she left the hotel, collecting a lemon magdalena and another strong espresso in the lobby on the way out. She took the coffee with milky foam this time, to ease the caffeine jolt.

Rafa Lopez had promised to follow up on Elden, but Jess didn't expect him to do her job. She could find Elden and ask her own questions.

Her Mini Cooper's navigation system had the Grupo Lopez location stored in memory. She followed directions through a maze of twists and turns to the plant. At the traffic lights, she nibbled the muffin and finished the last of the coffee after she reached the Grupo Lopez parking lot.

She parked close to the bus stops. A few workers were already arriving. She stood by the same lamppost as the day before, directly between the buses and the main gates. From here, she had a clear view of the workers who used this entrance. Since Elden left from this point yesterday, she might enter here today.

Fifteen minutes later, workers streamed in. The parking lot filled quickly. People walked fast, heads down, morning bodies on autopilot. Like yesterday, everyone seemed to carry a bag of some sort. Everything from plastic shopping bags to handbags to briefcases. Many bulged.

The young man Elden left with yesterday, the unshaven one, walked past. He was alone this morning. He paid no attention to Jess. She might have stopped him, but finding Elden was more important.

Fifteen minutes later, when the horn blast pierced the air three times to signal the beginning of the work shift, the last few workers rushed inside.

Debora Elden was not among them.

CHAPTER THIRTY-TWO

Friday, August 19
8:30 a.m. CET
Zorita, Spain

SHE KNEW WHERE DESIGNER Stubble lived. Maybe Elden was there. Or, maybe she could get a name from one of his neighbors to match with his handsome face. The idea was thin, but it was the only lead she'd managed to find.

She put her car in gear, and followed the route she had taken the afternoon before. It was more difficult than she thought. Following the bus was easy. Remembering the route now was a lot harder. She doubled back twice before she found the bus station.

Finally, she made it to the street where Elden and the man had left the bus. She drove farther on to the alley near his apartment and found a place to park.

The alley was deserted. She walked uneasily, checking behind her every few steps. A few small cars dashed across the alley's entrance now and then. She reached the apartment building. She saw no movement behind the windows.

She approached and entered the building. A row of mailboxes was set into the wall on the right. The stairs were on the left.

The mailboxes were secured by padlocks of various types, suggesting the locks were supplied by the residents. The boxes were numbered, and a few doors had names handwritten in black marker. She had no idea which number belonged to Elden's friend.

She climbed the stairs, the boards creaking underfoot.

On the second floor, a door opened a few inches, held in place by a security chain. A woman peered through the gap. She spoke in simple Spanish that Jess could understand. "What do you want?"

Jess struggled to reply. "I'm…looking for a man. Debora Elden's friend."

The woman shook her head. "No entiendo."

Jess mimed a beard on her face. "El Joven?"

"Ah." The woman pointed up the stairs. "Numero ocho."

Jess nodded. "Gracias."

The woman closed her door, and Jess climbed two more flights to reach number 8. She pressed the doorbell button and heard a whimsical tune play inside.

She pressed her ear to the door. Silence. She tried the bell again. When the music died away the apartment was soundless and still.

Elden wasn't here.

She descended the stairs.

She located the mailbox for apartment number 8. Felipe Cantor was printed on it. She grinned. She'd found a name, at least. It wasn't much, but it was more than she'd had five minutes ago.

Outside, morning foot traffic was thinning. The sides of the streets were jammed with cars parked nose to tail.

A man in a blue Fiat glanced up briefly as he fiddled with his phone.

She hustled through the alley, walked along a row of shops, and returned to her Mini. She made a few notes.

The man from the Fiat emerged from the alley. He entered a newsstand.

Jess looked along the row of shops. Elden had dropped off her laundry at the dry cleaner yesterday. Her Spanish was nowhere near good enough to ask the right questions. She shrugged. Playing dumb was the only approach she could master.

She set her phone timer to ring in three minutes, and set the alarm to the same sound as an incoming call.

Inside, the dry cleaner looked the same as in the US. Posters of smiling people wearing clean, bright clothes on the wall. A cash register on a laminated counter at the rear.

A woman behind the counter held out her hand. "Boleto."

Jess smiled. "I'm visiting my friend from home. Debora Elden. I've come to collect her things she dropped off yesterday."

The woman shook her hand. "The ticket?"

Jess shrugged. "She didn't give me a ticket. Debora Elden? She's an American."

The woman nodded. "The American. Sí."

She disappeared through a door behind the counter. She reappeared with hanging clothes covered with thin plastic. "Miss Elden's."

Jess took the clothes, paid the bill, and thanked the lady.

There was a small label pinned on the top of the hangers that

Jess figured was Elden's address. *C/ Santa Maria 45, 3, 2, 26101, Zorita.*

As scheduled, her phone's timer sounded. She pulled the phone from her pocket and held it to her ear, as if answering a call.

"Hi," she said. "Uh-huh. Uh-huh. Just now." She held up the laundry and glanced toward the lady at the counter. "Maybe I could just leave your stuff here and pick it up on the way back."

She mimed waiting for an answer.

"Okay," she said, and hung up on the non-existent call.

She gave the woman a sheepish grin. "I don't suppose I could give you these back, and pick them up later?"

The lady frowned.

"Later?"

The woman scowled a moment then held out her hand. "Later."

Jess handed over the laundry and left.

She looked up the address. Three streets away, in the opposite direction from Felipe Cantor's apartment.

She walked briskly to the small terrace house. The red brick that had faded in the sun and the heat. There were no front lawns. Brightly painted front doors opened straight onto the sidewalk. Elden's door was leaf green.

The curtains were drawn across the downstairs window, but a light bulb shined on the second floor.

When she rang the doorbell, she heard noises and a muffled shout inside. Cars drove by, and pedestrians nodded as they passed. She waited a full minute before ringing the bell again.

Footsteps thundered down the stairs. The door flew open and a teenaged girl stared at Jess.

Jess took a half step back.

The girl fired off a rapid series of sentences in Spanish that Jess couldn't follow.

The girl glowered.

"Debora Elden?" Jess said.

The girl seemed to soften a fraction. "Americano? A friend?"

Jess nodded. "I'm looking for Debora."

"Sí, sí." She gestured for Jess to enter the house and pointed her to a tiny living room. "I Olivia. I get."

Olivia raced up the stairs yelling for Debora. There was no reply. Jess heard a knock on an upstairs door then a few moments later a door creak.

Olivia raced back down the stairs and into the living room. "She gone."

"To work?"

She put her arms out, like wings. "Fly, I think. Her bag gone. South of here."

"I saw here yesterday."

The girl nodded. "She stay here last night. Gone now."

Jess shook her head.

Olivia shrugged. "Sorry."

"Do you know when she will be back?"

Olivia shrugged. "Days?"

Jess grimaced. She couldn't wait around Zorita that long. "You've no idea where she went?"

Olivia shook her head.

"Old tickets? Receipts?"

Olivia shook her head.

"Tags on her bags?" Jess knew she was reaching.

Olivia frowned. "Tags?"

"Labels. Stuck to her bags?"

Olivia thought a moment. "No sticky things."

Jess took a breath. "She works at Grupo Lopez, correct?"

"Sí. Scientist." The girl shook her head. "Secret work. She never say." She smiled. "A good thing. Yes?"

Jess smiled. "Do you work there?"

The girl shook her head. "Andros. Department store." She looked at her watch. "I start at eleven, and…" she gestured to her wet hair.

Jess stood up. "Of course. Do you know Felipe Cantor?"

"Sí. Debora's boyfriend. He works at Grupo Lopez, too. A computer man." She typed on an imaginary keyboard. "You know?"

Jess nodded. "Do they work together?"

She shrugged.

"How long have they been dating?" Jess said.

"Few weeks. Started at the same time, and…" She raised her eyebrows. "Maybe serious."

Olivia stood up and touched her wet hair. "I have to go."

Jess thanked her, they shook hands, and Jess left as Olivia raced up stairs.

CHAPTER THIRTY-THREE

Friday, August 19
9:30 a.m. CET
Zorita, Spain

KALE HAD A FRIENDLY face that served him well. Tiny lines radiated from the corners of his eyes and enhanced his smile, the result of years spent squinting in the sun of foreign lands.

His blond hair was medium length, neatly trimmed, and tousled just enough to suggest he'd spent little time grooming. He was tall and broad shouldered and looked like a man who could handle himself in a fight. Which usually deterred confrontation.

This morning, he wore a light patterned shirt, medium blue wash jeans, and a pair of eyeglasses. He adjusted the glasses on his nose.

Through the window, he'd watched the Kimball woman pick up clothes from the dry cleaner and then return them to the shopkeeper after receiving a phone call.

While she was inside, he had run a quick search on the shop

and its owners. They had lived in Zorita after moving from Barcelona several years ago. Tax returns showed the business was barely solvent. No indications they'd received large or irregular payments working as informants, or money laundering along with the dry cleaning.

Kimball left and walked determinedly to a house three streets away.

He knew the street and the house. He'd spent most of the previous night watching it.

Kimball had located Debora Elden's residence. Vanna Sánchez would not be pleased.

The front door opened and after a moment's conversation, Kimball stepped inside.

Kale found his phone. He pressed the speed dial button. He only had to wait two rings.

"What do you have?" Vanna Sánchez, her voice, cool and calm and sultry, matched her lithe figure and unshakable composure.

Her appearance screamed prima donna, but he'd seen her kick off those stilettos and heft a dead body into the trunk of her car, then drive off into the night, heels hanging from her upturned hand by the straps.

He shook the image from his mind. "Kimball is inside Elden's house."

"Who is there with her?"

"Presumably the house-mate, but I can't get a visual."

"And before?"

"Cantor's apartment. Stopped at a dry cleaner. Now here."

"What happened at the dry cleaner?"

"Picked up dry cleaning then gave it back to the shop keeper."

Sánchez waited a beat. "Why?"

"I don't know."

Sánchez said nothing, but Kale heard disapproval.

"I'll find out."

"Do that. One moment…"

There was a click on the line. Sánchez had muted her speaker. Kale stood still, calm and relaxed. He didn't pace or shift his weight to reveal the impatience burning his muscles.

Sánchez came back on the line. "Kill her now."

"No problem."

She hung up.

CHAPTER THIRTY-FOUR

Friday, August 19
10:30 a.m. CET
Zorita, Spain

JESS RETURNED TO HER Mini, and updated her notes.

Debora Elden's life was full of secrets. She had access to Kelso's labs and computers weeks after she left the company. Now she was working for a competitor in Spain on a secret project she didn't discuss.

She hadn't even told her housemate that she was leaving early this morning.

Although Elden traveled frequently, her bags had no claim labels from commercial airlines attached to luggage.

Elden was an activist, according to the Local World Action website. An activist. Not usually the kind of person who conducted secret research for a chemical company like Grupo Lopez.

Elden's profile was developing, but it made little sense to Jess.

Felipe Cantor had been Elden's boyfriend for most of the time she had been in Spain, according to her housemate. Jess might be able to get better information from him.

The clock on the Mini's dashboard read eleven o'clock. Maybe Cantor would leave the plant for lunch and Jess could catch up with him.

She searched the Grupo Lopez website for shift schedules. After digging through several pages, she found it. The usual lunch time was two o'clock. Could that possibly be right?

A quick web search returned articles explaining the work hours in Spain. A two o'clock lunch was traditional, and employees could take an optional two-hour siesta afterward. All of which stretched the working day to seven or eight in the evening.

Jess groaned. Her stomach growled, too. Her body hadn't adjusted to the time change. She couldn't wait three more hours for food.

She used her phone to find a restaurant that was highly rated by the locals. She put the Mini in gear, U-turned in a gap in the traffic, and followed the directions.

CHAPTER THIRTY-FIVE

Friday, August 19
11:00 a.m. CET
Zorita, Spain

KALE WATCHED KIMBALL PULL into the flow of traffic with her phone balanced on the dashboard.

He started his Fiat thirty seconds later, hanging back as he followed her distinctive Mini.

She headed toward the outskirts of town. Two miles of dual carriageway later, she turned off onto a road through an area with light industrial units.

The lights were flashing at a railroad crossing, and an air horn sounded nearby. The barriers were descending. The column of traffic slowed to a stop. She was six cars ahead of him.

He looked at the industrial units, pretending to be bored. The units had roll up doors and a uniform gray look. It wasn't difficult to be bored.

The car in front of him switched off its engine. He noticed several others had done the same. He left his running.

A minute later a train passed. It rumbled by at maybe twenty or thirty miles an hour. Kale felt the vibration through the ground.

There was a diesel locomotive with an improbably wide and square front that defied any notion of aerodynamics, followed by open bed trucks stacked with iron girders. The whole train clanked as the massive weight jostled against its couplings, and the wheels squealed as they scraped against the rails.

It took a full minute for the train to pass. It sounded its horn as it left. The lights flashed for another few seconds before the barriers lifted.

The line of cars drove on. He watched them bump over the tracks. The gap between the tarmac and the rail was wide. Poor workmanship and decades of wear. The Mini Cooper took a hard jolt.

The industrial area ended a few hundred yards farther on.

The street morphed into lines of grand old terraced houses, built in the early 1900s. The wealthy owners had homes maintained by servants. These days, the houses were converted into offices, shops, and trendy restaurants, all with apartments above.

Kimball squeezed her Mini through a break in the buildings into a rear parking lot. Thirty seconds later, he'd parked and followed her until she ducked into a restaurant called *de tapeo*.

This location wasn't good enough. The parking lot was hemmed in on all sides by buildings. Only one way in and out, a narrow lane that could be easily blocked.

Kale considered his options, and finally chose the most feasible one.

He needed a bigger vehicle.

CHAPTER THIRTY-SIX

Friday, August 19
Noon CET
Zorita, Spain

JESS ENTERED *DE TAPEO*, and took a seat near a window looking out on the main street. Brisk traffic dashed along the road out front and the sidewalk filled with pedestrians in a hurry.

A waiter handed her a menu. She glanced at it. "Do you have one in English?"

"Anything for you," he said with an Australian accent and a big smile. He returned with a handwritten menu.

"I'm David. You new in Zorita?"

She nodded. "I arrived yesterday."

"For work?"

"Yes, so if you're going to tell me all the great tourist sights—"

"Nah." He shook his head. "The scenery is good, but Zorita isn't much of a tourist center."

"So why are you in Zorita?"

"I wanted to live along the coast, but the pay over there is pitiful. Besides, it's nothing but bloody tourists," he said with a wink. "Light lunch? Spaniards go for a pretty heavy meal and a siesta."

She frowned. "Not for me. I hate napping in the afternoon."

He pointed to the handwritten menu. "Tapas? I could bring you a selection."

Jess looked down the list of small plates. "No mussels, okay?"

"Sure. Red or white wine?"

"I don't really want wine with lunch."

"You have to have a drink. Really, they just give the tapas away free. Like chips and salsa in a Mexican restaurant, you know?"

Jess nodded and looked again at the menu.

David said, "How about clara de limón? It's pretty refreshing."

"What is it?"

"Beer and sparkling lemonade." When she scowled, he grinned again. "Tastes a lot better than it sounds. Trust me."

She handed him the menu. "Tapas with beer and lemonade it is."

A few minutes later, David brought the clara de limón and food on a tray. "The potato ones with the red sauce are spicy." He put down a glass of water and pointed to it with another smile "Lots of ice. Because you're American."

The beer and lemonade mix was way better than she expected. The stuff could easily become addictive.

The conversation level in the room grew louder as more diners arrived.

She finished her food, put a twenty on the table, waved to

David, and dialed Henry Morris on her way out. He answered on the first ring, before she was outside.

"Jess, how's things?"

"Good."

"Sounds like you're somewhere noisy."

"I'm leaving a restaurant where I've been drinking lemonade and beer." The door closed behind her and she walked toward her car.

He laughed. "I'm not even going to ask. Making any progress?"

"I still haven't interviewed Debora Elden. But I did meet the Grupo Lopez CEO."

"Do tell," he teased as if she'd met a famous Spanish celebrity.

"He called me, or more specifically, his assistant called me. Which was strange. The only person I talked to at Grupo Lopez when I went there looking for Elden was a receptionist and I'm pretty sure she doesn't chat with the CEO very often. If ever."

"So what did he want?"

"I'm not sure. He's intense. His staff knows exactly what he wants. Like telepathy or something."

"Probably they've been explicitly drilled on his preferences, don't you think?"

"He made an effort to seem modest, but it was too rehearsed to be genuine. He's obsessed by what he calls great ideas. At first I thought that was an act, too. But by the time he'd finished talking, I had the feeling he meant it."

Morris asked, "To what end?"

Jess replied, "He wants to be famous."

"Being the CEO of a multi-national company that bears his name isn't enough?"

"That's where the obsession comes in, I think. He wants his name to last for centuries. Like Aristotle, he said."

Morris snorted. "Sounds like he thinks he's going to get even richer."

"Right. I suspect Rafa's working on mosquito control, in particular." Jess waited for a car to pass. "He said a million people die each year from malaria transmitted by mosquitoes."

He whistled. "Maybe he has a point."

"The thing is, Alex Cole said almost the very same words to me. And Rafa knew all about the explosion at Kelso Products, too."

He paused. "Kelso is one of his competitors. I'd be more surprised if he didn't know."

"Rafa mentioned Alex Cole specifically," Jess said.

Morris sounded more thoughtful. "The bombing attack has been getting more news coverage over there than we knew, I guess."

Jess shook her head, exasperated. "Henry, when I used the word *bomb* he linked it *directly* to the explosion at Kelso Products."

"Perhaps security has been on his mind since Kelso is in the same business as Grupo Lopez. Maybe he thinks his company might be next."

Her patience for Henry's perfectly reasonable explanations had run out. "He spent the whole evening ignoring my questions about Debora Elden, Henry. The whole time. He claimed he didn't know her or know anything about her."

"Like the responses you got from Kelso's CEO."

"Exactly. And I had the feeling that Rafa had been alerted. He knew I expected Elden to join us for dinner because I told his assistant when I accepted the invitation. And he didn't even ask one of his minions to give him basic information about Elden?"

She shook her head again, even though he couldn't see her. "Sorry, Henry. But no. That simply doesn't pass the smell test for me. Does it for you?"

He grunted, all business now. "No. What else?"

"Lopez said he would locate Elden for me today. But this morning, she didn't show up for work. Her housemate said she's gone. She travels often, never says where she's going or when. And Elden is working on something secret that she won't talk about."

"Sounds like she'd meet the secrecy requirements for the CIA." He sounded like he was only half joking. "Have you tried the boyfriend?"

"I'm hoping to catch him when he leaves for lunch. Any news from Remington about the Kelso investigation?"

"Nothing much. I'd say you've made them a little twitchy about Cole's lack of solid motive."

"They could put some pressure on Winter. She knows more than she's telling."

"They'd like to, I'm sure. Until they have something concrete to confront her with, they've got no real leverage."

"And what about Alex Cole in the meantime?"

"Still suspect number one, I'm afraid."

"Can you find out where Debora Elden has been traveling these past few months?"

Henry sighed. "Probably. But this is starting to sound too dangerous, don't you think?"

She held her annoyance in check. "I'll find out anyway, Henry. You know I will."

"Or you could let us do our jobs and you could wait to report the news." He took a deep breath that she could hear halfway around the world.

She waited.

Finally, he said, "Remington asked the local police to talk to her. They'll find out. If the boyfriend tells you first, you'd make a few points with Remington if you shared that information."

The mention of Cantor reminded her of the time. "I have to go, if I'm going to catch him. I'll call you later."

CHAPTER THIRTY-SEVEN

Friday, August 19
1:00 p.m. CET
Zorita, Spain

KALE HAD TRADED THE stolen fiat for a stolen Mitsubishi Shogun while Kimball was having lunch. He waited on the main street by the alley to *de tapeo's* parking lot with the engine idling. The sidewalks were busy because the lunch rush had started.

He wore a baseball cap and oversized sunglasses to conceal his features.

On the passenger seat, under the blanket he'd found in the back, he'd stashed a stolen Skorpion vz 61, a Czechoslovakian machine pistol with twenty rounds. Not the best gun in the world, and definitely not his first choice. But it was untraceable. On short notice, the Skorpion was the best he could do. It was wedged between the passenger seat and the center console with the grip at the correct angle for an easy grab.

The Kimball woman had eaten lunch at a table by a window.

He watched her leave, talking on the phone as she walked toward her car.

He put the SUV in gear and released the brake. He'd selected the four-wheel drive, which in the Shogun was a traditional brute force solution that applied motive force to all the wheels without electronic compromises.

He lowered his window and listened for the Mini Cooper's raucous engine as it bounced off the walls in the narrow alley.

The Mini emerged from the alley. He kept one eye on the Mini and watched the busy traffic in his side mirror.

Kimball edged the Mini forward, craning to see around the Shogun's bulk.

A traffic gap approached. He held the SUV on its handbrake as he brought the clutch up to its biting point. The gap in traffic was alongside him.

The Mini moved another couple of inches forward.

Why didn't she move? He revved his engine a fraction.

Kimball edged out another couple of inches. Low down in her Mini she couldn't see oncoming traffic as well as he could, but she obviously realized there was an opportunity. She burst into traffic just as the gap closed.

Kale swore. He rolled the Shogun away from the curb. A passing Fiat honked. He rolled further. The next car slowed, warily. He stomped on the accelerator and engaged the clutch. The big tires chirped as the SUV lurched forward.

The Mini was a good distance ahead.

The Shogun was woefully underpowered. He kept it in a low gear for better acceleration, but a full thirty seconds elapsed before he caught up with the Fiat and the Mini.

The stately terraced houses petered out.

The Fiat pulled closer to the Mini and veered in and out, the driver impatient to pass before they reached the rough ground at the train tracks.

Kale wanted the Fiat out of the way. Twenty rounds in the Skorpion seemed like plenty until he took into account firing single-handed from a moving vehicle at a moving target. The last thing he wanted was to run out of ammo before he completed the kill.

The Fiat changed down a gear, and pulled out to pass the Mini as they were both headed for the train crossing.

An approaching train sounded its air horn.

The lights at the railway crossing began flashing.

The barriers descended to block the passage across the train tracks.

The Fiat had no choice. It slowed and pulled back in behind the Mini to wait for the train to pass.

Kimball applied her breaks and stopped ten feet short of the barrier, the first in line.

The Fiat stopped behind her at an angle, its nose pointed to the right shoulder. The Fiat had insufficient space to pull in straight behind the Mini.

Kale stopped close behind the Fiat and slammed his palm on the steering wheel. "Dammit!"

Beyond the tracks, most of the industrial buildings looked as if they had closed up for lunch and siesta, exactly as he'd planned.

A straight, unobstructed killing zone in a near-perfect location.

Afterward, he could reach the freeway in mere seconds for a clean escape.

By the time authorities arrived, he would be five miles away. Maybe more.

Dump the Shogun, steal a better vehicle, and collect his money.

But none of that would happen now.

Not with the Fiat in the way.

The Shogun simply couldn't pass the Fiat on the other side of the crossing and close fast enough on the Mini.

In fact, with the Mitsubishi's sluggish acceleration, the Mini could simply outrun him when the barriers lifted.

Time to improvise.

He glanced down the track. The train was still a ways off to the right.

The Fiat turned off its engine to conserve fuel during the wait.

Kale lowered his window and listened carefully. The Mini's engine had gone silent, too.

He grabbed the Skorpion and placed it in his lap.

A rumble and a faint vibration moved the big Shogun. The train was closing the distance. Time to deal with the Mini or be forced to abandon his plan.

Kale was no quitter.

He pushed back the gun's side lever to chamber the first round. It moved, but only with a good bit of pressure and not with precision. It stopped on the return path, an inch short of the firing position. He rammed the lever back and forth, but the lever didn't move forward.

The roar of the train's diesel engine grew louder.

He angled the gun to look into the chamber. The bullet was wedged in the space forward of the chamber.

He smacked the bottom of the magazine ensuring it was fully seated into the gun, but the bullet remained stuck.

He tapped the gun against the door, trying to use shock to free the obstruction.

It didn't work.

The force he'd applied to the lever had jammed it for good. Only stripping the gun down would make it operational.

He glanced toward the train. The locomotive was a few hundred yards away and approaching inexorably.

No time to deal with the Skorpion now.

He had another gun. A pistol. But a drive by shooting with a pistol would be foolish.

The train's horn sounded. Much closer.

Now or never.

He shook his head violently. He refused to be beaten by Kimball's dumb luck.

He slammed the Shogun into gear and rammed into the car behind him to move it out of the way.

He shifted to low gear and put his foot flat to the floor.

The train was three hundred yards from the crossing.

CHAPTER THIRTY-EIGHT

Friday, August 19
1:10 p.m. CET
Zorita, Spain

JESS HAD STOPPED WELL short of the barriers and turned off the Mini's engine to wait for the approaching train. The Mini was low to the ground. The big passenger train would tower above her and shake the very ground beneath the Mini's wheels when it passed.

An engine revved. She glanced in the rearview mirror.

The Fiat that had been trying to pass her to beat the train was parked at an angle behind her Mini. The driver glowered in her direction.

Behind the Fiat was a big SUV.

The SUV lurched backward and hit the car behind. A loud crash of metal-on-metal reached her ears.

The SUV rocked back and forth after the impact before the engine revved again and it leaped forward.

The SUV veered the short distance around the Fiat, engine screaming.

She cringed when the SUV's front grille filled the Mini's tiny black window and kept on coming.

She had no room to move out of the way.

She pressed both feet hard on the brake in an attempt to avoid being pushed onto the tracks in front of the oncoming train.

She braced her head against the headrest for the impact a moment before the SUV hammered into the Mini's trunk.

Events unfolded in rapid succession.

The Mini jolted forward.

The impact threw Jess against her seatbelt.

The seatbelt locked in place and imprisoned her torso against the seat back.

The Mini bounced into the air.

All four wheels left the ground.

The Mini dropped to earth like a lead balloon.

And bounced again.

The SUV's engine coughed like it might stall.

Jess twisted to look at the SUV in the side mirror.

Did that idiot really believe he could maneuver through the barriers before the train arrived?

Jess shook her head. People died trying stupid stunts like that.

And killed others in the process.

The train was bearing down. Surely, he could wait until it passed.

Instead of waiting, the driver pushed his foot down on the accelerator to try again.

The SUV revved up.

A flash of heat ran over her skin as she watched in the mirror.

The front of the Shogun obscured most of the Mini's rear window.

The glass broke into a million pieces under the strain.

She snapped her eyes closed for half-a-second just in case one of the shards landed up front.

Which was when she knew for sure.

He was deliberately trying to push her into the path of the train.

Her heart rate picked up to almost a hundred beats a minute.

Car vs. train? No contest.

The car would be a mangled mess.

The car's driver, if she didn't die of fright, would be killed.

The Mini slid forward, pushed from behind by the big Shogun.

She inhaled deliberately and exhaled fast, trying to think past the panic.

The SUV kept pushing, but the Fiat rested between the two vehicles.

The Shogun's off-center angle was awkwardly connected to the left of the Mini's center.

The SUV's asymmetric force twisted the small car sideways as it moved.

The Mini turned almost ninety degrees.

The SUV was no longer pushing her car forward onto the tracks.

The driver adjusted his attack.

With a crunch of gears, the Shogun quickly reversed a few feet and then angled around to bring the Shogun up against the Mini's passenger door.

The locomotive sounded its air horn. A long blast. The train moved slowly through the urban area, but it was still a thousand times the mass of the Mini.

The SUV's engine screamed and its radiator grille crushed against the Mini's passenger door.

Jess kept both feet on the brake pedal. The Mini bounced as it skipped across the tarmac toward the barriers.

She braced for the car to roll over.

The Mini smashed through the crossing barrier almost sideways. She heard the scraping of metal, and the SUV's tires scrabbling for grip.

The Mini bucked and rocked wildly.

She clutched the door handle. The Mini's wheels bounced over the first of the tracks, which jerked her hand away from the door.

The train's air horn sounded. Blast after blast. Louder and louder.

The horn's tone fell as the train slowed, but it gave her little comfort. Even a slow impact would crush the tiny car.

The Mini had been turned so its front bumper pointed directly at the train.

Jess saw the train's engine bearing down.

The locomotive was enormous. Square and unforgiving. Sparks fairly poured from under its wheels as the engineer attempted to stop.

Her heart slammed against her chest.

She stabbed the Mini's start button and the motor burst into life.

The Mini's relentless slide came to an abrupt stop.

The tiny car was tilted at an angle. The wheels on one side had dug into the rut beside the track.

The SUV slithered past the Mini, metal grinding.

She caught a flash of the monstrous beast as it headed across the tracks.

She was close enough now to see rust and peeling paint on the locomotive's front. The sound of metal squealing on metal was deafening as the engineer applied the brakes, attempting to stop the heavy train.

The train had insufficient stopping distance.

She felt like a deer in headlights. Her eyes widened. The big locomotive was about to hit her head on.

"Move, Kimball, move!" she shouted.

She shoved the Mini into reverse and stomped on the accelerator again and again, fighting the wheel to lever the tires clear.

The train's air horn sounded again, raising her blood pressure to near-bursting.

After three tries, the Mini lurched sideways, popping out of the rut.

She spun the wheel, keeping her foot on the accelerator pressed it all the way to the floor.

The Mini hurtled across the street in front of the industrial units, and she stomped on the brake to avoid hitting the far curb.

The train pounded past.

Metal ground on metal as the driver put everything into slowing the behemoth.

Sparks flew in all directions like fireworks.

The squeal was louder than dragon nails on a giant chalkboard.

The ground shook, and even though she kept a death grip on the steering wheel, her hands shook, too.

Her arms were locked rigid, and her mouth hung open as she

watched the carriages pass, each one moving ever more slowly.

Passengers gaped from the windows. Despite the battered Mini's unusual position on the road, they weren't staring at her.

She steadied her breathing and looked around for the SUV.

The Mitsubishi sat thirty feet from her on the wrong side of the road.

The driver stood beside the big Shogun, arms outstretched, holding a big black gun.

Pointed directly at her.

She'd survived the train only to be killed by a maniac with a gun?

Not a chance.

She revved the Mini and slung it around the Shogun.

The Mini's steering wheel shook. The wheels were damaged and not running true, but Jess kept her foot down hard.

She recognized the crisp sound of gunfire.

The side window behind her burst, showering the Mini's interior with glass.

She accelerated along the empty road.

The car pulled to the left and she leaned her weight against the pull, fighting to travel straight.

She glanced down at the speedometer. Her eyes widened. She was doing eighty.

In the rearview mirror, she saw the Shogun turning around. The SUV was a lumbering beast compared to the Mini. As long as he had no accomplices, she would easily outrun him.

The steering wheel shook wildly, rocking her in her seat. She eased off the accelerator a fraction. If something broke now, she'd be a sitting target. The shooter's aim was surely good enough to hit her.

The road angled right, hiding her from the gunman's view.

She braked hard, took a right off the main road, and looped around the block. She slowed to a stop beside a building where she could watch the main road without being noticed.

A few minutes later, the Shogun sailed by, engine still screaming to bring the SUV's weight up to speed.

The driver's face pressed forward, searching for her through the windshield.

If he found her, he'd surely finish the job he'd started.

She waited, the car in gear and her foot hovering over the accelerator, checking through the shattered rear window, her heart pounding painfully through each passing second.

CHAPTER THIRTY-NINE

Friday, August 19
1:20 p.m. CET
Zorita, Spain

POLICE SIRENS WAILED IN the distance. Minutes passed.
The Shogun didn't come back. The shooter could have made it to
the freeway by now. He'd be long gone.

Could she possibly be that lucky?

She sank back in her seat, and waited until her hands stopped
shaking. The monstrous metal front of the locomotive was vivid
in her mind. The big train had come way too close to being the
last thing she ever saw.

When she could stand without collapsing, she assessed the
damage to the sturdy little Mini Cooper.

The rear of the vehicle was seriously dented and deformed.
But the crumple zone had done its job. The energy of the impact
with the big Shogun seemed to have been diffused without
damage to the integrity of the car.

The passenger side was dented and scraped, and the front

alloy wheel was a mess. Mercifully, the car's high-tech run flat tires were tougher than normal tires. They had retained their shape, enabling her to get away.

She grinned, insanely grateful for the little car's fighting spirit. Her next big story would be all about the heroic Mini Cooper, if she could talk her boss into running it.

She drove carefully back to the railroad crossing, keeping her speed under thirty.

The scene was chaotic. The train had come to a stop with its carriages blocking the junction. Cars lined up on either side waiting to cross, and their passengers were milling around, trying to figure out what happened. Two police cars were parked on the far side, their lights flashing.

Passengers on the train were hanging out of the windows, trying to find out what had caused the emergency stop.

She shivered. If it had been a freight train, it would never have slowed enough to give her time to escape.

She shoved the thought to the back of her mind, and parked on the hard shoulder. Several people recognized the beat-up Mini, and pointed. As she walked the length of parked cars, rumors spread in front of her.

She made straight for one of the policemen. He left organizing the milling crowd to the others, and studied her as she approached.

"Someone tried to push me in front of the train," she said.

He frowned, and held up his hand. "Wait, wait."

He spoke rapid fire Spanish into his radio, and a few moments later a man in a white shirt and black slacks ducked between the carriages. He beckoned to Jess, and ducked back to the other side of the carriages.

Jess followed, keeping her head low under the couplings.

The mass of metal above her head an ominous reminder of what she had escaped.

Several officers were taking photographs and collecting samples. The man in the white shirt was inspecting tire marks where the Mini had been pushed sideways and the Shogun's wheels had spun.

"Someone in an SUV tried to push me in front of the train," she said to the man in the white shirt.

"So I see," he said in clear English. He held out his hand. "Subinspector Pablo Garza, and you are?"

"Jessica Kimball. I was in my car, waiting at the barrier when a Mitsubishi Shogun drove into the back of me and pushed my car onto the tracks."

"You're American?"

"Yes."

"Tourist?"

"I came to see someone."

"The person in the Shogun?"

"No. I have no idea who the driver was. I didn't get a good look."

"Did you cut them off? Drive in front of them?"

"No. I pulled out from *de tapeos*, drove to here and stopped at the barrier. They just attacked me."

"Forgive me, but people don't just attack anyone. There's always a reason."

"It wasn't road rage. There was a Fiat behind me, and the Shogun behind him. We were all stopped for almost a minute before the Shogun decided to shove me in front of this train."

"You drove off."

"I was in the middle of the tracks. I managed to start my car and back out," she pointed, "over there."

"And the Shogun drove off?"

"No. He pointed a gun at me, so I went around him and drove away. He tried to follow, but I got away and doubled back. He went straight by. Probably onto the dual carriageway."

He nodded. "We have a helicopter searching."

"He's probably gone already."

Pablo shrugged. "We will search anyway." He looked up and down the length of the train. "You were lucky."

"That wasn't the first thought to cross my mind."

He grunted his agreement. "But as you stand here now?"

She laughed. "Yes. I guess I was lucky."

A man in a blue uniform stepped off the train and stood between Jess and Garza. He had a conversation with the subinspector which involved a good deal of arm waving.

Garza took one more look around the tracks, and nodded. The man in blue thanked the subinspector, and walked back to the locomotive.

Garza shouted instructions to the officers around the crossing. People were pushed back behind the broken remains of the barrier.

The locomotive's air horn sounded twice, and the train started to move. The wheels squealed and the couplings clanked as they took up the strain. The train moved away at a walking pace.

The noise made hearing impossible. Garza waited with his arms crossed until the last of the carriages had rolled by.

He remained in the middle of the crossing. His officers held back the waiting lines of traffic.

He tilted his head. "Who did you come to visit?"

"Debora Elden." Jess didn't see any point in trying to hide the name.

Garza stared at her. "An unusual name for Spain, yet it is the second time I have heard it today."

Jess narrowed her focus on the man. "Is she okay?"

"I have no idea. I was asked to interview her today."

"Why?"

"I am an officer of the Cuerpo Nacional de Policía, so obviously it was police business. Equally obvious, I am not at liberty to discuss it."

He looked between the carriages at Jess's Mini. "Your car is okay?"

"It's covered in dents, but it drives."

"One of my men will take it."

"I need it."

"Forgive me, Ms. Kimball. Someone just pushed you in front of a train and tried to shoot you when you escaped. Your embassy, your government, and more likely your press would have what I believe you call a *field day* if I did not take your safety seriously."

He was right. She had no weapon, and even if she did, if her assailant wanted to take a shot at her, she was completely exposed.

"What do you have in mind?"

"In the near term you will be safe at our station while we conduct enquiries."

"And in the longer term?"

"Perhaps you will have to leave Zorita."

"I need to talk to Debora Elden."

"And why is that?"

She stared at him. She knew she was about to ratchet up his unwanted interest, but he would find out eventually, and honesty always was the best policy.

"I'm a journalist investigating an explosion in America. Debora Elden's ex-boyfriend is the prime suspect."

"Really? And you didn't think to tell me this?"

He clucked his tongue against his teeth, and pointed at the tire marks. "Tell me what happened here one more time then we will go to the station."

CHAPTER FORTY

Friday, August 19
1:30 p.m. CET
Zorita, Spain

KALE LET FORTH A torrent of obscenities and expletives until his throat was sore.

He had failed.

He didn't care about the likely snide comments from Sánchez. He didn't care about his pay. He didn't care about professional pride.

He just hated losing.

Hated, hated, *hated* losing.

He picked the jammed Skorpion from the seat, threw it into the passenger footwell, and repeated his obscenities.

She should have been easy to kill. One good shot. That was all he needed. Pushing her car onto the tracks was an impulse, and impulses were the downfall of winners. And he was a winner. Time and time again, planning had made him a winner.

He slowed the Shogun and parked it on a quiet street.

He picked up the Skorpion and tucked it into a flammable canvas bag and placed it on the seat.

Behind the passenger seat was a gallon of gas in a plastic container. He emptied it over the rear carpet and upholstery.

He opened all the windows for maximum oxygen, and dangled a slow fuse from the driver's seat into the gas.

He lit the fuse, closed the door, and walked away.

He took a left at the end of the street and ran to catch a bus.

Standing on the steps of the bus, he heard the thump of an explosive start to his gasoline fire. He paid the fare with the anger in his blood still raging, even beyond the heat of the fire.

He didn't know how, and he didn't know when, but Jessica Kimball would die young.

He would make damn sure of that.

CHAPTER FORTY-ONE

Friday, August 19
1:45 p.m. CET
Zorita, Spain

HADLOW WANDERED ALONG THE side of the railway tracks, hands resting in his pockets, pulse elevated, working through events in his head. What had he missed?

He glanced back at his car, waiting in the line of vehicles held up by a train stopped in the middle of the crossing. No one was going anywhere. Not yet, anyway.

The morning began badly and went downhill from there.

He'd followed Elden from her home to the airport well before dawn. For the first time since this assignment started, Hadlow wasn't the only one following her. He spotted the six-foot-tall man with blond hair and glasses within the first two minutes.

His face was friendly enough, but his shoulders and the muscles in his neck suggested serious menace was packed into his jacket, along with the unmistakable bulge of a gun. Hadlow tagged every contact with a name for ease of reference. This one was Rock.

As soon as he had the chance, Hadlow snapped photos of Rock until he got one shot clear enough to run through facial recognition.

Rock carried himself like a soldier. Along with his build and the gun, Hadlow marked him as ex-military. The relaxed smile was a practiced fake, meant to belie the kind of training that made him formidable.

But Rock's training wasn't special ops. He'd displayed several examples of the kind of ham-handed surveillance no covert operative would employ. He stood on open street corners, stared way too long, and he jogged to catch up to his target as quickly as possible. Any good operative applied patience and a longer stride to achieve better results.

Elden boarded a business jet before sunrise. From a distance, he'd peered through binoculars to identify the tail number.

Fifteen minutes later, Hadlow acquired the flight plan. The pilot chose a reasonably direct route to a small airfield two-thousand miles south in Chad, a landlocked country in Central Africa.

Hadlow assumed this flight plan was a subterfuge, just like the last one. Hadlow had used the pilot's formal plan for Elden's previous flight, but the aircraft never arrived at the planned destination.

In the two-week gap since Elden had last traveled on the jet, Nash had earned some of his fat salary. He'd made arrangements to record the jet's radar track on subsequent trips. This was the first chance to deploy the device.

Hadlow requested a private jet to follow Elden immediately.

Nash refused. "Sorry. Not in the budget this time, Hadlow," he'd said, with unmistakable malice in his tone.

Hadlow refused to protest the stupid decision, which meant he was forced to wait until Elden's jet landed. Only then would he know where she'd set down. At which point he could follow in a commercial plane. And make the best of conditions on the ground.

Nash said, "You've got other chores to complete this morning while you wait, Hadlow. Get going. We're not paying you to dawdle."

Hadlow ground his teeth waiting for Nash to stop chortling and hang up.

Then he spent the morning on chores.

Bugging the American's hotel room while she was out with Rafa Lopez had been easy. Two voice-only devices. One in the center of the main room. The other in the bathroom. Because Americans never went anywhere without their mobile phones.

Overnight, she'd neither made nor received phone calls. He'd heard a lot of keyboard noises, which made sense after Nash had verified her employment at *Taboo Magazine*. By secure satellite, Nash delivered a short dossier that included her son's tragic abduction and Kimball's unrelenting but, as yet unsuccessful, search to rescue Peter.

Nash's conclusion about Kimball, underlined three times with a fat red line: Threat Level Zero.

Which, of course, made Hadlow determined to prove him wrong, simply for sport.

Kimball was certainly focused on her job. He had to hand it to her for the subterfuge at the dry cleaner. A clever way to find Elden's address.

If pressed, his report would describe her as determined and

creative. Not a great combination for a civilian dealing with the likes of Rafa Lopez.

The smart play was to let the professionals handle Lopez and Elden and the others. Kimball, however, had yet to defer to anyone. Not even her FBI boyfriend, if that's what Agent Morris was.

Hadlow grinned. He admired Kimball's spirit, even as he wondered if she had a secret death wish. He'd seen it before. Passion that strong could lead to tragic consequences in the blink of an eye.

After the dry cleaner, she hit several snags that slowed her progress. She'd learned about Elden's boyfriend. Which wouldn't help much.

Cantor was employed by Grupo Lopez, but he was isolated from Elden. They weren't doing the same work and he should have known almost nothing about Elden's research.

Of course, pillow talk being what it was, Cantor might know more than he should.

Perhaps Nash had a point. Possibly, Hadlow should direct his meager resources to Elden instead of Kimball. Before Hadlow made the decision, another player turned up outside Elden's home and followed Kimball. Rock.

Two women in the same day. Both the subject of Rock's awkward surveillance. Why was he following them? And for whom?

At *de tapeos*, the restaurant where Kimball ate lunch, Rock was armed, but he didn't make a move against her. Instead, he simply followed her on her way back to Grupo Lopez, driving a stolen SUV.

When Rock shoved Kimball's car onto the train tracks into the path of the oncoming train, Hadlow jumped from his car, reaching into his jacket for his gun.

He watched in horror as the locomotive barreled down on the Mini, unable to change the course of the collision. Rock was on the other side of the train where Hadlow couldn't reach him.

Kimball had cleverly maneuvered her car from the train's path at the last second. Maybe less than a second.

The rapidly braking train cut him off from Kimball and Rock. It took another forty-five seconds for the train carriages to halt so he could get to the far side of the tracks. By that time, they had raced away.

Hadlow played the shocked bystander for a few minutes. He checked out the passengers in every car at the crossing. He scanned the nearby buildings, especially the upstairs windows where a sniper might be located. If Rock had a partner, Hadlow didn't find him.

The whole incident was puzzling. It was clear who Rock was working for, but why the assassination attempt? Elden had already left Zorita, and Kimball wasn't likely to hang around with Elden gone.

He pondered the question while the police arrived. A few minutes later, Kimball returned in her damaged Mini Cooper. She approached the police officer in charge.

Hadlow whistled softly and ambled up and down the tracks. He passed Kimball and the officer twice.

Her demeanor was remarkably calm, given that she'd almost been flattened by a train. The officer's questions Hadlow overheard were unremarkable. Almost as if he hadn't, or couldn't, comprehend the situation.

He overheard Kimball connect the dots for the nearly clueless police. She was investigating links between Elden and an explosion in the US.

The police knew about the explosion at Kelso Products, but to them, it was one piece of data in a sea of noise. Hadlow preferred to keep it that way. One thing he didn't need was interference in his operation from Spanish police.

Unfortunately, Kimball's presence in Spain meant the bomb wasn't noise any more. He could almost see the police officer conclude that the information could be important.

CHAPTER FORTY-TWO

Friday, August 19
5:00 p.m. CET
Zorita, Spain

JESS WAITED IN PABLO Garza's office alone. A glass
porthole in the closed door provided a clear view of the hubbub
on the other side.

They'd reviewed the details of her investigation to date. The
TATP bomb in Chatham, Alex Cole, and the link to Debora
Elden. She left out any mention of Henry Morris and Elden's
unauthorized access to Kelso Products.

Garza took copious notes, stopping her frequently to catch
up with her words. He used a yellow lined notepad, and filled
each page with small, precise handwriting before he placed the
pages into a three-ring binder. His old-fashioned style was slow
and frustrating.

He'd left her alone twenty minutes earlier for reasons he
didn't share. He'd provided a third cup of coffee to keep her
occupied. For cop shop coffee, it wasn't bad.

Garza's office was carefully arranged. Instead of a desk at the center, he worked on four large tables, one pushed against each wall. Hung behind each table were corkboards containing file materials for four different cases. Four cases might have been his limit. Jess glanced at the gruesome photographs pinned to the boards and understood why four cases were plenty of work. She certainly wouldn't want to be any of the victims hanging there.

Two wheeled office chairs rested in the middle of the room. While Garza interviewed her, he'd wheeled himself around the room, like the movement comforted him the way a child might rub a favorite blanket.

His investigation technique was tepid. He seemed merely curious about the attempt to kill her. What she wanted him to demonstrate was a lot more of the famed Latin temper she'd heard so much about. So far, he hadn't.

She'd long finished the coffee by the time Garza returned. He closed the door and settled into one of the empty chairs. Thoughtfully, he resumed rolling backward around the room, as if he still had much to figure out.

Mustering as much patience as possible, Jess waited for his epiphany.

After too long, he finally stopped the chair facing Jess. "A man tried to kill you. Agreed?"

She nodded without snarky commentary, which she figured wouldn't help prod him along.

"And we don't know who he was or why he wanted you dead."

The blunt words caused a painful tremor low in her belly. "I've never seen that man before in my life."

"We've used your description to search our computers, but

haven't located him yet. If he's in our databases, we will identify him." He cocked his head. "You are investigating a deadly explosion in America. Which brings you into contact with violent people, don't you agree?"

"I don't agree. No. Not like this guy." Jess shook her head. "Ramming my car and shoving me in front of an oncoming train is significantly different than creating, planting, and detonating a bomb."

"Perhaps." Garza nodded while he pursed his lips to think. "A deliberate attack on a particular target by a ruthless killer is usually not the same as anonymous behavior designed to kill and maim innocents. That's true."

"Not even close to the same," Jess said, with more force than she intended.

Garza's eyebrows arched. "But since we don't know who committed either act, we are in the dark, are we not?"

"You found CCTV? What about witnesses?"

"Unfortunately not." He shook his head sorrowfully. "My officers have scoured the area for cameras. There is no useful footage. Witnesses identified the SUV but not the driver."

"Surely you found the SUV, didn't you?"

"Burnt out. We'll do what we can, but there will be little usable evidence due to the intense fire." He sighed and shook his head.

"So now what do we do?"

"Given the failed attempt on your life, you should leave Zorita. Preferably return to the US." He nodded, his mind apparently made up. "That is the prudent thing to do. It is likely this man will try again and next time, you may not be so lucky."

"I can't go yet." Jess disagreed before he finished his maddeningly slow delivery. "I came here to find Debora Elden, and I won't stop till I'm done."

"I thought you might say that." He unfolded his hands and reached into his jacket for a sheet of folded paper. "Which is why I will share this."

He rolled the chair closer and extended the paper.

"You may know that your FBI requested that we find and interview Debora Elden. We were not asked to keep the information confidential." He paused and smiled. "And you would find out all this yourself, I am sure."

She opened the one sheet of plain white printer paper. No header, no identifying marks of any kind. And no signature at the bottom of the page.

He smiled. "A slight sanitization. No facts have been withheld, I assure you."

Quickly, she read through the paragraphs, which were printed in English.

Elden's neighbors believe she left Zorita early in the morning of August 19. She travels often, and has done the same before. She usually takes a gray suitcase. When she is expecting to be away for a week or more, she asks her housemate to water her plants. She has not done so on this occasion.

Grupo Lopez is unaware of her whereabouts. She has not arrived for work. She has several unexplained absences in her file. Human Resources is considering disciplinary action that may include termination of employment. If her employment is terminated, Elden's work visa will be revoked and she will be required to leave Spain. Elden is a US citizen and it is presumed she will return to her home.

Felipe Cantor is not a fiancé, though he is her current boyfriend and spends considerable time with her. He does not know her whereabouts. He confirmed that she travels occasionally.

A search of airline records shows several trips to the US, landing each time in Chicago (which the FBI is in a better position to investigate further). No additional flight records for her have been located despite a diligent search. She owns no vehicle and we located no vehicle rentals in her name.

Cuerpo Nacional de Policía will continue to monitor Grupo Lopez and Elden's housemate, and will inform the FBI when she returns.

"She can't have simply vanished." Jess frowned.

Garza shrugged. "We found no departing airline reservations."

"What about buses or trains?"

"We are checking, but I hold little hope that we'll find anything useful. Buses and trains accept payment in cash. If Elden wished to keep her travel activities secret..." he shrugged again.

"Do you believe her employer doesn't know where she is?"

"Grupo Lopez is an old and established company in Zorita. We have no reason to doubt." He cocked his head. "Which leaves me with a worrying conclusion."

"Something has happened to her. Foul play." Jess nodded slowly.

"It is a logical answer." He took a deep breath. "However, it is not uncommon for visitors and tourists to travel without properly advising friends and colleagues."

Jess nodded. She traveled frequently herself. He was right.

"If we learn that Elden has met with foul play, we will investigate and find the ones responsible." He gestured toward the papers on his corkboards. "For now, I have much work to do for these families. Surely, you understand."

She did understand. The story was the same everywhere.

Too many crimes and too few resources to deal with them.

She'd had the experience herself when her son was abducted. Her *Taboo Magazine* investigations were almost always about families seeking justice when the system failed.

Jess Kimball knew better than anyone that not every story has a happy ending. The evidence against Alex Cole seemed overwhelming. Debora Elden's actions were extremely suspicious. She might even have been the one who actually bombed Kelso Products. But if Elden had actually disappeared without a trace, Garza was right. Jess had no reason to remain in Zorita.

CHAPTER FORTY-THREE

Friday, August 19
5:30 p.m. CET
Zorita, Spain

PABLO GARZA HAD OFFERED her a security escort and it seemed prudent to accept. Jess waited on the ground floor of the Cuerpo Nacional de Policía building while he made arrangements.

She dialed her cell phone. The line clicked and whirred before connecting.

"Morris," he groaned.

She groaned back in sympathy. "Sorry, Henry. I forgot the time difference."

He grunted and she heard rustling sheets in the background.

She glanced at the clock. Denver was eight hours behind Zorita. What was he doing in bed? It was nine-thirty in the morning in Denver.

"Long night. I only just got to bed." His voice was returning to normal.

250 | D<small>IANE</small> C<small>APRI</small> & N<small>IGEL</small> B<small>LACKWELL</small>

She shook her head. Henry Morris was one of the hardest working men she'd ever known. "You can sleep. I can call later."

"No." He cleared his throat. "I haven't heard from you for too long as it is. I was starting to worry."

She grinned and a pink flush warmed her cheeks. Having a good man like Henry to worry about her wasn't half as annoying as she'd feared.

"How's the investigation going?" he asked. "Progress?"

"Oh, I had an exciting day." She clenched her teeth. But she put a little humor in her report. "I missed Elden's boyfriend because of my date with a locomotive."

His voice went up an octave. "What?"

"Someone tried to push me in front of a train. At a railroad crossing. And when I got my car off the tracks, he shot at me."

"You're serious?"

She could hear something close to panic in his voice coming across the miles. She didn't want him to freak out. Everything had turned out fine. "Well, it didn't work, obviously. I'm not calling you from the great beyond or anything."

She heard more rustling. Henry must have given up on sleep for the moment.

"You've just as obviously tapped into something very dangerous. You can't stay there."

"Says the guy who stands in front of killers every day with a gun in his holster." She said it lightly, but he was being totally unreasonable now. Concern was one thing. Bossing her around was a whole different thing she wasn't willing to accept. Even from a good guy like Henry. "Look, everything's okay. I'm at a police station and they're arranging protection for me. I'll be fine."

He paused a long time and she knew he wasn't happy with

her answer. He had the good sense not to press her any further, though. "Are you coming back here?"

"Soon," she said. "Can we talk about something else for a minute?"

"Be reasonable, Jess. Please." Henry sighed. "Look, you're a great reporter. But you're not a detective. You don't have any authority over there and no backup. You have no support. No police assistance, nothing. And you're operating in a foreign country with little or no intel. Hell, you don't even have a gun with you. And you'd be arrested if you had one."

She waited until he ran out of steam. And then she laid it out for him. "I appreciate that you're worried about me, Henry. But I've been doing this work a long time. A lot longer than I've been dating you, actually. I don't need or want you to protect me right now. I told you I'm fine and I am. I'm being careful and I'll have an armed guard."

At that point, he had the good sense to remain silent. Even without Miranda warnings, he must have figured out that anything he did say might be used against him.

Finally, he exhaled. "I do have something for you. The Italians have come back with a bit of a bombshell on our Marco Benito inquiry. Turns out he's dead."

It took a moment for the name to register with her and then to wrap her mind around it well enough to ask an intelligent question. "The actual Marco Benito? The man at the University of Turin?"

"Yes and yes. Car crash." He paused. "Two days after the explosion at Kelso Products."

Jess frowned and she considered the possibilities. "Is there a link between the two events? Did Benito know something about the man using his identity?"

"Hard to say. I guess so, without being a mind reader or a medium." She heard the grin in his voice. "But we've told the Italians about the visa irregularities. I expect we'll get more feedback in a day or two."

"Was the car crash suspicious?"

"Italians didn't think so at the time. Given what we've told them, they're going back to review the evidence."

"So the man that impersonates Benito is dead, and now Benito is dead, too?" She shook her head. "Seems incredible, doesn't it?"

"And if your locomotive dodging skills weren't up to scratch, maybe you would be dead. Really, Jess, leaving this whole thing to the professionals is the smart thing to do."

She sighed. He was right, of course. As he should be. This was his field, and one he'd worked in long enough to know when to press ahead and when to call for reinforcements.

Elden had left town, the Spanish police agreed to watch for her return, and any further contact Jess might have with Rafa Lopez was likely to be through email with his assistant at best.

She sighed. Tenacity was one thing. Idiocy was something else. "You're right. I'll check with the airline."

Morris was silent a beat. "I know that's not what you wanted to do, Jess. But thank you. I'll feel better knowing you're on your way home."

After they hung up, Jess checked with her airline, and booked a 7:00 a.m. flight out of Valencia. She sent travel details to Morris by text. He sent back a smiley face.

When she looked up, Garza was walking toward her with a hulking bodyguard.

CHAPTER FORTY-FOUR

Friday, August 19
6:30 p.m. CET
Zorita, Spain

IT WAS STILL DAYLIGHT as Kale threaded his way through the streets in a blue Peugeot he'd stolen thirty minutes earlier.

He stopped four blocks from his destination and backed into a parking space. He grabbed the duffel bag and left the car unlocked.

He crossed the street, and zigzagged to the rear terrace of a mixed-use four-story building. The ground level was retail shops. Dumpsters were out back.

He donned a pair of gloves and walked up and down the street twice, checking doorways and recesses for places to establish a nest. Several units had gates. He checked the latches and noted which ones opened easily.

Confident he had the area mapped out in his mind, he returned to one of the empty shops in the first building.

The courtyard behind the once-thriving shop was filled with

mangled cartons. He moved boxes and other obstructions to clear a straight path between the back door and the rear gate that exited to the road behind it.

The back door's recess provided cover from prying eyes, should anyone bother to look. The building was secured with a large industrial padlock. It weighed a good pound or two in his hand, and the thick steel hoop wrapped through the equally thick clasp on the door. Despite its weight, the steel yielded to bolt cutters on the first try.

Inside, he turned on his flashlight. It had a weak red beam that glowed instead of shining, but it was bright enough to avoid the debris on the abandoned shop floor.

A car approached, engine wheezing. He stood still, easing the flashlight closer to him until the lens was pressed against his body to extinguish the glow.

The car passed by.

He waited fifteen seconds. The engine's noise faded.

He released the flashlight's soft beam for a quick look around. He saw one large rectangular space. Cheap painted plywood boarded off one corner.

A door was set into the side wall, secured by a deadbolt. He pushed aside two broken chairs, clearing his path to the door.

He waited, listening to the building creak as the stresses and strains shifted with the wind. He heard no identifiable human activity.

He sprayed oil on the deadbolt and hinges, and gave it a full minute to work.

The door opened silently.

On the other side was a corridor with wooden stair treads that led upward. No basement.

He climbed the stairs gently, walking on the edge of each old tread, deftly shifting his weight from foot to foot to prevent a rapid creak, or worse.

At the top, the stairs were tucked between the pitch of the front and rear roofs.

He ducked his head to pass.

A low door, maybe five feet high or so, was set into one wall. He used a generous quantity of the oil on the handle and hinges, and it, too, opened silently. He ducked lower as he passed through into a room that hadn't been used in years.

The odor of old books and rotting vegetation assaulted his nose. A thick layer of dust covered the floor and the furniture left behind.

A ragged and dirty lace curtain sagged over a single casement window. He brushed the grime from a stool with the back of his glove, sat beside the window, and lowered his duffel bag to the dusty floor.

He oiled the window hinge and allowed it a full minute to penetrate the rusted mechanism. He was in no hurry.

He bumped the window with his shoulder as he pried it open. It gave only a slight creak the nearest occupants one floor below wouldn't have heard.

The curtain was suspended on a thin wire across the window. He unhooked one end. The other end unhooked itself and sprung outward through the window to the open air. He yanked the wire back inside, but the filthy curtain slid off the wire outside.

He lunged forward, grabbing for the curtain.

It fluttered and danced in the air.

His fingers snapped onto the delicate fabric, but it slipped through his gloved hand.

He made one last grab, clenching his fist around the center of the fabric, and wrenched it back inside.

He knotted the fabric to the leg of the stool, and sat with a thump. The escaping fabric and the noise he'd made retrieving it rattled him. At this point, he could only hope no one had observed the ridiculous comedy.

He took a few deep breaths to regain control of his frustration.

He waited. He heard no alarms.

After a few minutes of silence, he returned to his work.

He pulled a black case from the duffel bag and unclipped its two latches. Inside was a matte black gun, a VSK-94. It looked more like a prop from a futuristic movie than a lethal weapon.

He grinned. Appearances were deceiving.

The VSK-94's stock was square and hollowed out. The magazine jutted out at a right angle to the body. The barrel was a thick plain cylinder.

Seemingly, the only concession to ergonomics was the grip, sloped and shaped for a human hand in stark contrast to the rest of the design's rigid geometry.

The sight was a separate piece. It clipped on with a precision click. He rocked it back and forth. No free play. Perfect.

Finally, he screwed on the sound suppressor.

He adjusted the position of his seat, rested the barrel on the window frame, and tuned the scope to focus.

The view from the window wasn't perfect, but good enough for his purposes.

Felix Cantor wasn't home from work yet. He would be soon.

Kale needed only one shot.

One swift kill would restore his employer's confidence.

And Kale's pride.

CHAPTER FORTY-FIVE

Friday, August 19
6:30 p.m. CET
Zorita, Spain

JESS SUPPRESSED A GRIN. Inspector Garza's idea of a
suitable bodyguard was built exactly like a man Morris would
have selected.

Bulky, muscular body, jet black hair. And smoky green eyes,
she noticed. Morris might not have been too pleased with how
hot this guy looked, though.

His dark blue uniform was covered by a bullet-proof vest.
The submachine gun strapped in a holster across his chest made
him look even bulkier. In a good way.

"I'm Bruno Toscani." He shook Jess's hand with a solid
grip.

"Toscani? Like the famous photographer?" she asked him,
smiling.

"Call me Bruno," he replied, all business in front of the boss.
Or maybe he simply had no sense of humor.

"My flight departs at seven in the morning, so I have time to interview Elden's boyfriend." She checked her watch. "He should be home from work."

Garza frowned a moment and then nodded. "After the interview you will remain in your hotel? I don't have the manpower to guarantee your protection if you're wandering around the city."

"Agreed." She scribbled Cantor's address on a page from her notebook, and handed it to Garza who relayed it to Bruno. "I'm not interested in any more excitement while I'm here, either."

"It's been a pleasure meeting you. I hope your return home is less eventful than your stay in Zorita," Garza said, shaking her hand one final time.

"Trust me, I do, too." She smiled at him and this time, he smiled back.

Bruno led her to an underground parking garage and a white Hyundai hatchback. He handed Jess the keys and patted the gun on his chest. "You drive, I watch."

The Hyundai's door clanged as she closed it. She fought with the lever to shift the manual seat close enough to reach the pedals. The external mirrors were easily adjusted with a small stalk.

She started the engine. It buzzed to life with a sound that suggested the motor was housed in a tin box. She grimaced. A far cry from the jazzy little Mini Cooper.

Jess backed out of the parking space. She slipped easily into first gear.

Bruno pointed to the left.

She merged into traffic.

Bruno was quick with hand signals, and they weaved their way through some busy streets without a single U-turn.

After ten minutes, she recognized the dry cleaner where she'd learned Elden's address. She slowed to find a parking space.

Bruno shook his head, and pointed farther down the road. She turned right and doubled back to Felipe Cantor's apartment. Bruno directed her to park outside the apartment building beside a sign that read *estacionamiento prohibido*.

"Wait here." He climbed out and hammered on the apartment's outer door with the flat of his fist. Twenty seconds later he shouted "Policía," and hammered again.

He spoke briefly with a resident. She backed away and he propped the door open with what looked like a garden gnome.

He gestured for Jess to get out. He led her into the building, shielding her from the street with his body.

The woman who had talked to Jess on her previous visit was there. She nodded her recognition. "Numero ocho."

Jess smiled. "Sí."

The woman disappeared into her apartment on the ground floor. Bruno led the way up the stairs.

He scanned constantly, checking the area for threats, Jess assumed. He waved her to the third floor. The stairs continued upward.

The third floor had four doors off the corridor. Bruno stared at them each in turn.

Jess followed his gaze. His intensity unnerved her. Did he know something terrible about this building? Or this area? Surely local police didn't enter all buildings using these procedures. Or maybe they did. She shrugged.

He looked outside the window, and gave her a nod.

She pressed the doorbell to number 8. The happy tune echoed in the apartment behind the door. Jess gritted her teeth.

No matter what she'd said to Garza, if she missed Cantor here after what she'd been through, she'd barge into Grupo Lopez and demand to see him. She'd take Bruno along. He didn't look like a man who would be refused entry anywhere.

She stabbed the doorbell again. The music played. Footsteps clicked on a hard floor.

Bruno stepped up to the door. He held his badge in front of the spy hole. "Policía."

The door opened two inches, held by the chain. Felipe Cantor's bearded face peered through the gap.

Bruno held his badge up. "Policía."

Cantor said something in Spanish much too rapidly for Jess to catch. Bruno replied, and Jess caught her name.

Cantor grunted, and pulled the door open. In English, he said, "Welcome to my home."

CHAPTER FORTY-SIX

Friday, August 19
7:00 p.m. CET
Zorita, Spain

HADLOW YAWNED AS HE drove. Elden's early morning
flight didn't fit well with the Spanish fondness for late nights. He
breathed deeply to help focus.

His target was a white Hyundai, three vehicles ahead.
Kimball had finally emerged from the police station with an
officer who could be nothing but her bodyguard carrying a
CETME-C2 strapped across his chest. He shook his head. Better
than letting her roam the streets alone, but did this mean the CNP
had abandoned the search for the man who had tried to kill her?

As an exercise, Hadlow challenged himself to guess her
destination. He smiled when she parked at Felipe Cantor's
apartment.

He parked a hundred yards down the road. He watched as
they entered Cantor's apartment building. The bodyguard looked
formidable enough to intimidate civilians, at least.

At the shop on the corner, Hadlow bought a newspaper and an espresso to go. The clerk handed him a tiny paper cup.

He pressed an earbud into his right ear. The recording device he'd placed in Kimball's bag clicked on and her voice burst into his ear.

He wandered toward Cantor's apartment, sipping from the cup, and holding the folded paper in front of him as if he was reading.

Kimball talked to a woman. From the footsteps, he heard them climbing the stairs. The musical tune from Cantor's doorbell that Hadlow heard last week when he used it to confirm that Cantor was out sounded.

A trio of mopeds raced by. Screaming tiny engines blotted out the conversation inside.

A bird fluttered from the roof opposite. Hadlow looked up. A window was open on the top floor of the building. A window that hadn't been open when Hadlow was here before.

He was approaching Cantor's apartment block. He could walk past and double back, or loiter. Neither were good options. There were shops across the street. They were closed, but he could look in the windows without drawing too much attention.

He stopped ten feet from Cantor's building and waited to cross the street.

He glanced again at that open upstairs window. From this angle something looked different.

He blinked to focus and stared intently.

Which was when he saw it.

A thin black cylinder poked from the window.

His blood ran cold.

A rifle barrel.

He dropped his espresso and newspaper, and bolted for Cantor's door.

He hammered his boot on the lock and raced inside.

He took the stairs three at a time.

Three floors.

Climbed fast.

Well aware that the rifleman could squeeze the trigger any moment.

CHAPTER FORTY-SEVEN

Friday, August 19
7:15 p.m. CET
Zorita, Spain

BRUNO LED THE WAY into Felipe Cantor's apartment. Jess
followed through the front door, which opened into a small
hallway. To the rear was a bedroom with a bedside lamp
illuminating a messy bed. To the front was a living room with
two small sofas on either side of a coffee table. The curtains
were closed. Somewhere there had to be a bathroom.

The small kitchen smelled of strong coffee. A machine
gurgled in the corner. A two-cup carafe, but only one mug
waited on the countertop. Beside it was a half-eaten sandwich.

Cantor waved toward the kitchen and closed the front door
when Bruno moved out of the way.

The kitchen's single garish light bulb wasn't bright enough
to banish the shadows. Bruno and his equipment overwhelmed
the confined space. Cantor's gaze returned repeatedly to the big
gun.

"Do you speak English?" Jess said.

Cantor nodded. "Some."

She gestured through a small archway to the living room. "Can we sit?"

Cantor stepped into the room and flipped on the light.

The coffee table was covered in magazines. Jess noticed *Taboo* among them. An empty red wine bottle and a wine-stained glass lay beside one of the table's legs.

He picked up the glass and bottle, stood them beside each other on the table, and gestured toward the sofas.

Jess sat and Cantor took the opposite sofa. Bruno remained standing in a corner of the room, just inside the archway leading from the kitchen.

She held up a small recorder and flipped it on. "Do you mind if I record our conversation?"

Cantor looked at the recorder and then at Bruno. "Whatever."

She placed it on the magazines in the center of the table.

"I'm Jessica Kimball with *Taboo Magazine*." She tapped the issue of her magazine on the table. He glanced down briefly. "You're Felipe Cantor, correct?"

"Sí. Yes." He nodded. "What's this about?"

"Debora Elden. I need to find her. Do you know where she is?"

"Why? What's happened?" He frowned and glanced sideways at Bruno. "Is she in trouble?"

Jess said nothing.

"So you come in here with RoboCop to what? Frighten me?"

Jess leaned forward. She stared at him for a moment.

He lowered his gaze and slumped back against the sofa.

"A friend of hers has been arrested in the US."

He shrugged. "She has lots of friends."

"A bomb exploded. Four people are dead. Many more are injured."

He whistled. "What friend?"

"Alex Cole."

He nodded. "Oh."

"You know him?"

He swung his head, slowly. "I... No."

"I don't think he did this. But I need to talk to Debora."

"Because she knew him."

Jess nodded. "He was her boyfriend."

She waited for Cantor to show some response, but he didn't. "Do you know where Debora has gone?"

He shook his head.

"I saw you leaving Grupo Lopez together."

"We live close to each other. We're not...you know." He shook his head. "We're just friends."

"Debora's not your girlfriend?"

He stood and opened the drapes. "I guess she will be back soon."

"What kind of work is she—"

The front door crashed open.

Instantly, Jess and Cantor turned to look.

Bruno raised his submachine gun.

A large man with jet-black hair Jess recognized from her hotel burst into the room.

Without pause, he launched a jab to Bruno's chin, rocking his head backward.

Bruno's arms flailed in circles. His knees gave way.

The man ran for Jess. He grabbed the front of her shirt. She twisted to lever his hand away, but he half-lifted, half-dragged her off the couch and toward the kitchen as she struggled to break free.

"Get down!" he yelled toward Cantor.

"What the—" Cantor sputtered without moving from the sofa.

The living room window exploded.

Chunks of glass spewed through the air.

Cantor screamed. He lunged forward from the sofa.

The man threw Jess into the kitchen. "Stay there," he said.

Two more dull thumps hit the soft furnishings in the living room.

The man dived in, grabbed Cantor with one hand and shoved him on the floor at Jess's feet.

He pulled the unconscious Bruno along next, and dropped to his knees.

"What the hell's going on?" Jess said. "Who are you?"

Cantor struggled to reach his phone on the kitchen counter. His arm was bloody. "I've been shot."

"Damn lucky you weren't all shot," the man said, with a British accent she hadn't noticed initially.

Chunks of wood splintered off the arch between the kitchen and the living room with the next shot.

The Brit jerked his thumb toward the window. "Sniper's nest on the other side of the street. Seeking to kill Cantor. Maybe he wants to kill all of you, who knows?"

CHAPTER FORTY-EIGHT

CANTOR HAD REACHED HIS phone. "I need the police," he said. "A man broke into my apartment. Someone's shooting at us."

The Brit grabbed Cantor's arm, jerked the phone away, and ended the call. He stuffed the phone in his pocket. "Can we get out the back?"

Cantor glared but didn't answer.

"We're sitting ducks here." The Brit shook Cantor by his wounded arm.

Cantor screamed.

"Is there another way out? Fire escape? Anything?"

Cantor's eyes were wild. He shook his head. "No."

Police sirens sounded in the distance.

The Brit crouched low and peered around the corner of the archway into the living room. "He's gone."

"Who? Who is gone?" Jess demanded.

"The sniper." He looked around. "He may be on his way here to finish what he started. We've got to get out."

Cantor darted between Jess and the Brit, and ran out onto the landing.

"No!" the Brit yelled.

Cantor ran flat out down the stairs. A few moments later, Jess could no longer hear his footsteps.

Bruno groaned. The Brit leaned down and gave him a solid punch on the temple, not hard enough to kill. Bruno grunted and his head rolled sideways. The Brit took his submachine gun.

"He'll be fine. We have to go out the rear," the Brit said.

"The police are on the way," Jess said.

"Exactly. We don't want to be here when they arrive." he replied. "You're in over your head, Ms. Kimball. When we get out of here, take a flight stateside and forget about this."

Jess frowned. "How do you know my name? Who are you?"

The Brit dashed into the bedroom. He dropped low and checked outside the bedroom window.

She grabbed her recorder from the coffee table, followed him into the bedroom, and glanced through the window. There was a roof jutting out from the floor below.

He twisted his head from side to side, straining to scope out as much of the street as possible. "Just call me a concerned citizen."

"You're British." Which probably meant neither Morris nor Remington had sent him, which had been her first thought.

"No fooling you." He opened the rear window and gestured toward it.

She made no move to join him.

He looked directly at her. "At lunchtime you were shoved in front of a train and by dinner time someone is shooting at you."

She stared at him. "Why have you been following me?"

He checked the street again. "You want to hang around here and let him finish the job, that's up to you."

He slung the submachine gun over his shoulder and braced it between his elbow and his ribs.

"Look." He nodded toward Bruno, out cold. "He's probably a good man, but you're a target and he can't protect you while he's unconscious. Hell, he didn't do such a great job for you anyway. He didn't even try to duck when I hit him, did he?"

Shouts were exchanged on the ground floor. Two shots fired.

"That's not the police shooting down there. And this isn't a good place for a firefight." The Brit ran into the kitchen, and dragged Bruno back with him. He slapped the man in the face.

Bruno groaned and opened his eyes.

Screaming from downstairs.

The Brit shoved Bruno out the window. Bruno groaned and mumbled, but he was in no state to resist. The Brit rolled out of the window after him.

"Last chance." He looked at Jess one more time. "Come on."

Jess glanced at the open apartment door and then followed.

The roof was steep, but the old tiles were rough and her shoes gripped well enough.

The Brit held Bruno as he staggered along the top of the roof beside the wall then down the slope. At the end of the roof, a wall below separated Cantor's building from its neighbor.

The Brit dangled Bruno over the edge, and lowered him onto the top of the wall.

Out of view, Bruno fell to the ground. She heard the heavy thud when he landed. But he didn't scream.

The Brit held his hands out to Jess. "Keep moving."

He swung her out over the edge and dropped her onto the wall.

She crouched down, grabbed the top of the wall, and lowered herself to the ground near Bruno.

The Brit made it from the roof to the wall and the wall to the ground in two jumps.

He lifted Bruno by his collar, and hurried to an alleyway opposite.

Bruno's boots bounced as his legs were dragged across the road.

Jess followed. She glanced back at the apartment window.

Halfway down the alley, the Brit stopped and propped Bruno against the wall. He was slowly regaining consciousness.

The Brit waved the submachine gun in his face. "Count to a hundred before you do anything. Understand? Cien, cien. Understand?"

Bruno nodded.

The Brit stared at Jess. "You got your passport?"

Jess held up her bag. "Yeah."

"Good. Because you're leaving the country." He nudged Jess forward. "Uncle Sam is calling. Let's go."

CHAPTER FORTY-NINE

Friday, August 19
7:30 p.m. CET
Zorita, Spain

SIRENS FILLED THE AIR. Shouting followed the screech of car tires. Jess looked back along the alley. She had no clue about the Brit. But someone had shot at them and Cantor, at least, would have died without his intervention.

"Let's move." The Brit walked away. "The shooter might still be active in the area."

Bruno was vertical, but still dazed. He seemed to be trying to count on his fingers.

"You okay?" she said.

He nodded, and his eyes wobbled with the effort.

A blue Peugeot screeched to a stop at the end of the alley. The window buzzed down and Jess caught sight of a large black gun.

She wrapped her arm around Bruno's, levering him to his unsteady feet, and ran. Bruno had seen the gun, too, and did his stumbling best to move.

The Brit was down on one knee, leveling Bruno's big gun down the alley at the Peugeot. Jess shoved Bruno to one side of the passage and out of the line of fire.

The Brit fired three single shots in rapid succession. The submachine gun jerked in his hands and the sound pounded off the alley's concrete walls.

Jess kept moving.

All of it brought Bruno fully back to consciousness.

The Peugeot raced away with a squeal of tires. Never fired a shot.

The Brit jumped up, stopping Jess and Bruno with outstretched arms. "Back, back." He shoved them back the way they had come.

"But—" Jess said.

Quickly, he said, "He's going round the block to try and cut us off. We can go either way to my car. Move!"

Bruno grabbed for his gun.

The Brit fought back for a moment then let go. "Save the complaining."

Jess wasn't sure Bruno understood until he ran flat out ahead of them to the end of the alley, and dropped to one knee to check to see if the road was clear.

Jess and the Brit lined up behind him. Bruno waved them out.

The Brit ran to a silver Ford Escort, waving the remote control in the air and stabbing at the unlock button. The car bleeped and its lights flashed.

Jess took the passenger seat as the Brit pressed the start button. The engine burst into life with a snarl. The car was moving by the time Bruno jumped in the rear.

The Ford was quick, but the Brit drove without revving hard

or torturing the tires. He took a right to avoid red lights and back left onto a parallel road.

Behind them was a sea of official vehicles and flashing lights.

Bruno pointed the submachine gun at the Brit's back.

"Don't even think about it," the Brit said as he took a ramp to a freeway.

Bruno held the gun on him. "Stop!"

The Brit kept his foot down. "Shooting the driver at seventy miles an hour is a good recipe for disaster."

He looked at Bruno in the rearview mirror. "And you're not even buckled up." He mimed using the seatbelt.

Bruno shuffled back in his seat and buckled up. He kept the gun in one hand and took out his radio.

The Brit shook his head. He held up two fingers. "Two minutes. Dos minutos."

His accent was terrible but Bruno seemed to understand. He looked from the Brit to Jess and back again. He held onto the radio, but took his finger off the transmit switch.

"But we do need the police," Jess said.

"We're on the way. I know just the place," the Brit replied.

At this point, she had no choice but to trust him. Nothing had deterred him from his own plans so far. And if shooting the driver at seventy miles an hour was a recipe for disaster, jumping out of a moving vehicle at that speed would be even worse.

He turned off the freeway and worked through a few blocks to a small police station. It was an industrial looking building, probably built on the lowest budget. The small amount of parking was all labeled for police cars.

The Brit went around to the other side of the building where an area had been cleared for construction.

He parked neatly in one corner, pointing, the car toward the police station. "We're here."

Bruno nodded.

They all stepped out of the car.

Bruno kept his gun on the Brit.

The Brit held his hands up in front of him, his fingers outstretched. "I'm sorry I had to do what I did back there, but there was no way I was going to explain it all before someone got shot. So, I did what I had to do." He lowered his hands. "You would have done the same."

Bruno nodded his head and slowly lowered his weapon.

The Brit smiled. He lashed out a straight arm punch that landed solidly on Bruno's jaw. His other hand wrenched the gun away from the collapsing police officer.

Adrenaline and anger fueled Jess to step toward Bruno and lash out. "What the hell is wrong with you?"

The Brit blocked her way. He nodded toward the station. "They'll come and get him in a few minutes."

"We left the scene of a crime. Shots were fired. Someone tried to kill us. Deliberately, if you're right about the sniper. This is a matter for the police."

"Trust me, you don't want to tell all this to the local police."

"Or what?" She stuck her chin out so he'd have a clear path to her jaw. "You'll knock me out cold?"

He knelt and folded Bruno into the recovery position. "You need to be out of the country before anyone else gets hurt."

"Like I'm going to trust you after you've laid out a police officer with one punch, and won't tell me who you are or why you're here?"

The Brit circled back to the Ford. "We can talk on the way."

Jess looked at Bruno and then the police station. She'd spent several hours with Garza today. She knew what would happen if she went inside. And this time, she wasn't so clearly the victim he might feel a duty to protect.

She was tempted to simply walk away and get the hell out of the country.

But then she'd never know what was going on here.

And what about Alex Cole? She'd promised Marcia McAllister. After all she'd been through already, she wouldn't simply give up and quit now.

"I've got to go before they come out here for the big guy." The Brit opened the car door and put one foot inside. "Are you coming or not?"

She held her hand out, over the top of the car. "Give me the gun."

He frowned.

"Give me the gun."

"Why?"

"Because I don't like being in a car with an armed stranger."

He rolled his eyes, and held out the stock to Jess.

She grabbed the gun, and rolled it over, cycling the magazine out to confirm it was loaded.

He got in the car, and the engine barked to life.

She clicked the safety on, and held her hand over the mechanism. No reason to advertise that it would take a moment longer to shoot him.

She took the passenger seat, laying the gun across her lap with the business end pointed at the Brit.

He backed the car out of the building site, and rejoined the highway.

"Let's start with the basics," Jess said. "Tell me your name and why you've been following me."

CHAPTER FIFTY

Friday, August 19
7:45 p.m. CET
Zorita, Spain

TRAFFIC ON THE FREEWAY was lighter as rush hour faded. The Brit stayed in the middle lane, going with the flow, and keeping a good distance between him and the car in front. He turned the radio on low. The female host had a British accent.

"Why don't we start with you?" he said. "Jessica Kimball. Reporter with *Taboo Magazine*. You live in Denver. Your boyfriend is FBI. Came here because Alex Cole is accused of blowing up a biochemical plant in Chatham, Iowa. Kelso Products, to be specific. You suspect he's not guilty, but don't have any evidence to back that up."

Jess barely blinked. "Am I supposed to be impressed?"

"You're supposed to realize that there's more going on than you know."

"So fill me in."

"We're heading to Gibraltar."

Jess waited for the rest.

"It's a British territory and possession," he said.

"I'm well aware." She ground her teeth while she waited.

He turned up the radio a fraction. "Gibraltar is adjacent to Spain and joined to the mainland. We can drive there. It has an airport. You'll be able to fly to the UK and on to the US."

"So you've not only been following me, you're spying on my conversations, too," she said, through gritted teeth.

He shrugged.

This was ridiculous. She should have stayed at the police station. "Just drop me off. I have already booked a flight home from Valencia in the morning."

"And no one knows that besides me and Garza and Bruno and your FBI boyfriend and the guy who tried to kill you and who knows who else by now?" He arched his eyebrows and glanced at her for a long moment.

She said nothing.

"I'm not a babysitter. I'm here because you're messing with people who don't give a rat's ass about justice or due process, or anything else you care about, for that matter." He glanced at her again. "They've killed others already and they won't care about one more."

"Tell me who was shooting at us." She ran her fingers through her hair. "Help me understand this."

"I didn't see the shooter." He paused and nodded once, as if he'd made up his mind about something. "I was on the street watching Cantor's place when you and Bruno went inside. I saw the barrel of a gun directly opposite your flat. Just be grateful I did, and leave it at that."

Jess squeezed her lips together. He was probably right, but

there were so many open questions. After a while, she tried a new approach. "Do you know Felipe Cantor?"

"No better than you do."

"How about Debora Elden?"

"Not personally."

"Professionally? Whatever your profession is."

He shook his head. "I was keeping tabs on her for two weeks before you arrived."

"Where is she now?" Jess frowned.

"I lost track of her."

She waited but he didn't elaborate. "Look, I can't keep thinking of you as the Brit. What's your name?"

"You can call me Hadlow."

"Because that's the name you're going under this week?" she snapped.

"Longer than a week, but yes." He grinned for the first time in a while. "Gary Hadlow. You might be surprised to know that I'm pretty impressed with you, by the way. You've brushed off more stuff than a lot of the guys I know. And trust me, I know some mean guys."

She knew he was trying to divert and disarm her, but as long as he was talking, she had a chance to bring him around. "Thanks for the compliment, I guess."

"I was at the train crossing when you talked to the inspector. Not many people can talk that calmly five minutes after escaping an oncoming train. In fact, not many people can talk at all after facing an oncoming train." His smile was broader this time. "Nice reversing, by the way."

A phone buzzed in Hadlow's pocket, but he ignored it.

"Want me to answer that?" she said.

He fished the phone from his pocket. "Just tell me who it is."

She looked at the display. "Grupo Lopez." She adjusted her grip on the gun. "You work for Grupo Lopez?"

He shook his head. "Not even close."

"But they're calling you." She stared at the name on the display. "Should I answer it?"

"No."

The buzzing stopped and the words *Missed Call* appeared. She groaned. "This is Felipe Cantor's phone, isn't it?"

He shrugged.

"Why would someone from Grupo Lopez be calling him at this time of night?"

The music on the radio stopped. The host came back on with the news. Her Oxford accent sounded like an old-time BBC announcer. Hadlow turned up the volume.

"Reports are coming in of a multiple shooting in Zorita. Details are hazy, but initial reports indicate one gunman chased people from an apartment near the center of the city. One of the gunmen was shot and is now in custody. It also appears that one or more hostages were taken by another gunman."

"That would be me." Jess raised her hand.

"Must be me." Hadlow laughed. "Because you're the one holding the gun."

Ms. Oxford accent finished the report. *"Police are establishing roadblocks around Zorita. We will keep you updated as this story unfolds."*

Another song started on the radio and Hadlow turned the volume down to a murmur. "No deaths reported. Hopefully, that means Cantor is okay."

"I hope so." Jess turned the phone over in her hands. "You've been following him, too."

He shrugged.

Cantor's phone rang again. *Grupo Lopez* appeared on the display again.

"Don't answer it," he said.

"They'll just keep calling. Besides, we need all the information we can get." She pointed to a freeway exit. "Let's find out who it is, at least. Pull over and stop the car."

CHAPTER FIFTY-ONE

Friday, August 19
8:15 p.m. CET
Zorita, Spain

HADLOW ANGLED OFF THE freeway and pulled into a rest area.

Jess cleared her throat, and answered the phone. "Hello?"

"Felipe?" said a young man's voice.

She opened her mouth to ask the man his name, and stopped.

"Felipe?" the young man said. "That you?"

"Sorry. Felipe left his phone at my place last night. I thought it might be him calling."

The man umm'd and err'd. "Debora?"

"No, it's Alice. Felipe's girlfriend," she said. "Who's Debora?"

Hadlow frowned at her. She shrugged.

The young man's voice tightened. "Girlfriend?"

"Who's Debora?" Jess said.

"I... I—"

"I'm sure he'll come back soon. Can I have him call you?"

"Sí. Tell him security came by."

"Came by? At work? Is he in trouble?"

"Tell him it was like with Camilo."

"What happened with Camilo?"

"He'll know. They emptied Felipe's desk and took his computer. Just now."

"Do they want to talk to him?"

"They didn't even talk to me, and I've got the desk next to his. So, tell him. Tell him it's serious. Make sure Felipe knows. Okay? Like Camilo."

"Okay. What's your name?"

Jess heard other voices on the line. "I must go," the young man said. The line went dead.

Jess leaned back in her seat. "Wow."

"So, tell me," Hadlow said.

"Felipe Cantor's desk has been cleared out at work. Grupo Lopez's security took his computer, too. They're looking for him. The guy said it was just like Camilo."

He nodded slowly. "Who's Camilo?"

"He wouldn't say." She scowled. "Why would Grupo Lopez security clear out Cantor's desk? The timing seems like it might be related to me, doesn't it?"

"That would be my guess. They expected the sniper to kill him and were preparing for the inevitable police inquiry by eliminating everything. If I had to guess, I'd say something similar happened to Camilo. I'll ask my desk jockey boss to check it out." He glanced toward her. "Besides his association with Elden and now you, Cantor's not been up to anything that would get him erased like that."

Jess shook her head. She might be an outsider. She might

have stirred things up. Investigations always did. Maybe it was wishful thinking, but the timeline felt wrong.

"You said you saw a gun pointing at Cantor's apartment before you came busting into the place."

He didn't reply.

"You were following me."

"So?"

"The shooter wasn't following me." She cocked her head and talked it through. "I didn't plan to go to Cantor's apartment at that specific time. It was a spur of the moment thing. When I made the decision, the only person I told was Garza. And I only mentioned it on my way out of the police station. If the shooter had some way of overhearing my plans, he still didn't have time to get there ahead of me and get set up in his nest before you came along and saw me walking into the building."

Hadlow nodded, frowning.

"So, the shooter was already on the third floor opposite when I arrived. He'd brought his rifle. He was already set up." She paused for a breath. "He was there for Felipe."

Hadlow's frown deepened. "Perhaps."

"The caller said they didn't ask for Cantor before they cleared out his desk. They already knew he wasn't coming back."

His eyes scanned the almost deserted rest area. "We need to keep moving."

"Grupo Lopez tried to kill off one of their employees."

He pulled out of the rest area and merged onto the freeway.

When they were once again up to speed, she asked, "Why would they do that?"

"Rafa Lopez is fighting for control of Grupo Lopez. He has his own secret organization running inside the company." He glanced across the cabin. "Rafa is a ruthless son of a bitch. I believe he'll do just about anything, including deep-sixing employees."

"That's what you're doing, isn't it? Something about Rafa Lopez."

He glanced at the clock on the dashboard. "We'll be in Gibraltar in an hour and a half."

She found her phone and checked the signal strength. She dialed her editor and long time friend, Carter Pierce.

"Who are you calling?" Hadlow said.

She angled the gun toward his torso. "My office."

"Why?"

"I don't know what alphabet soup organization you work for, but I'm sure as hell not going to be *deep-sixed*. For all I know, you could be one of Rafa Lopez's men. Someone needs to know where I am."

"Jess?" Carter's voice was groggy because it was three in the morning in Denver, but he snapped the word like he was awake enough.

"Listen to me. I'm in a car with a Brit calling himself Gary Hadlow who is investigating Rafa Lopez but is desperate to stay away from the local police."

"Jess—"

"His people may come there to—"

Carter groaned. "They've already been and gone."

"What?"

"You've stumbled into something, Jess. Whatever it is, it's got people alerted. They promised me Hadlow would get you safely out of Spain. So I agreed."

"You agreed to what?"

"To drop your Kelso Products bombing story in return for getting you back safely."

What the hell? Jess's mouth hung open. In all the years she'd worked with *Taboo*, Carter had never undermined her like this. Not once. Exactly the opposite. He'd always been her staunchest supporter.

"They came to my house a few hours ago," Carter said. "I knew one of them."

"What do you mean you knew them?"

"This has happened before, Jess. Sometimes, we have to play the game. I hate it, too. Maybe we can get the story out afterward. Whatever it is."

Her nostrils flared. "And what about Alex Cole? He could be executed, Carter. Can you live with that?"

"Let it go for now, Jess."

"What about all the people who got killed in that explosion? And Debora Elden? She's at the center of all this. I know it like I know you're not really agreeing to this, Carter."

"Jess. Please. We don't know what's going on and we could screw this up and put other lives at risk. Not only your life, Jess. There are more innocents to consider here. Go with Hadlow. He'll get you out of Spain. We can discuss the rest when you get back."

"What did they say to you?"

"This is bigger than any one person, Jess." Carter's sigh sounded old all of a sudden. "Do it for me, will you? Just this once. I promise I'll never ask you again."

She looked across at Hadlow. "Of course. This is bigger than any one person. I think you're right."

She hung up.

CHAPTER FIFTY-TWO

Friday, August 19
8:30 p.m. CET
Zorita, Spain

HADLOW CONTINUED WITH THE flow of traffic, keeping to the inside lane.

"Congratulations," she said sourly. "You've persuaded my boss. I've been called back. I've got to face a woman I really admire and tell her I've failed. An innocent man will go to prison forever and the terrorists responsible for the Kelso Products bombing will get away with murder. You can be very proud of what you've accomplished."

"Sarcasm now? Look, I don't steer the ship. I'm only chained to an oar. Besides that, a lot of people are working damn hard on this case, putting our lives on the line, if you hadn't noticed." He shrugged and his tone was more than a little edgy. "How does your FBI boyfriend deal with your low opinion of us professionals?"

"You know that's crap." She scowled right back at him.

They held the silence for quite a while. Finally, he asked, "Why is all this so important to you? Why can't you wait until we get the situation handled?"

"Because no one seems to care about Alex Cole except me. He's being framed. I know it as well as I know your name isn't really Gary Hadlow." Jess sighed and ran both hands through her hair. "Now that I'm leaving, don't you owe me some answers, at the very least? What exactly do you think is happening at Grupo Lopez?"

Hadlow shook his head.

"Well, what do you think happened to Debora Elden?"

He seemed tempted to answer, but the moment passed.

"Are you going back to find Cantor? Try to keep him alive, at least?"

He gave an exasperated sigh. "*Will you* give it a rest? I've got enough to deal with as it is."

"Driving along the expressway doesn't seem all that difficult to me."

"I have to get us through to Gibraltar." He gave her the side eye. "We can't just turn up and sip tea with our pinkies in the air to prove we're British, if that's what you were thinking."

Hadlow slowed at the next junction, and stopped at a public payphone. He spent a while on a call and then returned to the car.

"You're cleared to fly from Gibraltar," he said, as if that had been her desire all along.

"And you're going back to Zorita?"

He rejoined the freeway without answering.

Jess sighed. "So let's recap."

"Please. Let's don't." Hadlow frowned. "There is nothing you can rephrase or attack from another angle that I can answer. Don't you get that?"

His phone buzzed and he glanced at the display. "I'm sorry. I know you're trying to help your friend. I wish I was at liberty to say more. But I'm not."

"Damn right I'm trying to help my friend. But that's not all. I've been shot at and pushed in front of a train by whoever is behind all this." She paused with a big dose of exasperation of her own.

He grinned. "Next you're going to tell me you were abducted at gunpoint by a mysterious stranger who made you jump off a roof."

She renewed her grip on the gun. "You're making fun of me."

"Actually not." He sounded a little surprised. He cocked his head and his eyes narrowed. "It's refreshing to find a civilian who can take care of herself and think under pressure."

She glowered at him. "Tell me the truth. If you were in my shoes, would you simply accept all this and go home without a fight?"

He said nothing.

"Exactly as I thought," she said, nodding. "So you want me to do what you, yourself, would not."

He kept quiet for a mile or so before he took a deep breath, having made some sort of decision. "I saw Debora Elden board the Grupo Lopez company jet this morning at 4 a.m. We didn't know her destination at that point. The jet made two stops. No one deplaned at the first stop. The second was Quatro de Fevereiro Airport." He held up his phone. "I just got notification."

"Where is that?"

"Africa. Angola, actually. Luanda, the capital."

"That's a big place."

"Yes, it is."

She searched on her phone. "Grupo Lopez doesn't have any facilities near there."

"We're trying to get further intel."

"Are you going there?"

"Why would I be going there?"

"Why would you be watching her get on the company jet at four in the morning, and why would you be trying to get *more intel* otherwise?"

He sighed.

A road sign indicated another thirty miles to Gibraltar.

He took the next exit, and pulled into a large gas station with a mini-mart. He filled up the car while Jess stretched her legs and used the restroom.

When she came back, he took his wallet out, and pointed to the car. "Stay here, I'm going to pay."

He disappeared into the mini-mart. A minute later he returned with two bottles of water and a magazine.

He gave one of the water bottles to Jess and they headed back onto the freeway. "I talked to my boss. As I suspected, the mysterious Camilo worked at Grupo Lopez in the same department as Cantor. He died a couple of months ago. Car crash."

"Yeah, right." She glanced at the magazine. He picked it up, and shook it over her lap. Two British passports dropped out. One with Hadlow's picture, the other with hers. She read the names. "Harry and Julia Beaumont?"

He grinned. "And you're British. Just like that."

"As long as I don't open my mouth and ruin the cover."

"Haven't you heard? Lots of Brits marry Americans these days."

Her eyes widened. "We're married?"

"Oh, thanks," he said with mock indignation.

She laughed. "I still have a boyfriend. Maybe I should let him know."

"Trust me, it's a marriage of convenience."

"At least we agree on something."

"At the very least, someone on the Spanish side of the border will have our pictures from the incident at Cantor's apartment," he explained. "The photos will be traced to the names and passports we used coming into the country. It might have already happened."

"Won't these new passports be suspicious then?"

"If they were new passports they'd be suspicious as hell."

She read the text next to her picture. "It's dated two years ago."

"Wonderful things, computers," he said with a grin.

Cantor's phone chimed with a text message. Unlike answering a phone call, the messages could only be accessed by unlocking it with a fingerprint or a PIN number. She had neither, but she read through the snippet of message on the display. "Booking reference BQC90P. Southern Europe Airways."

"I can get someone to look that up," Hadlow said.

Jess brought up the Southern Europe Airways website and typed in the booking reference. The website asked for the surname. She used Cantor and the site promptly gave her the flight details. "He's going to Tangier, then Luanda, then Kitande."

His eyebrows popped up. "I'm familiar with the other two, but where's Kitande?"

She looked up Kitande. "Small place. Five hundred miles south. Borders Namibia. Inland by about a hundred miles." She zoomed in on the map. "Doesn't look like there's much industry there. Doesn't look like much of anything, actually."

She ran a couple more searches. "Step on it and we could make the 9:43 p.m. to Casablanca with a connection to Luanda and Kitande. Twenty-four-hour trip, and we'd be two hours after him." She whistled. "Like you said. Big place, Africa."

She turned off her phone.

They passed a sign that announced they were entering the town of La Línea de la Concepción.

Hadlow navigated the town's streets like a local. He hadn't even objected to her use of the word *"we."* Which she should have realized was suspicious on its own.

What was he planning?

They reached a series of low modern buildings. Signs pointed to Gibraltar.

The famous rock rose up behind the buildings. It was smaller than she'd expected, but there was no mistaking it from the flat land around it.

Hadlow took a right turn, and the border post was in front of them. It had an arch and three small lines of cars. Hadlow chose the lane marked *British Passport Holders.*

A guard with a British accent asked for their passports, checked them with a scanner, and waved them through.

Moments later she was on British soil without so much as opening her mouth to answer a single question and reveal her Midwest accent in all its glory.

"Wonderful things, computers." Hadlow grinned. "Welcome to Gibraltar, Mrs. Beaumont."

CHAPTER FIFTY-THREE

Friday, August 19
9:00 p.m. CET
Gibraltar, Iberian Peninsula

ON THE OTHER SIDE of border control, Hadlow stopped at an intersection behind a barrier and flashing lights similar to the train crossing back in Zorita.

"Remind you of anything?" he said with a grin.

"I'd rather not be reminded, thanks." She peered through the windshield. In front of them was a massive open area. "Is that what I think it is?"

"Unlike Africa, Gibraltar is a small place. There's no land to waste." He gestured out of the windshield. "That's the runway."

As if to make his point, a twin propeller aircraft thundered by.

The lights stopped flashing and the barrier rose automatically after the plane passed.

Jess checked her watch. "Nine forty-three? We could make it."

"Suppose I agreed to take you along with me." He glanced at her and crossed the runway. "You realize that worse things could happen than you've already been through?"

"I can take care of myself."

"I don't doubt that for a minute." He paused and looked at her again. She looked straight back. "Look, the truth is that I could use a partner and your cover as my wife would work fairly well on this. But I've been to these places before and I know a lot more about this situation than you do. Things I can't tell you. So can you take orders and do what I say?"

He veered off the marked route across the runway, and drove along the rear of a line of jets parked at the terminal. He curved in around the last aircraft in the line.

Jess grinned. "Why, Mr. Beaumont, after all the time we've been married, how can you question my fidelity?"

"This is no joke, Jess. Yes or no? You'll do what I tell you or I'm leaving you here."

"I hear you," she replied. Which wasn't the same as a promise. He probably didn't have anybody for backup. Otherwise, he wouldn't be asking.

A set of stairs led up to the departure level of the terminal. A man in a suit paced at the bottom of the staircase.

Hadlow screeched to a halt, hopped out of the car, and tossed the keys to the guy.

Jess followed him.

"Arnold Chapman. Nice to meet you." Chapman shook hands and then offered an envelope. "I have one ticket for the UK, made out in the name on your passport. The American embassy will have someone meet you at Heathrow. They'll sort things out from there. Just don't leave the terminal, either here or at Heathrow and everything will go smoothly."

She took the envelope.

Hadlow took the gun from her, and handed it to Chapman.

The man handled it like a live snake. "No one said anything about guns."

"Then it's your lucky day," Hadlow said.

"What am I supposed to do with it?"

"If you're feeling generous, you could wipe it thoroughly to remove any identifying prints or DNA and return it to the police in Zorita," Hadlow replied.

The man opened his mouth, but Hadlow held up his hand. "There's a flight for Kitande in Africa in thirty minutes."

"Kitande?"

"Via Casablanca and Luanda. You have a credit card?"

"Well…of course."

"Then let's move."

Chapman frowned at the gun. "Is this loaded?"

Hadlow ripped the gun from his hands, pulled out the magazine, ejected the round from the chamber, and shoved the parts back into his chest. "No."

He pushed Chapman up the steps. "Now move. Mrs. Beaumont and I need tickets."

Jess grinned.

Hadlow grimaced. "I need to have my head examined."

CHAPTER FIFTY-FOUR

Saturday, August 20
11:30 p.m. WAT
Kitande, Africa

THE FLIGHT TO KITANDE was long and delayed. During the layover in Casablanca, Hadlow chatted on a satellite phone that was as large as a brick. He connected Cantor's cell phone to the satellite phone with a cable and spent the better part of half an hour watching a small blue bar grow across the screen.

"Don't ask," he said as she watched him.

Jess ate in Casablanca and Luanda, figuring she better make the most of every opportunity. They had long layovers, and took turns sleeping and keeping watch.

In Luanda she used her credit card to buy the local currency, which came in the form of five- and ten-thousand Kwanza notes. She split a couple of the larger denomination notes into thousands, and ended up with a bundle an inch thick.

The Casablanca and Luanda flights were pure luxury compared to the aging Cessna Caravan they flew to Kitande, where the seats were tiny and the ceiling so low that Hadlow was practically folded in two. Even Jess had to duck as they found their way to their seats. They were in the back row, and eight of the nine spaces were occupied.

The flight was delayed for two hours on the runway. The pilot turned the engines off to save fuel, and the temperature in the tiny cylinder soared. He had a small supply of sodas in an ice chest, which rapidly ran out.

Jess was filled with questions. She wanted to discuss everything with Hadlow, partly to make sense of what she already knew, but he remained quiet all the way to the approach to Kitande.

"We'll see if we can find a way to trace Cantor. If not, we'll find a room and make an early start tomorrow."

"If Cantor is following Elden, why? What's he worried about?" Jess mused aloud.

"Good questions. But it seems like Grupo Lopez employees are dying at a rather rapid rate to me."

The nighttime approach into Kitande was easy. The town was small. Light spilled from houses sprawled haphazardly along its half dozen streets. Desolate looking roads led to all four points of the compass.

The pilot landed smoothly but braked hard on the short runway. The aircraft rolled to a single-story terminal building that was not much longer than the Cessna. Two large lights illuminated the aircraft and a patch of tarmac.

The passengers filed out. A few stood by the cargo hold.

"Wait up," Hadlow said.

The pilot wrestled bags through a door at the rear of the aircraft. Hadlow picked up a small dark gray canvas suitcase. Jess contained her curiosity.

He pointed to the terminal. "We have a car booked."

The terminal was basically a room with a single counter at one end. Behind it was a man who, according to the sign, handled tickets, food, and rental cars.

Jess checked her phone. She had cell phone service, but no connection to the internet.

She left Hadlow at the counter and wandered out the front of the building to a line of taxis. She counted three, an optimistic number given the number of passengers on the plane.

The drivers sat in a group around a table sporting an oversized umbrella that would have looked at home on the waterfront at Monaco. They watched her approach.

"English?" she said hopefully.

A bald man stood up. "Where to?"

Jess smiled. "I'm afraid I don't need a taxi." She pulled a thousand Kwanza note from her pocket. "I was just wondering if any of you saw a young man on the earlier flight. Tall."

The man frowned, and rattled off rapid-fire Portuguese to the rest of the group. They shook their heads, and talked among themselves.

"Felipe Cantor? Spanish."

One of the men clicked his fingers and said something that seemed hopeful. The bald man relayed his comments.

"There was a man from Spain. Three hours ago." He laughed and patted his head. "Black hair. Beard."

"Yes." She nodded with a big smile. "Where did he go?"

There was more discussion before the bald man spoke. "Rooibank. On the coast."

She handed over the note, and withdrew another from her pocket. "What's in Rooibank?"

The bald man shrugged. "Fishermen. Maybe he goes to fish. Like the others."

Jess frowned. "Others."

The bald man conferred with the group for a moment. "Usually when Spanish come here, they go fishing." He gestured to the group. "But they don't use our taxis. They have a Land Rover. Big. Expensive."

"But Felipe used one of your taxis?"

The bald man nodded and pointed to the driver.

"Exactly where did he take him?"

The bald man scribbled an address on the corner of a cigarette packet. "A hundred miles." He pointed west. "A good road."

Jess thanked them and handed over a five-thousand note, for which they rewarded her with big grins and happy nods.

Hadlow exited the terminal building, jangling a set of keys. "We're set."

"I have an address. Cantor went west. Rooibank. A hundred miles. On the coast."

Hadlow looked west. "What's over there?"

"Fishing, they say."

Hadlow sneered.

"We won't know till we get there," Jess replied.

The car turned out to be a five-year-old Opel. It had dents all over it, and its ash tray had been well used. The stale cigarette smoke was noxious but the car started right away and the tank was full.

Hadlow drove. He took the road west. They kept the windows open for the breeze so they could breathe.

"What's in the bag?" Jess asked.

"I'm sure you can guess." He pulled a gun from under his

jacket and handed it to Jess. "I did some work out this way before. If you're going to risk your own life, least I can do is give you the chance to protect it. You can shoot, right?"

"Want to challenge me to a contest?"

He laughed. "Something tells me I'd be way out of my league."

She grinned. The pistol was heavy with a *V* engraved on the grip and she wondered who it had belonged to.

"Vektor. It's South African," he said. "Fifteen rounds. Nine-millimeter. Rugged. Safety's at the back. Just one rule here. You only draw it when all other options are gone, and you only shoot when you have a solid chance of hitting your target." He waved his hand in the air. "There's a lot of civilians around, and no matter what, this isn't their fight."

Jess smiled. "I think we're going to get along fine, Hadlow."

In the middle of an African night, the sky filled with a million stars, and the milky blue of a lonely moon.

The Opel's engine hummed along like a windup toy. The lights of the town faded fast. The road became rougher the farther they drove. Jess was tired, but she refused to go to sleep and kept her gaze probing the dark. But she saw no sign of human activity.

CHAPTER FIFTY-FIVE

Sunday, August 21
2 a.m. CAT
Kumbha Airbase, Zambia, 150 miles inside the Zambia-Angola border

TEBOGO KNELT IN THE bushes. The sun had long gone and the new moon that had replaced it offered no help to unaided eyes.

In front of him lay Kumbha airbase. It wasn't an important airbase. But it was in Africa where there was no shortage of land. So the government had erected miles of fencing to secure the property they had claimed.

He laughed to himself. The government forces of most countries were fools. They always assumed their opponents would carry out the most obvious attack, they never put themselves in their opponents' position. They never looked to see how they could be defeated, they simply stopped thinking after their first possible solution.

The government's solution was an eight-foot-high chain-link

fence topped with a barbed wire roll. His answer was bolt cutters. His team would be through the government's illusion of security in seconds.

Kumbha airbase might have occupied acres of land, but its buildings were clustered to one side of the runway. The buildings were separated by a taxiway, hangars closest to the runway, offices, and the control tower on the other side. The control tower was a good three hundred yards from the offices. It probably wasn't ideal to be so far from the aircraft, but the land rose in that direction, and the government had economized by building a shorter tower than normal.

The offices were in two rows of five decrepit buildings erected in the seventies, most likely by the son of a corrupt government official.

The only building that looked cared for was the fire station. It had a single large roll up door, and therefore a single fire engine. Perhaps no surprise for a small airbase, but soon it would be revealed as a glaring mistake.

There were six hangars in a straight line, parallel to the runway. The aprons had been arranged for the aircraft to roll into the hangar at the rear and exit from the front. Exiting the front of the hangars put the aircraft onto the taxiway beside the offices. At the far end of the hangars, the taxiway turned right onto the runway.

It was probably an efficient layout for the operation of the base, but it made Tebogo's job more difficult.

Between the fence and the hangars was two hundred yards of open ground. It was the shortest distance from the fence to the hangars, and therefore the entry point that carried the least exposure time. But they would be easily visible to anyone in the control tower with night vision equipment.

As ordered, Tebogo placed the final call for authorization. "We are in place."

"Excellent." Sánchez, the cold-hearted bitch, seemed to smile across the connection. "Call back when your mission is completed."

She disconnected. He returned the phone to his backpack and then checked behind him.

His men had formed up into their teams. There were three groups of three. Each group consisted of two of his fighters and one pilot. The pilots were Angolan, and he considered them mostly as more baggage his team would be required to carry.

His was the fourth group. His second-in-command, Umi, a mountain of a man called Mort, and two more Angolan pilots.

His men were heavily armed. They carried Heckler & Koch G36 assault rifles with night scopes and suppressors. They were excellent pieces of engineering, and he'd been lucky to get them at a bargain price.

Besides the H&K, each team carried an MC60 mortar from a defunct South African company. The mortars were extremely simple and lightweight, a tube with a small shock absorbing brace, and an inclinometer to judge range.

Each team had eight shells carried in a pack on their backs. It was a heavy load, but the ability to spread firepower over a wide range always disoriented an opponent, usually pushing them into defensive positions, fearing they were fighting a much larger force.

The pilots had been given handguns. They carried them wearily, and he wasn't sure they knew how to use them. The airmen were in poor physical condition. Jogging through the bush from their drop-off point had been difficult, but his men had done it while also carrying a fifty-pound load.

They had to stop numerous times for the pilots to catch up and recover. He had no respect for their lack of ability, but he needed them for one critical aspect of the escape.

The means of escape was also their prize. Each of the six hangars housed a single Antonov An-12, a fifty-person transport aircraft. They were old, but the design had held up to the test of time in the harshest of environments. Of the six aircraft, two were hangar queens that had been cannibalized to keep the other four flying. The four flying aircraft were farthest from the fence and closest to the route through to the runway.

Launching any aircraft was a prolonged process. Even if one wasn't concerned with details such as flight plans and tower control, the big issue was fuel. Fortunately, their employer had deep pockets. Two tankers of aviation fuel had arrived at the base gates the day before. Paperwork showed the fuel was for the base, but Tebogo knew the base's storage tank was already full.

No base commander was going to turn away fuel, so the tankers were directed to brim each aircraft, even the two hangar queens.

All that was left was the two minutes for the engines to come up to speed. Two minutes was both fast and slow. To him and his men it would be agonizing. He had prepared a distraction.

Tebogo wasn't a bloodthirsty killer. He'd been involved in all sorts of battles, but given the choice, he would always take the path of stealth and distraction rather than weapons and violence.

He tapped Umi on the shoulder, and showed him his watch.

Umi keyed the microphone on his radio, twice. The click, click of static alerted the teams. They had practiced the operation. They all knew what to do. And if the plan had to be improvised, they'd planned for that, too.

They checked their equipment and switched off safeties. Except for emergencies, they would maintain radio silence and communicate with hand signals.

With a thumbs-up from every man in the group, Umi extended an antenna from a plastic box, and glanced at Tebogo for final approval. Tebogo nodded, and Umi pressed a button on the box.

A second later, a mile away on the other side of the airbase, a blinding flash lit up the sky.

The earth trembled and a pounding explosion rent the air.

The first explosion was followed by a second, and a third.

The blinding flashes were joined by a flickering glow that grew stronger by the moment.

CHAPTER FIFTY-SIX

AS THE FOREST FIRE raged, a commotion started on the base. People ran in and out of the offices in a frenzy. Tebogo's night vision, the type used by the US military, couldn't bring the tower closer. He could distinguish nothing but movement. He hoped from the better vantage point, the air traffic controllers would be directing the base response.

Seconds later, a siren wailed and flashing lights lit up on the fire station. Its metal door clattered as it rolled up. The fire engine revved hard and began its labored exit. It turned away, lumbering along the apron and onto a road out of the far side of the base.

What looked like two school buses painted with camouflage stopped outside. People poured out of the buildings and the buses left a few moments later. A ragtag collection of vehicles loaded down with men and equipment followed.

Tebogo rotated his arm over his head and pointed forward. The teams approached the fence, bolt cutters ready, and thirty seconds later they were through. The last team zip-tied the ruined fence into something that would pass a first glance before separating to head for a small hut between the office buildings and the fence.

Tebogo led the way to the first hangar, He ran hard, the base's wailing siren blotted out most noise. The tarmac taxiway was far easier going than the rough open ground.

At the hangar, the teams spread out, using the barrels and boxes littering the area for cover. Tebogo peered around the side of the hangar. The taxiway was empty, but plenty of lights were on in the buildings. He had to hope they had simply been left on as the bulk of the personnel evacuated.

Through his night vision he could see the team at the hut. One man remained on guard while the others went inside. He counted off the seconds. At sixty he began to worry, but they emerged before he reached ninety. The guard raised his hand and yanked it down. He repeated the gesture twice to make sure it had been seen, and then the team headed toward the hangars.

When the team reached the taxiway, Umi pressed a second button on the remote-control detonator. The small explosion it caused could barely be heard above the wailing siren, but the effect was immediate.

The lights in the offices faded. The larger sodium floodlights that illuminated open areas flickered and went dark. The control tower's lights were replaced by a dim blue glow from computer monitors and emergency lighting backed by local batteries. The siren's wail descended the scale, growing quieter with each octave.

Within seconds, the camp was encased in the pitch-black night.

The last team was crossing the taxiway, assisted by the night vision gear.

Shouts came from around the fire station. Flashlight beams

flickered and danced inside the offices. Across the base, the convoy's headlights still bounced along the roads as they headed for the growing fire.

Timing was everything. It was something that couldn't be planned. Judgment was required, and he judged the time had come.

The base's focus was concentrated at the source of the explosions. More than half of the soldiers had already left to fight the growing fire. The fire truck had left. The leaders would be struggling to organize. Even if they realized what happened next, it would take minutes to turn the men around and get back to reinforce the few they had left guarding the base.

He keyed his microphone twice. The teams moved out, keeping low by the walls, and running hard in the spaces between. They each had a designated hangar and aircraft. Each would go through the same procedure simultaneously. If all went well, they wouldn't meet again until they landed, far from Kumbha.

The hangars' large multi-segment doors were closed. They would be electrically operated with a hand-crank backup, but there would be no way to open them from the outside.

He led his team around the side of the building, following his nose to the latrines. His night vision showed the short path between the latrines and the side door into the big building.

Umi sprayed the hinges with oil, counted to ten and whipped the door open. Tebogo was first in, rotating his head to look across the wide floor of the hangar, his gun following his gaze.

The area around the aircraft was empty. The door to the aircraft was open, and the steps were in place.

There were several mechanics tables with a man trying to feel his way from one to the next. In the far corner was a small office, like a ranch house built inside the bigger building.

He gestured to the mechanic. Mort ran full pelt in the pitch dark, and took the man out with a single punch.

Tebogo ran for the ranch house. There were two men inside. One of them was searching a cupboard. Before Tebogo reached the door, the man had found a flashlight and the beam darted around the room.

Tebogo opened the door, pointing his gun at the man. The flashlight beam settled on the Heckler & Koch. Neither man made a noise.

Tebogo used his gun to gesture for them to lie down. They eased themselves to the floor, their eyes fixed on the weapon. Umi gagged them, and zip-tied their hands and feet.

Tebogo cut through every wire in the room, and smashed both men's cell phones.

The two pilots had made it to the aircraft. One was inside and the other remained on the steps, waving the OK signal to Tebogo before disappearing inside.

Mort worked at the opening mechanism by the right-hand door, spraying the rusty mechanism with oil.

Umi followed Tebogo back outside to the front of the building. An iron ladder led up to the roof. Tebogo settled the mortar across his back before making the climb.

The roof was metal. Their feet made dull thumps as they walked.

Umi climbed the shallow sloping roof to the top, and took position beside a rooftop vent to scan the runway behind the building.

Tebogo stayed by the front ledge. From the top there was a good view of the entire taxiway, the office buildings, and the control tower beyond.

He removed the mortar tube from his back, and unloaded five shells from his backpack, keeping three stowed in case he was forced to relocate in a hurry.

Moving flashlights indicated people were still busy in the offices, but the taxiway was quiet.

He heard and felt a deep rumble. He knew the noise. To his right, the massive hangar doors were being wound open.

The metal roof shook. The trembling came in bursts. The hangar doors below him were being opened, but Mort was struggling to do so.

Tebogo heard a jeep before he could see it. He adjusted his night vision to get the best image. An open-top military police vehicle with two men in front. They were armed, but they looked casual in their seats.

He had three choices. Drop them now, scare them off, or create a distraction. At this distance, hitting them could be difficult, which meant they would simply retreat for reinforcements. He also wanted to avoid being the first to take a shot that would announce their presence.

His best choice was distraction.

He aimed the mortar over the buildings and used the inclinometer to set it for three hundred yards. Holding the weapon steady, he dropped the round into the tube.

There was a small explosion and a whooshing noise. From the corner of his eye, he saw a white streak disappear into the night. He counted. The shell was invisible in the dark. On the count of three, a blast shook the air and a flash of light illuminated the rough ground to the left of the control tower.

Several men came out of the offices. The jeep stopped, and the passenger stood on his seat to get a better view.

He shouted, and pointed to the faint billowing cloud of

smoke rising from the mortar's detonation. The man struggled to get seated as the jeep turned ninety degrees.

Headlights blazing, the jeep raced between the buildings and out into the open ground toward the control tower and the plume of smoke that was dissolving into the night.

Tebogo saw movement below him. One of his men ran from hangar to hangar, racing inside for a moment before sprinting to the next. After the last hangar, he turned and ran back with both hands in the air.

It was the signal.

Each pilot would count down and start their engines simultaneously to reduce the risk of attracting attention before each aircraft was ready to start.

The normal power-up procedure had the pilot start one engine to bring up the electrical power, let it stabilize, then start the other engines. Tonight, they would start two engines at the same time. It would strain the batteries, but batteries could be replaced.

The first engine whirred as an electric starter turned over the heavy rotor. The whirring became faster and was drowned out by the roar of the half jet, half propeller turboprop. The second engine caught moments after the first.

Down the line of hangars came a cacophony of squealing and roaring as the other aircraft started their engines.

This was where the mission really got dangerous. Until now, concentrated fire or the appropriate use of the right weapon would give him and his men all the advantage they needed to make an escape. Despite the weight of the weapons they carried, his men were strong and light on their feet.

But aircraft changed everything. The lumbering beasts announced themselves unmistakably. Sheer size made them easy targets. A few well-placed rifle rounds would bring down forty-thousand pounds of airplane. An accurate or lucky shot could take out the pilot.

He scanned the tarmac. His night vision revealed a clear view for several hundred yards. Jeeps and anything else using a light were easily seen. But a man-sized figure was harder to spot. A man could easily come much closer without being seen in the dark.

The military police jeep was still heading across the open ground. Tebogo wondered what they thought they were going to do when they got there. The mortar had exploded a safe distance from the control tower, and the tower's occupants had returned to their building.

He sensed a light, and snapped his head up. The windows of the control tower glinted in the dark. The glow was air traffic control displays reflecting off the glass.

His night vision goggles bloomed, the green and black images became almost white. All the detail and shapes were lost.

He ripped the goggles from his head. The night was black. No light visible with his naked eyes meant someone had trained an infrared illuminator on him.

CHAPTER FIFTY-SEVEN

HE MOVED POSITIONS, SHIELDING his goggles as he went.
It took a few moments for the image in his goggles to recover.
He spun around to look at the tower. The goggles saw through
the glass.

Three men were pointing at the hangars.

One was on the phone.

Another had a large set of binoculars trained on the hangar.
Big ones. Not ordinary binoculars but old generation night-
vision gear. The type that used infrared illuminators. The man
swept his binoculars along the row of hangars and gestured
wildly for his colleagues.

With those older night vision binoculars, the watcher was
too far away to make out human-sized figures, but the open
doors and roar from eight engines would be unmistakable to
anyone.

A klaxon sounded, its hash monotone wail pulsing into the
night.

The military police jeep abandoned the mortar explosion and
turned back for the hangars.

Far down the apron Tebogo noticed movement that showed as speckles and blobs in his goggles, and raised his adrenaline. But the fact that it was noticeable meant it was large enough to be a serious threat. A vehicle was approaching.

He set another mortar for five hundred yards. At that distance, aiming was uncertain, but a quick barrage would slow all but the most determined soldiers or well-armored vehicles.

He lined up four shells. He'd use three as a rapid salvo, and keep one in reserve. He laid his backpack down. He had three more shells, but he left them in the backpack. Long ago he'd learned to keep plenty of ammunition for whatever might happen after the opening shots.

The military jeep was closing fast. It would arrive well before the larger vehicle. He had no choice, he would have to deal with the faster one first.

He brought up his G36, settling it onto his shoulder and lining his eye up against the night scope.

The jeep bounced over the open ground.

He waited.

The jeep rolled onto the smooth tarmac.

He watched.

It reached the far side of the line of buildings and kept coming.

Closer.

Before the wide open space of the taxi apron.

As good as the target would get.

He fired two shots.

The driver bucked.

The jeep swerved violently left throwing the passenger sideways.

The jeep hurtled out of view, heading straight toward the rear of a building.

Over the roar of Antonov engines he didn't hear the inevitable crash, but he was sure it would have hit full tilt, and both occupants would have been thrown from the vehicle.

With luck, they'd be dead.

At least, they'd be sitting out the rest of the night.

To his right, the first of the Antonovs rolled out of its hangar.

Tebogo swore. The pilot was using the taxi lights. The plane turned, its lights illuminating itself and highlighting the open hangar doors.

The speckles and blobs in Tebogo's goggles were resolving into a tall, square shape. The features on the front of the approaching square told him it was a Nyala armored personnel carrier of South African design. There was something moving on the top, which he guessed was a gun.

The goggle's resolution of the vehicle told him it was coming in range, and it was time to take action.

He braced the bottom of the mortar with his foot, and dropped a shell into the tube.

The percussive blast rattled the weapon on the metal roof, and a white streak disappeared into the air.

He surveyed the buildings and taxiway as he picked up the next round. The jeep hadn't reappeared from behind the building, and the apron was still clear.

His first round impacted the vehicle. The sound of the explosion was muted by distance, but the blinding flash and the instant cloud of smoke left no doubt as to the damage it had caused.

The flash illuminated the apron and the angular bulk of the personnel carrier. He saw movement on the vehicle's roof. It was a heavy .50 caliber machine gun that would do serious damage to the aircraft's thin skin.

Unless he stopped the vehicle.

The second aircraft exited its hangar with its lights off, as planned. It followed along the apron.

The third followed close behind the second.

The first plane was about forty feet in front as it turned ninety degrees, and disappeared between the hangars toward the runway.

Tebogo breathed a sigh of relief. Even without their lights, the others moved faster than the first.

He kept the mortar's range the same, and dropped the next round in the tube. The natural variation in rounds and wind speed would give it a spread pattern.

There was the same launch blast, the same white line scorching into the darkness, and three seconds later the same blinding flash. The personnel carrier had turned to avoid the first explosion, and the second shell missed by a good hundred feet.

He checked the ground below and saw no sign of the fourth aircraft. What was keeping them? With the previous three aircraft headed out to the runway, the team had only two means of escape, the fourth aircraft or a hard slog on foot.

Tebogo adjusted his arm and dropped in the next round. The explosion was much closer this time. His night vision revealed no detail, but the carrier would have been peppered with debris. It diverted off the apron and sheltered behind a building.

The metal roof began to vibrate. The aircraft below was revving its engines at last.

Behind him, Umi fired onto the runway using his H&K. Not a good sign. Someone or something was close.

Umi hunched low, and crossed the roof. "Company on the runway. We gotta go."

Tebogo caught a glimpse of the personnel carrier crossing behind the buildings. He picked up another shell, adjusted the mortar's range, and dropped the round down the tube. The shell arced into the night. Three seconds later it exploded in front of the vehicle.

Tebogo slung the hot mortar over his shoulder and followed Umi down the rusty ladder.

The fourth Antonov rolled out of the hangar, Mort at the side door, gun ready for covering fire.

Umi sprinted for the door, leaping through and rolling on his back to clear the way for Tebogo.

The tarmac in front of Tebogo erupted into a cloud of dust and shrapnel. He turned back for the hangar wall.

The armored carrier had come to a stop half out on the apron between the gap in the buildings. Its front was caved in, probably closer to the last mortar than he had judged, but the explosion hadn't taken out its heavy machine gun.

He dropped to one knee. They hadn't fired on the aircraft. They meant to block his team's escape.

He lifted the Heckler & Koch night scope to his eye. Once he fired, they would sight his muzzle flash. He had to get his shots in first and empty the magazine before they had a chance to get their heads up.

A metal shroud protected the gunner. The top of his head was visible, but it'd be a lucky shot to take him out. Tebogo aimed and fired. He had twenty-six bullets. He fired five-shot bursts. The sixth and last burst had one extra bullet for what he hoped would be luck.

CHAPTER FIFTY-EIGHT

HIS NIGHT VISION GOGGLES lit up as his rounds smashed into the vehicle's armor. The gunner's head disappeared with the first round, but Tebogo was pretty sure he hadn't hit him.

Tebogo raced to the next hangar, slamming his back into the wall. He ripped out the empty magazine and slammed in another.

The fourth Antonov's engines revved. Tebogo's eyes widened. The aircraft had turned away from the route through to the runway. It was moving farther away from him.

The .50 cal fired on the spot where he had been. The ground and the wall blossomed into a deathly cloud of dust and hot metal.

The Antonov was a couple of hundred feet from him. The .50 cal would never let him cover that ground. He had no choice.

He laid the mortar down low. Judging the shallowest angle he could risk. The shell would lack gravity's assistance, and the recoil would fight back on the tube without being braced against the ground, but he would improvise.

He gripped a shell. He would have to fire and move. He knelt low and peered around the corner of the hangar. The armored carrier was disabled, and armed soldiers were grouped around the side of the vehicle. The Antonov was out of the line of fire.

The hangar wall was made from heavy precast concrete. The end of the wall was flat and solid. He gripped the mortar in his left hand and the shell in his right. In one movement he stepped out from behind the wall, jammed the rear of the mortar tube against the wall, angling it low across the apron, and hurled the round into the tube.

The mortar jerked in his hand and the shell flew from the tube. He saw nothing, but he heard the almost instant explosion. He dived behind the wall, catching sight of a fireball where the carrier had been. Screams and sporadic gunfire erupted.

He repeated the action with the mortar, bending low and hurling the shell into the tube. The explosion was instant. The personnel carrier was engulfed in flames.

He didn't dive for shelter.

He dropped the mortar and shells to lighten his load, and sprinted across the open apron after the disappearing Antonov.

The aircraft was reaching the end of the apron. It had nowhere else to go. If the pilot thought he could take off on the apron, he was an idiot.

Tebogo glanced behind him. A second armored vehicle was thundering down the taxiway.

The aircraft turned. The side door was still open. Umi jumped out, dropping to his knees and launching a salvo of mortars as Tebogo barreled past. He dove in through the doorway. Umi followed a second later.

Tebogo levered himself to his feet and ran for the cockpit. The two pilots were at the controls. They had switched on the taxi lights. The aircraft was pointing across open ground, an expanse of rough and bare earth.

"What are you doing?" Tebogo yelled over the roar of the engines.

Neither pilot replied. The captain pushed the throttles full forward. They had started all the engines.

The lightly loaded Antonov responded immediately. It leaned back on its rear wheels and accelerated. The aircraft jostled and bounced across the rough ground. The captain fought with the pedals to keep the aircraft straight, but the lurching terrain threatened to throw the aircraft over.

Tebogo held onto the bulkhead that separated the cockpit from the passenger area.

The bouncing aircraft buckled his knees and slammed his head against the aluminum wall.

The engines screamed and the rotors thrashed the air.

Along the side windows, dust swirled, but ahead was nothing but blackness.

The pilot pulled back on the yoke.

Tebogo's stomach felt the acceleration. He held a fearsome grip on the bulkhead and stared out the dark windows.

If there was anything out there to hit, a fleeting glimpse is all he would have before they were all crushed in a raging fireball.

The rear wheels left the ground.

The pounding the undercarriage had taken on the bare earth stopped.

The smoothness was uncanny.

The pilot kept the yoke back.

Tebogo felt the acceleration as they climbed higher.

He abandoned his deathwatch on the windows, and saw the altimeter reading grow.

They passed five hundred feet, then leveled out below a thousand to keep under the radar.

Once across the border they would climb to twenty thousand to give the engines the thinner air they needed for best efficiency and range.

Tebogo breathed out. He looked back down the length of the dark aircraft.

The side door was closed. Umi sat beside it, watching the airbase disappear behind them.

Mort's huge body filled two seats. A cigarette glowed red between his fingers.

The captain banked for the border.

The man in the copilot's seat tapped Tebogo on the arm. "I thought you said there were five aircraft?"

Tebogo shook his head. "Four."

"Then why five of us?"

Tebogo laughed. "We didn't think you'd all make it."

The copilot's mouth was still open when Tebogo took a seat in the passenger compartment.

CHAPTER FIFTY-NINE

Sunday, August 21
1 a.m. WAT
Rooibank, Africa

AFTER HADLOW HAD DRIVEN for an hour, Jess took the wheel. The road's washboard surface pounded the car's entire frame and bounced her around like a rag doll. Whatever suspension had once existed on the battered Opel was long gone. The headlights shook and shivered, sending light beams vibrating erratically over the dusty surface.

At fifty miles an hour, the steering grew light, and the car weaved from side to side as if it was about to take control of its own destiny. Jess eased off to forty-five miles an hour and held it there.

They passed no towns or villages. Two hours after they set off, the lights of Rooibank glowed on the horizon. Ten minutes later they rolled across the city limits.

The homes were dark at this early hour, and she saw only an occasional street lamp. The road led them straight to the harbor.

A square building with a flat roof had a neon sign that read *Nova Cuca*.

Hadlow said. "Well, the bars are open."

It took five minutes to circle the town and find Cantor's address, which was a sketchy hotel off the main drag. The Hotel Africans was as dark as the other buildings around it. Hadlow hammered on the door with an iron fist, but no one answered.

When he returned to the car, he said, "There was a place on the seafront. Let's try there."

Jess found her way back to the harbor and Hadlow pointed a route to The Seaside Inn. Plenty of parking spaces at the entrance and, like the bars, its lights were on.

Hadlow carried the gray bag. Jess still had no idea what was inside, but at least it suggested they were a traveling couple.

"Two rooms?" Hadlow said.

Jess shook her head. "If anything happens, we'll be better off together."

"Fair enough."

When they reached the front desk, Hadlow requested three nights in the largest double, facing the water. The clerk seemed unfazed by travelers arriving in the middle of the night. He made a note of Hadlow's fake passport number and handed over a key on a heavy key ring.

"Why three nights?" she said as they climbed the stairs to their room.

"One night is a plain giveaway if anyone is searching. And a longer stay makes us seem less suspicious. This isn't the kind of place for a one-night stopover."

She nodded and wondered how long it would be before Morris, and her editor became alarmed by her failure to get on that flight home from Valencia. And what they would do once they found out.

The room was clean and had an air conditioner in the window. She adjusted the dials and buttons, and ten minutes later the temperature was comfortable.

The bathroom had two plastic toothbrushes in plastic wrappers and a thin tube of toothpaste. The mint flavor was heaven in her mouth, and the water washed today's grime from her face.

Hadlow said, "I'll sleep in the armchair."

"Okay." She placed the gun on the bedside table, and checked the safety. "Did you get another weapon from Chapman?"

"Yeah. You keep that one." He balanced a glass on the lower sash of the window, testing it to see if it fell with the slightest movement. Satisfied, he wadded up a towel, and wedged it under the door. Finally, he dragged a chest of drawers behind the towel to brace the door.

She watched with a reporter's eye for observing odd behavior. "What are you doing?"

"Habit." He folded himself into the armchair and shrugged. "If anyone tries to break in while we're sleeping, we'll have a bit of warning and a brief opportunity to shoot him first."

She pulled the gun from the nightstand into the bed and closed her eyes.

CHAPTER SIXTY

Sunday, August 21
4 a.m. WAT
Rooibank, Africa

JESS WOKE WITH A start. The room was pitch black. A sliver of light escaped from the thin drapes around the window. Long shadows illuminated the hunched Hadlow, peering outside between the drapes.

A siren started in the distance, rising and falling as the emergency vehicle moved.

"Police," he said.

She picked up the Vektor and joined him at the window. She saw no one moving around outside. "What did you hear before the siren started?"

"Some sort of sharp noise loud enough to wake me up." He shrugged.

"I heard a helicopter. In the distance. About an hour ago," Jess said.

The siren stopped, and everything went quiet.

Hadlow gestured to his satellite phone. "I got some bad news. They can't get around the encryption on Cantor's phone."

"Not at all?"

"They have his number, and they're trying to get access through the Spanish government, but that's likely to be a slow process. Meaning months, at least."

A car drove through the center of town, then the quiet returned.

He checked both ways along the street then moved to the door, pressing his ear to the woodwork for a minute before returning to his crouched position at the window.

"I might be paranoid," he said.

"Now you tell me."

He checked his watch. "Four o'clock. Catch another hour's sleep. I'll keep watch."

Jess returned to bed with the Vecktor, but there was no way she could sleep. The noises and the police sirens were probably nothing related to them or their mission, but her nerves tingled like she'd been electrified.

CHAPTER SIXTY-ONE

AT FIVE O'CLOCK, HADLOW left the window and showered. He came out a few minutes later, clean-shaven and dressed in different clothes from the gray bag. He tipped it upside down to show it was empty. "Sorry. I didn't know you were coming when I asked for the clothes."

"Mrs. Beaumont can buy a new outfit later." She offered a flat smile. "I always travel with a few things in my handbag. Stake out Cantor's place? See if Elden shows up?"

"Yup."

She rolled out of bed and showered. The bar of soap was tiny, and the bottle of shampoo was absurdly large for a single use. She had clean underwear, but not a fresh set of clothes. She shook out the ones she'd been wearing and dressed. She felt revived a little.

The window air conditioner rattled, working hard to bring down the humidity in the room, but with the steam from the shower, it was a losing battle.

She checked outside. The sun was still below the horizon, but a faint golden light was making its way into the world.

The harbor was to their left, and a narrow strip of fine-sand beach to the right. On several boats, men were assembling the nets and paraphernalia for the day's fishing.

The seawall had seen better days. The road that ran along the seafront was covered by patches of sand blown in by wind or washed up by storms. Steady breakers rolled in and lapped gently at the shore, but she suspected this ocean also had a cruel side.

More important than the geography was the fact that no one stood idling, watching the hotel.

Hadlow cleared the chest of drawers and towel from the door, and they went downstairs.

A tall, thin police officer was talking to the receptionist. He wore khaki shorts and a white short-sleeved shirt. An Uzi hung from his belt, and a radio was suspended from webbing across his chest.

His eyes followed Jess as she grabbed coffee in a paper cup and a couple of pieces of fruit from the breakfast bar.

Hadlow filled a paper bowl with a thick porridge and ate it standing up, staring out the window to the front of the hotel. Jess stood beside him, sipping the hot coffee.

The officer approached them. "Mr. and Mrs. Beaumont?"

Jess went on alert. He knew their names, or at least the names on their passports.

Hadlow turned. "That's us," he said with a jaunty lilt.

The officer held out a silver badge with writing too small to read. "Captain Yano. I need to talk to you."

Hadlow smiled like a carefree tourist might. "Nothing serious, I hope."

Yano didn't smile. "You arrived late?"

"Our flight was delayed."

"And which flight was that?"

"The one from Gibraltar to Casablanca. We had two connections. Miss the first one, and well, you know how that goes."

"You had no booking here."

Hadlow shrugged. "Spur of the moment thing."

Yano grunted. "And now you're leaving early?"

"We're not leaving. We just want to get a head start on the day."

"And what are you planning to do? Here in Rooibank?"

"Relax. Unwind. Walk around. Soak up the atmosphere. We have a friend who made his way down here as well."

"I see." Yano shifted his weight. "Your friend's name?"

"Felipe Cantor."

"When did he come here?"

"He was on a flight before us."

"You didn't want to travel with your friend?"

"We couldn't get seats on the same flight."

"I see." Yano took a deep breath. "You'll need to come with me."

"Why? What's wrong?"

He held his arm out, gesturing to the front door.

Hadlow picked up an apple and tucked it in his pocket. He held up his paper cup. "I'll just get a refill." He topped up his cup and walked out in front of Jess.

CHAPTER SIXTY-TWO

CAPTAIN YANO'S CAR WAS a white Audi from the late nineties, with a dark blue hood, and the word *Policia* in dark blue along the sides.

He opened the rear door. The passenger compartment was separated from the driver with a dense wire mesh. There were no door handles on the interior doors.

Hadlow looked at Yano. "Exactly what are we doing?"

"I have a matter that needs investigating."

Hadlow glanced at Jess. "Does my wife need to go?"

"Get in. Both of you." Yano put his hand on his Uzi and flashed a lopsided taunting grin. "Please."

Hadlow folded himself into the rear of the car. Jess slid in beside him.

The wire mesh barrier between the seats was secured to the sides of the car with large crude bolts. The barrier ran from the ceiling to the floor, blocking the space for feet under the front seats. Hadlow and Jess twisted sideways to relieve the stress on their ankles.

As Yano, drove, the car labored unevenly, and the engine

misfired. He looped around several blocks, ignored a no entry sign, and parked in front of The Hotel Africans. Cantor's hotel.

Another empty police car was parked in front of the entrance.

Jess's skin prickled. Sirens in the night and now two police cars at Cantor's hotel. Nothing good could come of this. "What's going on here?"

Yano didn't reply. He opened Jess's door and pointed to the hotel's entrance. "Inside."

The front door led directly into a corridor with a service window cut into the wall.

A tired woman wearing a flowered dress sat behind the counter. She rose as Jess and Hadlow entered. Yano stood behind them, his hand resting on the Uzi.

She spoke with an accent that sounded vaguely Spanish, but Jess didn't recognize any of the words.

Yano turned to Hadlow. "She says you were here late last night. Banging on the door. She didn't answer because it was too late."

Hadlow nodded. "We were looking for a hotel. No one answered so we went to the seafront."

Yano grunted. "You're the only strangers in town."

Hadlow shrugged. "Rooibank is off the beaten track, that's why we came here."

Yano repeated his grunt. "And you say you came with Felipe Cantor. I think I have bad news for you."

Jess frowned. "What?"

Yano shifted his weight. "A man was killed last night. Here. In this hotel. He may be your friend."

Hadlow's shoulders sagged.

Jess's mouth hung open, and she covered it with her palm.

Yano nodded. "It would be helpful if you are able to identify the body."

Jess swallowed. "Why don't you know who it is?"

"There are no personal belongings in his room and," he glanced at the woman behind the counter, "there is no signature in the register."

The woman shrugged.

Jess guessed that Cantor's late-night arrival had been a good opportunity for the woman to make some extra money without letting her employer know by making a record in her register.

"Follow me, please." Yano led them upstairs. At the end of a long corridor, an officer sat on a window ledge. He jumped up and hustled back to room five.

Yano spoke to him briefly before putting his hand on the doorknob.

He looked at Jess and Hadlow. "Are you ready?"

Jess nodded.

Yano opened the door.

One glance was enough to see the entire room. A single low-wattage bulb hung from a wire in the middle. A chest of drawers and a sink filled one corner. The small window was covered with a thin drape that could barely keep back the faint dawn light. The room would be sweltering long before midday.

Most of the floor space was occupied by a single bed. A naked man lay across it on his stomach. His torso was twisted over the far side. His head and shoulders hung out of sight on the other side.

Large dark stains on the white sheets testified to the fact that the man had died from knife wounds. Nothing else could have generated so much blood.

Hadlow and Jess stood in silence for a good thirty seconds.

Tears sprang to Jess's eyes, and she turned her back on the body. Only yesterday, she'd been in the same room with, talking to this handsome, virile man.

Hadlow put his hands in his pockets and squeezed himself with his arms as if trying to ease the pain of losing a friend.

"Can you identify Felipe Cantor?" Yano said.

Hadlow took a deep breath. He put his hand on her arm and squeezed. "Let me. Wait here with Captain Yano."

Jess shook her head. "I want to see him."

Yano studied her.

"He was my friend, too," she said.

Yano nodded.

Hadlow went first.

Jess picked her way around the bed. From the moment she glimpsed the dark hair she was sure this was Cantor.

There were only a few marks of blood on the carpet around the upper half of his body.

Hadlow dropped to his knees to lift Cantor's head a few inches. The muscles in his neck were stiff, and the movement lifted his shoulders and the upper half of his body, but his face wasn't visible.

He lowered the body back onto the bed and twisted down close to the floor, to look at Cantor's face.

From his position at the doorway, Yano said, "Is this Felipe Cantor?"

Hidden from Yano's view on the far side of the bed, Hadlow placed Cantor's phone on the floor by the dead man's hand. He eased the thumb onto the device's fingerprint reader.

Jess fought back the desire to look at Yano for any sign he realized what was happening.

The phone displayed the words *Print Not Registered*.

Yano stepped into the room. "Well? Can you recognize him?"

Hadlow slid the phone to the other hand and pressed it against the thumb. The display showed *Try Again*.

Hadlow lined up Cantor's thumb one more time, but Yano was leaning closer, perhaps close enough to see.

Jess stood and began panting. She turned to Yano. She held her hands in front of her. "I…" She breathed hard. "I think I…" She held her hand across her mouth and made choking noises.

Yano backed out into the hallway.

She stepped to the doorway, placed a hand on either side of the frame, and gulped air.

Yano looked at her with a sneer of disgust on his face. "You are going to be sick? Go outside."

She took deep breaths. The oxygen dizzying her brain. She slowed her breathing and nodded. "I think… I'm going to be okay." She exhaled long and slow. "Sorry. I'm not… I'm not used to seeing…" She waved her hand in the air toward the bed.

"Yes, but can you confirm it is Felipe Cantor?" Yano said.

"I think so." She gazed at the floor. "I couldn't look too closely."

Hadlow came up behind her and put his hand on her shoulder. "It's him all right. No question."

Jess moved into the corridor. "Where are his things?"

Yano shook his head. "Everything was taken. Clothes. Wallet. Passport." He nodded to the room, "We found his body and nothing else."

"Who killed him?"

Yano shook his head. "We have very little evidence to work with. Fingerprints all over the room, but this is a hotel. Many people have been here. It's not likely we will find the killer unless something unexpected turns up."

"You have no witnesses or security cameras here?" Hadlow asked.

Yano shook his head. "He arrives late in the evening, and that very night someone breaks in, kills him, and takes all his possessions." He stared at Hadlow and Jess. "*Almost* no one knew he was here."

"Except us," Hadlow said. "But why would we want to kill and rob our friend? That makes no sense, does it?"

Yano grunted what sounded like agreement. "You will have to leave your passports and car keys with me for the time being."

"You can't seriously think we killed him?" Jess said. "Have you asked the clerk at our hotel? We didn't leave all night."

Yano held his hand out.

Jess raised her eyebrows and turned to Hadlow. In a tone she hoped resembled a very worried British wife, she said, "Shouldn't we contact our embassy first, Gary? This doesn't seem right to me at all."

"I'm sure we don't need to do that." Hadlow patted her shoulder and handed the passports to Yano. "This is just routine, isn't it, Inspector? We'll get these back soon?"

Yano nodded. "They will be returned to you later today."

CHAPTER SIXTY-THREE

JESS LEANED ON THE metal railing along the seafront. Waves rolled in, breaking on the dark sand beach. The sun crept higher above the horizon behind her, casting gold and silver streaks across the sand and glinting off the surf.

Hadlow looked up and down the deserted sidewalk. "Good move in there, keeping Yano out of the room. The second attempt did the trick."

"Why didn't we simply tell him who we are and what's going on here? We don't know that he's corrupt, which is why you didn't trust him, I assume."

"I can't tell you everything I know, Jess. You signed up to that compromise when you came along. I did warn you before we started out."

She looked out to sea. "Yano came straight to us, which is weird."

Hadlow turned to follow her gaze. "Not really. Cantor arrived last night. We arrived last night. It would be a coincidence worth checking out to any cop."

"But how did he know we arrived last night?"

Hadlow sucked air between his teeth. "He probably knows everyone here. There's only two hotels to check."

She'd accept that answer. For now. "Cantor's door wasn't damaged. No sign of forced entry, and no sign of a struggle in the room. He was lying in bed. The sheets were knotted up, and all the blood was there, nowhere else. That's where the fight happened. So, his attacker had a room key."

"Possible. That place isn't very secure." Hadlow shrugged. "But did you see the lock? I could get through that without waking him up in a few seconds."

"So, Grupo Lopez cleared out his desk. He gets shot at in Zorita, he runs here…" she paused to be sure Hadlow was listening. "And he gets knifed while he sleeps in Rooibank. A place neither of us had ever heard of before yesterday."

"Someone really wanted to get rid of him. Or maybe he had more than one enemy. Who knows?"

"This was a close, brutal attack with a knife. In Zorita the sniper took shots from across the street. It's not even close to the same MO."

"If the radio report was right, the Zorita sniper is in custody. This was another professional with another style."

Jess shrugged. "In which case, the killer's gone. Not much reason to stick around after the deed has been done. Which brings us to the only new intel we have on Cantor."

"Yep." Hadlow grinned. "Cantor's phone is unlocked thanks to your quick thinking with Yano back there."

Down the street, in a single-story hut, a light came on, and the door opened. A rotund man with the last wisps of black hair on a bald head wrestled a sign onto the sidewalk and arranged the legs to keep it from toppling over. The sign had two pieces of paper fixed with thumbtacks, and the word *Café* painted in yellow.

Hadlow pointed. "Let's have breakfast while we look at Cantor's phone."

CHAPTER SIXTY-FOUR

JESS AND HADLOW WERE the cafe's first patrons. On her first glance of the place, she noticed six mismatched tables arranged in two rows. The mismatched chairs were an array of local construction and plastic moldings from nameless factories, but somehow the contrast was appealing.

Nautical paintings adorned the walls. Lights hung from the rafters with blue and yellow glass cones for lampshades. A small counter with a cash register and a shelf full of bottles was near the entrance.

The rotund man stood behind the counter. "Welcome. You must be the British." His French accent was pleasant enough.

Hadlow nodded. "Word travels fast."

"Don't be surprised. It's been a while since we had our last murder."

"We didn't do it," Jess said with a smile.

"I never said you did." He laughed, and all three of his chins wobbled. He leaned forward and whispered. "In Africa, murderers don't usually hang around waiting for the police to catch up."

Hadlow said, "We're hungry."

The owner held up one finger. "Let me guess, the full English breakfast, yes?"

"Two. With tea," Hadlow held up two fingers.

"And coffee," Jess added.

He nodded. "*Naturellement.* I am François, the best chef in Rooibank. Normally I would never cook anything English," he winked, "but for you, I shall make an exception. Please. Sit."

Hadlow worked his way to the tables at the rear, chose the most stable one, and sat down. He pulled out Cantor's phone and entered the unlock code. Jess sat next to him, and he held the phone angled so they could both see the screen.

Jess reached over and scrolled through the list of text messages, the greatest number of which were labeled *DE* and had a throbbing heart for an avatar.

The phone kept text messages for sixty days. The conversations showed a couple in love. There were moments that were sickly cute mixed in with notes to remember more liquid soap.

They had debated which movies to see on the basis of who chose the one they saw the previous week. He had extolled the virtues of a trip to the treasures of Barcelona, which Elden happened to notice coincided with Real Madrid playing the home team.

She leafed from oldest to newest, pressing the small gray *Info* button beside each message. The phone collected the date and time of the message, and a small arrow led to a page that showed the location on a tiny map.

It was a slow process, but Jess persisted, working all the way through to the last one.

Hadlow watched, grunting an occasional acknowledgment.

Jess stopped searching when she found a message sent to Cantor from Luanda. The date was two weeks earlier.

Hadlow tilted the phone toward him. "The flight plan for that trip said N'Djamena in Chad."

"How do you know that?"

"I was following her. She was on the Grupo Lopez executive jet. I had to take a commercial flight to N'Djamena, and surprise, surprise, she wasn't there."

"How can you be sure? N'Djamena's a big place."

"Because the route they actually took meant the pilot had to acknowledge crossing Cameroon airspace. It got listed in official records. I found out after I landed in N'Djamena."

"She could have stopped off?"

He shook his head. "Timeline doesn't allow it. They went straight to Cameroon."

"How nice to have an executive jet at your disposal, I guess."

"Tell me about it." He nodded to the phone. "Keep going."

There were several messages from Luanda, an hour's break, then one more message that said simply, *almost there.*

"He knew where she was going," Jess said.

"Here," Hadlow said.

She pressed the arrow to reveal the location. The small map showed a blue rectangle. The words underneath read *Near Rooibank.*

She zoomed in on the map. The rectangle stayed defiantly blue. She zoomed out. The Angolan coastline came into view on the right-hand edge of the rectangle. She dragged the map over to put Rooibank in the middle of the display.

"The GPS probably wasn't accurate enough for pinpointing more specifically," Hadlow said.

She dragged the map up and down the coast. Rooibank was the largest town until Kitande. Hell, it was the only town on this map.

"The location says it's near Rooibank. Could be only a mile or two. We could get a jeep and go exploring."

He said, "It could be five miles. Or ten. That's a lot of ground to cover."

She re-centered the map on Rooibank. "She has to be here. Cantor came here to find her."

"Maybe," Hadlow replied. "But if he knew where she was, wouldn't he have driven there directly? Why stop off at that sleazy hotel?"

Jess tapped her fingers on the table. "Where are you? Where?" She stopped tapping. "He arrived in the evening. It was dark."

Hadlow frowned. "So he couldn't find her place in the dark?"

"There's nothing over here but a small fishing port." Jess shrugged. She scrolled the map westward. The African coast disappeared. The rectangular map showed nothing but blue ocean. She moved farther west. A small dot came into view, and she zoomed in.

The dot became an island in the shape of a pear. The map showed two roads that circled the landmass, a town, and a port. The word *Gloriana* was written in bold in the center of the island.

Jess tapped her finger on the map. "He knew perfectly well where she was. He just couldn't get there last night. This was the end of the road."

CHAPTER SIXTY-FIVE

HADLOW TYPED FURIOUSLY WITH his thumbs on his satellite phone. Jess raised her eyes questioningly. He shrugged. "ET phone home."

Before she could ask him more, François brought their full English breakfast. The thick oval plates were white with a thin blue line around the edge and piled with bacon, sausage, scrambled eggs, toast, and tomatoes.

Hadlow's tea was served in the cup, and he turned down the milk that was offered. Jess's coffee was still brewing in a French coffee press. She assured François she could press the plunger herself.

Hadlow ate like he had never seen food before. He finished his meal a full five minutes before Jess finished everything on her plate.

Between bites, Jess checked her phone. She had better service here than she would in the wilds of Kitande.

She looked up Gloriana in *Taboo*'s files. She scanned the text and read the interesting parts aloud. "The island is eight miles by five and rises to three hundred feet above sea level in the center. Formerly a British colony, it was given to the Portuguese at the end of the 1800s, and finally became part of Angola during the long-running war of independence. It has a small port. The population is around two hundred fifty, mostly in the port town. It has landline access to the mainland, but no internet service. Main occupations are fishing, subsistence farming, and coffee harvesting. The island was largely protected from the civil war that gripped Angola through the early 2000s."

Hadlow's phone chimed. An image appeared. He studied it a few moments before holding it out for Jess to see. "Some of the residents are doing pretty well for subsistence farming."

The image was a bird's-eye view of the island. A direct overhead shot. There was a small cluster of urbanization around the port and two longer roads that looped around the island. Occasional light dots were probably the location of houses, but the picture was too small to distinguish much.

Hadlow put the phone on the table and zoomed in. The dots were small houses, a couple of them abandoned.

He tapped a button at the top right of the screen, and the color picture changed to one with a red hue.

Jess inched closer. What had seemed to be trees and vegetation was now a series of large ghostly outlines, squares, and rectangles. "Buildings? Under the canopies?"

"Looks like." He panned the image. The unmistakable outline of a helipad appeared, complete with a central *H*.

"Can we go back to the first picture?"

Hadlow tapped the button, and the color picture returned. The squares and the helipad vanished under a rich layer of green foliage. Minuscule text in the corner of the picture indicated it was a week old.

He placed his finger on the screen and swept left and right.

The image panned back and forth, slanting the camera's angle to show a sideways view. Hadlow whistled. "Those are some tall trees."

Jess zoomed in. "Big enough to fly a helicopter underneath."

"They're probably artificial. Russians used to do similar things."

"I take it you're not going to tell me how you got those pictures."

Hadlow did not reply.

Jess said, "Cantor was trying to get there because he knew Elden was there. Nothing else would have drawn him all this way."

"Possibly. He was worried about her. He should have gone to the police after someone tried to kill him. Any sane person would have, and he struck me as a very sane person."

"You think he realized she was in danger only after he was attacked?" she asked.

"Possible. Maybe even likely. But why not just call her?"

She shrugged. "Maybe he figured he was under surveillance?"

He shook his head. "He slept in that hotel without barricading the door, so he wasn't expecting anyone to attack him."

"But Grupo Lopez security was looking for him, and his desk was cleared out."

"We have his phone. Unless he talked to someone at Grupo Lopez, he might not have known that."

Jess stared at Cantor's phone. "He came all this way." She turned the phone over in her hand. "More to the point, he came straight here. Straight for Elden. So he must have known something that he thought was so important that he had to reach her, don't you think?"

Hadlow arched his eyebrows. "When someone is trying to kill you inside your own home, my guess is it's pretty easy to figure out you're a target."

"Right. So Cantor knew he was a target and immediately ran to warn Elden, probably. Which means he knew the threat was also to her. But why did he come here?" Jess cocked her head. "Grupo Lopez has no facilities near here."

Hadlow held up his phone. "Maybe, maybe not. And if I'm right, the very fact that Cantor knew where to find Elden is likely what got him killed." Hadlow looked around the room and took a deep breath. "This is why I was watching Elden and Rafa Lopez."

Jess frowned. "You want to elaborate?"

He looked around the empty room again and lowered his voice. "You know what sepsis is?"

"It's a reaction to an infection. Can be fatal if not treated. With treatment, people get over it, usually."

"Well, three months ago, there was a significant increase in the number of cases reported in a small, remote region in northern Botswana, around a thousand miles from here."

"I heard about that on the news."

"Nearly two hundred people inexplicably went into septic shock. Before Doctors Across Africa could get there, half of them died." He lowered his voice further. "A bunch of organizations, your CDC included, looked into the outbreak. They found nothing to explain it. No source, no common factor like bites or injuries or food. An entire area's population mysteriously became extremely sensitive to infections, and their immune systems went into overdrive causing sepsis and death."

She widened her eyes as the implications sunk in. "You think Grupo Lopez was responsible?"

"No one knows what happened, let alone who was responsible." He shrugged. "After a month the number of new cases dropped back to normal. Even in the wilds of Africa, they can trace infections, the spread of diseases."

She frowned. "And if they can't? What does that mean?"

CHAPTER SIXTY-SIX

HE TOOK A DEEP breath. "The collective belief is that a wide area reaction like that doesn't happen naturally. Which leaves only one option. Someone did this deliberately. Probably testing something."

"You mean a biological weapon?" She paused and then screwed up her face. "All those people died because someone wanted to test a weapon?"

He nodded. "That's the general consensus."

She exhaled. "What consensus? Who?"

He shook his head.

"Then who was behind the test?"

"There's a crowd of suspects from a number of countries."

"Including Grupo Lopez," she said, dully.

"One of dozens of possibilities. There are plenty of other people out digging for answers, your lot included."

"You mean the CIA?"

He didn't reply.

She sighed. "So. A biological weapon. Grupo Lopez is a biochemical company. So is Kelso Products."

He nodded as if she was an apt pupil, albeit a little too slow to grasp the obvious. "And development would have to be conducted away from prying eyes."

"But the place in Zorita isn't set up for that kind of development," Jess said. "That's a chemical production facility, with a little chemical research on the side. Totally different thing from biochemical."

Hadlow waited for her to figure things out.

"What if the sepsis wasn't caused by a biological weapon?" Jess bit her lip. "At least not intentionally?"

Hadlow frowned. "You mean, what if some crazy person in Botswana wanted to murder all his neighbors with poison or something?"

"Not exactly." She shook her head. "Rafa Lopez talked about mosquitoes and malaria and the need, his words, for big thinking and big experiments."

Hadlow stared. "You're thinking the sepsis outbreak could have been a side effect of something he's testing to kill mosquitoes?"

"That's what Kelso Products and Grupo Lopez have in common. And Elden is an experimental biochemist who has worked in the research departments at both companies. If she—" Jess snapped her fingers. "Let me see that picture of the helipad again."

He brought up the picture on his phone. She flipped between the color version and the all-seeing red one. The outlines of the buildings were easy to see, but other markings weren't as visible initially.

She zoomed in until the roof of one of the buildings filled the phone's screen. She moved on to the next building. It had the same marks and lines in the ghostly image. So did the next building.

She counted three buildings, all the same.

But the fourth building was very different. It had a smooth flat roof. As she zoomed in and out, she thought she saw steam billowing from the side.

"What?" Hadlow said.

"It's hot in Africa, right. So three of the buildings have air conditioning units on the roof." She pointed. "These small rectangular shapes are probably them. But the fourth building is completely different." She brought the building into view on the phone. "No air conditioning. And the side of the building looks to have steam coming from it."

Hadlow slipped back and forth between the red and normal photos. "Definitely. You can see the vegetation is greener around that building, too. Probably from the extra hydration. What do you think this means?"

She explained what she'd learned while she was working on the Kelso Products bombing story. "Biosafety labs have special air filtration systems to ensure nothing nasty accidentally escapes on unfiltered air."

He stared at the picture. "What you're saying makes sense. But it's hard to confirm that this building is a bio-weapons lab just because it has a different air conditioning unit."

She poured the last of her coffee from the French Press, which was cooler and stronger. "Debora Elden worked at Kelso Products where they have BSL-3 labs with air filtration systems similar to that building."

"I know. We made the connection, and someone stateside has been on top of Kelso Products," Hadlow said. "Kelso stopped the bio work because of the costs months ago. They planned to start up again. But they couldn't get the right personnel."

"Like a guy calling himself Marco Benito," Jess said, as that piece clicked into place for her. "The man who worked at Kelso Products wasn't actually the biochemist Marco Benito."

Hadlow's face hardened. "How do you know that?"

"I can't prove it. But it's a solid guess. The picture on his visa application wasn't the real Macro Benito. You could interrogate them both to confirm, but it turns out that both of them are dead."

"Yeah. We know." Hadlow stayed quiet a couple of beats. He cleared his throat. "Franco Olivetti was the first good lead we had that there might be more to this sepsis outbreak than a weird natural event." He looked down. "We put a man on him. Followed him everywhere. Including Johannesburg."

"So the man who died was a Brit. One of your team. I'm sorry. I didn't know." Jess sighed. "The police report said he was on vacation."

"We're all on vacation. I'm on vacation now. Foreign operations cover 101." Hadlow took a deep breath. "From his knife wounds, there were two attackers. South African police did us a favor keeping the lid on that. The one that got away doesn't know we're coming after him. I'll find him. And when I do…"

Jess put her hands together and breathed evenly to steady her fluttering nerves, which she hoped was caused by too much strong coffee. "I won't be involved in some kind of vendetta. All I'm trying to do is prove that Alex Cole is not the man responsible for the Kelso Products bombing. I'm willing to help you nail Rafa Lopez if he's responsible for the sepsis outbreak, whether or not the two things are related. But that's all. I'm sorry about your friend, but going after a killer like that is way beyond my skill set. I can't do it. And I don't want to. I have to find my son. I can't die out here on some kind of revenge quest you've got going, Hadlow."

"Vendetta? Where'd you get that idea?" he said, eyes widening as his mouth opened. His tone hardened. "This is all business for me, Jess. I'm going to find the guy. I'll turn him over and then he's someone else's problem. But I can't promise what kind of shape he'll be in when I do."

Her breathing returned to normal, and her nerves settled down. "I really am sorry about your friend."

He shook his head. "Right now we both need to have our heads in the game. No distractions."

"Cantor," she said. "He was killed with a knife, too. Seems very personal. Passionate."

"Yeah." Hadlow stood, took out his wallet, and tucked a few bills under his plate. "Like I said. Keep your head in the game."

CHAPTER SIXTY-SEVEN

JESS CHECKED THE VEKTOR before following Hadlow out of the cafe. She found him looking toward the harbor at the end of the seafront.

"Gloriana?" she said.

"Roger that."

"Can we get there without our passports?" she asked.

They walked, occasionally stopping, pretending to admire the view while periodically checking to confirm they weren't being followed.

A small Toyota pickup truck buzzed past, its tiny engine working hard. Jess made eye contact with the driver and watched the vehicle go.

Hadlow said, "Keep your eyes moving. Tourists don't stare at people in cars."

He walked with an ease she didn't feel, but she followed his lead. She'd finally accepted that the situation was much more complicated than even she'd believed. He was the professional here. She was feeling nervous about the whole situation, but she wouldn't let him know that. Not on a bet.

Kitande Harbor was as limited as the rest of the city. There were docks for a half-dozen boats, but only two were in port. She didn't know much about boats. These two looked like well-used fishing boats to her, one fairly small and one quite a bit larger. The tide was out, which placed the boats ten feet out from the stone walkway.

Two men were hunched over a trap door on the rear deck of the larger boat, which Jess guessed was the engine compartment.

The *Gelukkig*, according to the lettering on the front, looked about forty feet long. It had an open deck toward the front and a large wheelhouse. Thick paint testified to years of fresh layers applied in the off seasons. At the rear, an inflatable dinghy was tied down to a bench.

A man on the deck eyed their approach as he wound heavy-duty nylon thread through a tear in a fishing net.

Hadlow climbed down a rope ladder to the deck.

Jess noted the two men on the small boat were still occupied, then she glanced toward the seafront. No one seemed to be paying them any attention, which she knew by now, didn't necessarily mean no one was watching.

The man on the *Gelukkig* stopped working and stood to face Hadlow. "You looking for fishing?"

"You speak English," Hadlow said with a smile like any tourist would.

"We don't get a lot of visitors. Aussies mainly. But they all speak English," he replied. "If you're looking for sport fishing, you're too late. That boat's already sailed. Be sailing again tomorrow. Leaves at seven in the morning."

Hadlow shook his head. "What if we wanted to get to Gloriana?"

"Gloriana? That's a long way." The man's interest had been snagged, and he cocked his head, the better to examine Hadlow, presumably.

"We can pay," Hadlow said as if the man might think he'd been asking for a free ride.

"Usually visitors, rich people, they get a boat from farther up the coast. Luanda, even."

"We're not in Luanda, though," Hadlow said, reasonably, as he shrugged. "We're here, and my wife wants to go to Gloriana."

The man glanced up at Jess, and she did her best to plead without speaking. He blew air nosily out through his nose. "Takes a long time."

"It's thirty miles, according to the map."

"Ain't the miles. Current's bad around here." He looked at Jess again, and she offered him a blinding smile. He shrugged. "But I'm not fishing today, so if you've got the money..."

Hadlow pulled out his wallet and settled on a price.

Jess took one last glance around the harbor and climbed down onto the deck. The boat stank of fish. It wasn't just the usual smell of fresh fish in the local food store, but an odor far saltier and deeper and all-pervasive.

The fisherman held his hand out and flashed a big grin that displayed several missing teeth. "I'm Paavo."

"Jess," she said, shaking his hand.

Hadlow shot her a glance. Her skin tingled. Crap! "Beaumont," she added.

Paavo nodded. "Nice to meet you."

Paavo set about stowing his fishing net and lashing down anything loose.

Hadlow checked around the boat, beneath decks as well as

370 | DIANE CAPRI & NIGEL BLACKWELL

the wheelhouse. He came back and gave her a nod. "We're the only ones aboard," he said, quietly.

She took two worn but serviceable life vests from a plastic storage container and handed one to Hadlow.

Paavo finished tidying the decks. "You ready?"

"Ready," Jess said.

"I'll get the lines," Hadlow said.

Paavo stood in the wheelhouse in front of a simple dashboard arrangement. There was a traditional looking ship's wheel, complete with handles and spokes. It looked well worn. Between several archaic looking instruments, there was a large display with the letters GPS on the bezel, which improved her confidence.

The engine started with the first push of a button and settled into a steady rumble.

Hadlow unhitched the mooring lines front and rear, and Paavo powered the boat away from the harbor side.

Jess surveyed the harbor as the boat chugged out. She saw no one watching or following, and she wanted to believe Cantor's killer wasn't lurking.

As they passed through the narrow gap in the harbor wall, the boat began to rock. The movement was not uncomfortable, but given that they were barely away from land, she wondered what the ride would be like once they were out on the ocean.

A breeze blew on her face, faster and stronger than the movement of the boat alone would produce. The air carried a tang to her lips and tingled her senses.

She stepped inside the shelter of the wheelhouse.

"You been out on the sea in a small boat before?" Paavo said.

"Cruise ships, a couple of times." Jess shook her head. "Nothing this small."

"We're going to get some rough swells. The wind blows inland, and the currents twist and turn around here."

"How rough will it get?"

He grinned. "Nothing that bad, but it'll rock the boat for sure."

Hadlow stood outside the wheelhouse, staring back at the shore. She saw nothing worrisome back there and hoped he didn't either.

CHAPTER SIXTY-EIGHT

"YOU SAID RICH PEOPLE go to Gloriana?" she asked Paavo.

"Well, maybe not royalty, but rich enough to afford a big boat. There's one boat, it's so big it don't even pull into the harbor. They have to ferry people onto Gloriana."

"I didn't think there was much on the island to see." He glanced at her, and she smiled sheepishly. "That's why we want to see it."

He shook his head. "There ain't much. You're right about that."

"But rich people and big boats go there? Why?"

"Ain't no accounting for taste."

"Any businesses on Gloriana?"

"Just food and supplies and stuff." He shrugged. "It's an island, you know? They're selling to each other."

"You heard any rumors about the place? Anything unusual?"

He laughed. "Yeah, a couple of strangers just turned up and hired my boat to go out there." He gave Jess a sideways look. "Why you so interested in Gloriana?"

Hadlow stepped into the wheelhouse and leaned against the doorframe.

"Just curious. It looks interesting on the map, and the history seems interesting, too," Jess said.

Paavo grew quiet.

Jess changed the topic. "Have you been around the far side of the island?"

"Long time ago."

"Can you land around there?"

Paavo shook his head. "Just the port on the east. The side closest to us."

Jess pointed to the deflated dinghy on the back deck. "What about your dinghy?"

"Well, there's places. But—"

"We can buy it from you. Pay you extra for it if you want. Enough to buy a better one," Hadlow said.

Paavo shook his head. "I ain't going back to Kitande without a dinghy. Out in the ocean, never know what might happen."

The engine thrummed as the boat took on a steady fore/aft rocking motion.

"You could use it to drop us off," Jess said, pointing. "Your dinghy. And then bring it back."

Paavo stared. He looked over at Hadlow leaning against the doorframe. "You two sure don't act like tourists."

"It's because we're adventuring. Looking for something exciting," Jess said.

Paavo shook his head as if the whims of tourists were beyond his ken. The boat rocked, and waves broke against the hull, sending fine spray over the deck.

Finally, he grunted. "Okay. I know a place. But you got to pay."

"How much?" Jess said.

"Same as the trip out here."

Hadlow pushed himself off the doorframe "Hiring a dinghy to go a few yards costs the same as doing thirty miles in this whole boat?"

"I don't know what you're doing, but you sure ain't tourists. So yes, it costs the same." He gave a lopsided grin. "Or I can just drop you off at the port, where everyone will see you."

Jess dug into her bag and handed over a wad of bills.

She took a seat in the rear of the wheelhouse. An hour passed. The engine's vibration traveled through her bones. She thought she would never stop shaking.

Paavo pointed to a coffee pot. Despite the rolling of the boat, Hadlow made three coffees and handed them out. The aroma perked up Jess's senses.

She walked around outside with the coffee and was pleased to know she was gaining sea-legs. She was able to stand steady as the ship rocked and rolled. A fine mist doused her face, and the air helped blow away the worst of the fish smell.

As she stood on the bow, a small dot appeared dead ahead on the horizon. She stared hard. It took a good minute to confirm that it was land and not another boat.

She went inside the wheelhouse and pointed to the land. "Is that Gloriana?" she asked.

Paavo uh-huh'd his agreement as he moved the ship's wheel to adjust course. The island was no longer directly in the boat's path.

"Going round the island?" she said.

Paavo nodded. "I figured you weren't interested in announcing you're coming. No one can see us this far out."

They continued for another thirty minutes, the small dot of Gloriana on the horizon, working its way around from the bow to the side of the boat while it seemed to be getting neither smaller nor larger. Paavo kept checking the readings on the GPS display and making minor adjustments to the wheel before announcing he was heading for land.

Hadlow unclipped the dinghy on the foredeck. Jess helped him hold it down as they inflated it. The sea breeze battled to get under and lift it away until they had it tied down securely.

Paavo watched a sonar display as he approached close to the island. They crossed a shelf where the ocean floor raced up to a plateau that gently rose to the edge of the island. When the depth below the boat dropped to ten feet, he cut the engine. Hadlow helped drop anchor.

They were a hundred feet from the island. Paavo had brought them to a section with thick trees on either side of a narrow patch of sand.

He rigged a rope to help drop the dinghy into the water, and more importantly, help him drag it aboard when he returned alone.

He rummaged in a plastic box and pulled out two bottles of water. "You've got a long walk from here if you want to get into town. Better take these."

Jess thanked him and climbed into the dinghy. She sat at the front as Hadlow and Paavo rowed. The dinghy glided onto land, riding an incoming wave.

Jess and Hadlow jumped out.

Paavo held out a strip of worn paper. "My number, if you can find a phone. I can collect you. Tomorrow. Or whenever you decide you've collected enough nature."

"Aren't there boats here we can take back?" Jess said.

"Sure. Long as you don't mind explaining how you got onto the island in the first place," Paavo grinned. "Have fun."

He waded into the water, pushing the dinghy into the waves, and rowed toward his boat.

CHAPTER SIXTY-NINE

Sunday, August 21
2 p.m. WAT
Gloriana, Africa

JESS WALKED UP THE short beach. Rocks bordered the sand, and vegetation and stunted trees grew out of crevices. The only way off the beach was straight ahead.

The sand and rocks gave way to trees and a narrow, worn path suggesting that Paavo wasn't the only person to know about this spot.

The path twisted and turned as they climbed up from sea level. Looking back, the coastline on either side of the tiny beach was rocky with vegetation that ran right up to the island's edge.

As the ground leveled out, Hadlow tapped her on the shoulder and motioned for her to crouch down. He had a map on his bulky satellite phone.

"The buildings are west of here. There's a road ahead that curves around to them. My guess is the road is blocked off or guarded. That means we'll have to go cross-country and hope that the area isn't under remote surveillance."

"And if it is being watched?"

"We're just two lost tourists hoping to find some seclusion." He winked.

"Lovely," she said.

He grinned. "You think we're still married now we don't have the passports?"

She burst out laughing.

He slapped his hand over his heart. "You really know how to hurt a man."

She pointed forward. "Lead on, Romeo."

He moved up to the edge of the trees and checked both ways along the road before waving Jess to follow. The trail did not continue on the other side of the road. They walked a hundred yards to find a gap and then headed into the trees.

The ground was rough, but the trees and weeds were sparse. The terrain sloped gently upward. Those few trees provided a welcome relief from the sun, but Jess was soon sweating.

After thirty minutes, they stopped and drank water.

Hadlow checked their position on his satellite phone. "There's a ridge up ahead, then the ground drops to the far coast. The buildings are just over the ridge."

He checked his gun. Satisfied, he held it up. "Better safe than sorry, but a firefight is still a last resort. Okay?"

"Suits me." Jess checked her gun and set her cell phone for silent. It shouldn't be able to ring on an island without cell phone coverage, but she wouldn't take that chance.

Hadlow keyed a message into his phone. A few moments later, a small LED on the top blinked to indicate a reply. "Seems like I've been downgraded to reconnaissance."

"Meaning?"

"The Royal Navy wants a slice of the action. *HMS Buckland* is two hundred miles south of here."

She wrinkled her nose. "Two hundred miles?"

"A few hours or so."

She whistled.

He put his phone away. "It's not like we were going to storm a research lab, anyway. We just need to pick up any intel we can before *HMS* blow-your-cover turns up with a welcoming party."

"Did you tell them about Felipe Cantor and Debora Elden?"

"Of course, but my guess is they don't want to risk us. You know, since we're outnumbered."

"It's not just that, is it?" She stared at Hadlow. "We're outnumbered no matter what we do."

He shifted his weight. "You're a civilian."

"You mean the British navy is heading this way because of me?"

"No. They're the sensible option to deal with whatever's happening here. They were always slated to be involved." Hadlow nodded. "The big guns have been on the job all along. I've been talking to the boss for days."

"And me."

He sighed. "Your FBI boyfriend isn't happy. He's contacted your State Department, and now everybody is livid that you're not back on home soil already. Anything happens to you, and—"

"Oh, for cripes sake. I can take care of myself."

"You've said that before, and I believe you, but like so many other things, this is not my call."

They stood in silence a moment. "Elden is still in immediate danger, and a lot can happen in six hours' time."

"And you're a reporter. Recon should be right up your alley."

"This is—"

"What we're doing. Believe me, I hate being ordered to burn time as much as anyone, but just this once, my desk jockey boss is right. Overwhelming force beats depending on luck. Every time."

"Meaning?"

"Four-and-a-half inch guns, missiles, air power, and quite literally, a boatload of Royal Marines."

She smiled at his attempted humor. "But we've come this far."

He took a deep breath and nodded. "Yeah. I get you. But that overwhelming force that's arriving needs all the intel they can get. Trust me, I've been in their boots. Walking into a hostile environment isn't fun, and word from eyes on the ground beats all, okay?"

She looked at him. It was frustrating in the extreme, probably more so for him. But he was right. The two of them against whoever was on the island wasn't good odds no matter how she sliced them, and she was a reporter. There was still plenty she could do. She stood up. "Okay. Let's go reconnoiter."

CHAPTER SEVENTY

HADLOW LED THE WAY up to the ridge. The trees thinned
out. He kept below the peak and found an area that offered
plenty of undergrowth.

"Remember, we're tourists. Tourists don't hide in the trees."
He stood tall and strolled over the top of the ridge.

She followed, sweeping her gaze over the downslope's
majestic view. Thick green vegetation sprawled across the
undulating slope. More trees populated the slope as it ran down
to the crystal blue sea, a good two miles distant.

Even in the center of the island, she tasted the tang of salt in
the breeze. Occasional animal calls broke the silence, and she
wished she'd researched the native wildlife when she'd had the
chance. A few derelict wood structures dotted the landscape, but
they were not the structures they'd seen in the picture on
Hadlow's phone.

They searched for a wide swath of green toward the coast.
The buildings weren't visible, but a broad spur of tarmac that ran
inland from the road circled the island and disappeared into the
trees.

Paavo had been wrong. Indeed, there was a wooden dock on the western edge of the island. A small boat moored there, bobbing on the waves.

Anchored farther out was a luxury cruiser. Perhaps the big boat Paavo had mentioned. Its brilliant white hull contrasted with the ocean's blue. A rotating radar dish glinted on top of the superstructure.

Hadlow took several pictures and sent a message on his satellite phone.

"That's radar?" she asked.

He nodded. "*Buckland* is south of here, so they'll be masked by the island for most of the way, but anything we can tell them gives them an advantage."

Hadlow walked on, glancing around every time they passed a tree. He beckoned her beside him and wrapped his arm around her shoulder. "It's so quiet out here they might even have audio monitors, so talk quietly."

"Okay."

He slipped his arm from her shoulder. Moving downhill was easier than the climb, but under the shade of the trees, the heat stuck her clothes to her skin. She raked her fingers through her short, curly hair to fluff it away from her head. Hadlow untucked his shirt.

Just as she was about to wonder about a fence, one came into view. A flimsy collection of metal uprights strung with three horizontal strands of wire cut across the landscape, unhindered by the vegetation.

"It's been there a while," Hadlow noted.

Jess agreed. Vines coiled up around the uprights and along the wires. A hundred feet away, a sign dangled from the upper wire. She couldn't read the language, but the red triangle with an exclamation mark was an unmistakable warning.

"It's not exactly Fort Knox," she said. "So either they have nothing to hide, or they have a second line of defense."

He pulled apart the vines and ducked under the wires, holding them up for Jess to follow.

He strode on, seemingly unconcerned about being spotted. She kept up, but her unease grew with every step. Playing the lost tourist was easy enough, but the gun in her pocket would be difficult to explain, should the need arise.

A track big enough for a vehicle emerged from the trees on the right. Hadlow veered away and kept to the undergrowth.

Five minutes later he checked the location on his sat phone, which was indicated by a blue dot. He pointed to the buildings. "Five minutes and we'd be there, but we're going to angle off to the side. Gives a better stupid tourist impression, and allows us to get a good view of the place rather than just marching straight in."

As they walked on, Jess pointed out a cable running through the trees.

He nodded. "Security system, probably."

"You think they've already noticed us?"

He shrugged. "Been a while since we entered their property." He put his arm around Jess and hugged her. "Just two wandering tourists."

The trees and vegetation became thicker, slowing progress and forcing a new direction. Five minutes later it felt as if they were moving away from the buildings. A gap appeared in the undergrowth. They stopped short of an open area.

Jess looked both ways and whistled.

"No kidding," Hadlow said as he took more pictures.

In front of them lay a straight road, three lanes wide. It ran down toward the coast, and directly uphill toward the center of the island. The trees along the edges of the road had been cut back and piled into solid wooden barriers on either side. Camouflage netting was stretched between the tops of the trees to cover the road.

"A runway," she said, taking her own pictures with her phone.

"And a pretty big one. You could land a transport plane as big as a Hercules on that."

She pointed to the netting. "Is there enough height?"

"Might be tight. Depends on what planes they're using."

She looked left and right. The curve of the ground and the camouflage netting prevented her from seeing the ends of the road. "I don't see an aircraft."

He nodded as he sent pictures on his satellite phone.

They tracked alongside the runway, downhill, staying inside the trees. Several minutes later they stopped abruptly at the same time.

A couple of hundred yards ahead, Jess saw buildings through the trees. She hadn't noticed them at first because they were well-hidden. The walls were painted a brown color that blended with the terrain. Light shining through the windows was a giveaway. In the dark, or with all the lights off, she'd have run right into them.

Jess sidestepped behind a tree trunk. Hadlow followed and scanned the surrounding area.

"Nothing coming after us," she whispered.

"I don't like it," Hadlow said quietly. "Either nothing is going on here, or they're really lousy at security."

"I don't buy either of those options. Do you?"

"Not for a minute."

Nearby, an engine sounded.

She shuffled closer to the tree, a knot forming in her stomach.

A moment later an open-top Jeep drove up the runway, V8 engine rumbling.

Four armed men wearing camouflage suits stared straight ahead as the vehicle passed by.

She took a deep breath, then let it out slowly and completely, which did nothing to calm her nerves.

The Jeep disappeared up the slope.

Hadlow frowned. "What's going on? Those guys were solid soldiers. Special ops or mercs. Yet they cruised past as if they were on a pizza run."

The Jeep's rumbling slowed for a few moments before continuing into the distance.

"Subterfuge?" Jess said.

"Maybe." Hadlow nodded. He pointed across the runway. "Let's get moving. No need to make finding us too easy for them."

Hadlow checked both ways along the runway. "Let's walk across. Calmly. Nothing like running to attract attention."

CHAPTER SEVENTY-ONE

THEY CROSSED. JESS HELD her arms by her sides, her phone pointing down the runway's slope. She fired off a dozen shots without looking.

In the trees on the opposite side, she reviewed her un-aimed pictures. The buildings were just visible on the right of the runway. More visible on the left were light gray shapes that she couldn't identify.

They veered deeper into the woods and headed in the direction of the gray shapes. As they got closer, the shapes became clearer through the trees.

They knelt down, both snapping pictures. "Antonovs," Hadlow said. "An-12. The Soviet Union's answer to the C-130 Hercules, only cheaper and more likely to kill you."

"There's four of them," Jess said.

"That's a lot of lifting capacity."

On one of the aircraft, a man appeared to be crawling along the wings. "Maintenance," Hadlow said.

Jess used her phone's zoom to study the man. "He's got some sort of cable."

Hadlow stared. "That's a thick cable."

"Fuel?"

Hadlow shook his head.

She looked again. "Call me crazy, but I think it's a hosepipe."

Hadlow frowned. "See the farthest aircraft? They're loading drums."

He took a series of pictures and sent them out from his satellite phone.

Jess said, "Drums and a hosepipe? You think they're making a big crop sprayer?"

"Who knows?" Hadlow shrugged. "Why not just get a crop sprayer?"

She stared at the big aircraft and considered his question for a few moments before the answer occurred to her. "Range. If you're going to test something, you don't want to do it in your own backyard. You'd want to get pretty far away."

"And a conventional crop sprayer wouldn't have that kind of range." He nodded and then raised his eyebrows. "And if you're going to do a big experiment, you'd need a lot of the chemicals you're testing. So cargo capacity would be bigger this way, too."

While Hadlow typed furiously on his satellite phone, Jess moved away from him to get closer to the aircraft for a better view. Behind the Antonovs, a helicopter was tied down, also under the camouflage netting.

She shot a couple dozen photos with her phone and then turned back.

Shouts broke out. She heard punches being landed and a man screamed.

She reached for her Vektor, and raced back to where she'd left Hadlow.

One man wearing camouflage lay on the ground.

Hadlow was fighting another. The second man was armed with a serrated knife.

Jess circled the pair, the Vektor trained on Hadlow's attacker.

"Freeze," she said, loud enough to be heard.

He turned his head and stole a glance at Jess to assess the threat.

Hadlow made the most of the opportunity.

He lashed out with his boot, striking hard against the side of the man's knee joint.

Jess heard a sickening snap like a big tree trunk ripped apart.

The man screamed and grabbed his knee with both hands as he fell sideways to the ground, writhing in pain.

Hadlow pulled off the man's cloth hat and stuffed it into his mouth to stop his cries from reaching the others.

He landed a heavy punch on the back of the man's head, and the screaming stopped.

"We have to move," Hadlow said as he rolled the man into the undergrowth and picked up the knife.

Jess scanned the area. They were alone. "Which way did they come from?"

"They were already here." He pointed to a mangled bush. "Hiding."

She nodded. "So they know we're here."

Hadlow retrieved his gun from the undergrowth. "Yep, and this is the second line of defense. Which means we head out of here—"

He grabbed his neck. "Damn."

He fell to his knees, pulling a dart from his neck, already woozy.

She ran and knelt beside him and hefted her gun into shooting position.

Three soldiers raced from the trees.

Before she could squeeze the trigger on the Vektor, a strong hand gripped her arm, and a gun muzzle pushed into her temple. "Don't even think about it."

She lowered her gun to the ground. The soldier kicked it away.

Hadlow was face down. Three heavily-armed men stood around him.

Jess struggled free of the man's grip and knelt beside Hadlow. "What have you done? We're tourists."

"Yeah. Sure you are."

Hadlow groaned.

"We're tourists taking a walk. The gun was for protection. We're in Africa, you know," she said, doing her best imitation of the tourist she claimed to be.

An SUV shuddered to a stop on the side of the runway. More soldiers jumped out and headed in her direction.

The group of men parted, and her heart sank. Behind the soldiers, was a tall Germanic beauty with blonde hair and deep blue eyes.

"My, my," Vanna Sánchez said with a stare so cold it frosted the air between them. She scoffed. "The irritating Miss Jessica Kimball."

She turned and headed for the Jeep, raising her voice as she walked away. "Bring them."

CHAPTER SEVENTY-TWO

JESS WAS CUFFED AND thrown into one Jeep, and Hadlow into another. A guard held a gun aimed at her. Hadlow was handcuffed to a bar in the rear of the second Jeep.

The two vehicles traveled in tandem down the runway to the group of buildings they'd seen on Hadlow's map.

Hadlow was marched off, still drugged, barely able to walk.

Vanna told a guard to escort Jess to the building she had presumed was a biochemical lab. Vanna used a key card and a code to open the electronic door.

They passed through an airlock.

Inside, everything was white. White walls. White doors. Even white locks. The doors had no nameplates. A white camera stared from a corner of the ceiling.

Sánchez led the way to an elevator. The guard shoved Jess into the back corner, keeping his gun pointed at her. Sánchez pressed the button to descend four floors.

The decor four floors down was the same as the ground floor. But here the doors had nameplates. Warning signs along with emergency plans were posted at regular intervals.

They entered a control room. Large glass windows overlooked sealed laboratories on the floor below.

Several desks were lined up facing a wall of TV monitors. The screens showed columns of numbers and graphs, and views of the labs from various angles.

There was only one person in the room, Rafa Lopez. Seated at one of the desks, he typed furiously on a computer keyboard. He finished typing and turned to Jess.

"Miss Kimball." He simply stared for a good thirty seconds. "I can't say that I am surprised. I should have guessed you'd be so tenacious and troublesome after I read your background."

"Actually, Rafa, I am surprised." Jess ignored her pounding heart and spoke as calmly as she could manage. "I didn't know this was a Grupo Lopez facility."

"Strictly speaking, it isn't. There is no way I would have convinced the board to invest so much money down here." He smiled and folded his hands together. "But me? I have no such obstacles."

"Nice for you, to have enough money." Her only hope here was to hold off whatever they planned to do with her until the navy arrived. The only weapon she had at the moment was her brain. "If I'd known you owned this place, I'd have called and requested a tour."

"Yes, that would have been simpler for everyone." He waved to encompass the whole of his surroundings. "And do you know why I established this facility?"

She frowned. "Mosquitoes?"

He snapped his fingers and stood up. "Excellent! Exactly. At least you were listening the last time we met."

"I always listen. That's my job."

Vanna sneered. "You listen only to what you want to hear and disregard the rest."

"Now, now," Lopez said, with a dismissive wave in Vanna's direction. "Miss Kimball has shown remarkable determination to get this far. The least we can do is respect her efforts."

Vanna closed her mouth but continued the hard stare.

"You're looking into malaria?" she said, simply to keep him talking.

Rafa nodded. "That's right."

"A million people die a year from that disease," she said.

"Which is why I have invested so much of my own money here. This operation is state of the art. Even your CDC doesn't have some of the technology I have here." Rafa could not conceal his pride. Or perhaps he simply didn't bother.

Jess edged from the guard toward the windows and peered at the labs below. "It's a big operation."

Rafa stood beside her, proudly explaining his systems as if she'd been invited on a public relations tour. "Each lab is independent. The equipment is cutting-edge technology. Each is designed for a particular specialty. Samples can be transferred from one lab to another through secure portals. Sample testing is done robotically. The data is collected, and copies are stored at three off-site locations. Automated systems can perform hundreds of experiments simultaneously, each varying a single parameter. Then we use the latest detection and correlation software to make links between cause and effect. Our progress is ten times faster than everyone else."

Jess whistled almost involuntarily because it was true. "Most impressive."

"This is the future of biochemistry." Raffa nodded, this time wearing a genuine smile of pleasure.

She leaned closer to the window, peering into the empty labs below. "But there are no researchers?"

"Not at this time." Rafa shook his head. "These labs have been working hard for quite a while. But at the moment we are in a different test phase."

"Test?" she said, confident she knew the answer.

He nodded. "So we are waiting."

"Waiting?"

"For more data. Science is a data-driven business, Miss Kimball. Surely you know that, yes?" He cocked his head.

"Yes, of course. It's very, very impressive." Jess wanted to push him further, but she decided to wait until she had a better understanding of what was happening. "You're tackling the big problem. The big experiment you mentioned that night at dinner."

He smiled. "Precisely."

She sensed this was the time for a different approach. "You'll be famous forever. No one will forget your name or your contribution to humanity. Like Aristotle."

He bowed his head and offered a humble smile. "I will be pleased to have been of service to the world, Miss Kimball."

She opened her mouth to speak, but he held up his hand. "I have remembered that you are a reporter, aren't you?"

She frowned. "Yes. That's right."

"Reporters are always looking for the next big story, are they not?" he said.

She offered a cautious nod.

CHAPTER SEVENTY-THREE

HE GESTURED TO THE control room and the labs below. "You are here. The epicenter of the biggest story of our century. Very soon I shall know if we can save a million lives every year."

She whistled again. "That is a headline story, indeed."

"The biggest." He looked at her with some sort of calculation going on in his mind. She could almost hear the wheels turning. "I could give you access. To document my life's work. The risks and the effort and the triumphs." He smiled. "To document my success for the world."

She widened her eyes. "I'd be honored. But why not one of the science journals for a breakthrough of this magnitude?"

"The dry and dusty pages of academia? Hide my discovery amid their bickering and backbiting until one of them has a chance to steal it?" He shook his head. "I think not. Why not make it known to the world instead?"

"In a popular magazine." She cocked her head and pretended to consider the possibilities. "An international magazine like *Taboo* with a sophisticated readership. *Taboo* readers would appreciate your accomplishments. Certainly."

"Precisely! The world should know what I have achieved here." Rafa smiled and raised both arms to encompass the room and his work.

His motives were as clear as they were self-serving. His ego was even larger than his very impressive facility.

"Yes, that makes total sense. Thank you for the opportunity." Jess nodded as if the deal had been struck. Which, in a sense, if she survived, it had been. "My editor will first want to know he hasn't wasted his money sending me here to report on the Kelso Products bombing. Does Debora Elden work in this facility?"

Lopez's smiled faded. He folded his hands together again. "In the past."

"Where is she now?"

"She understood the goal. She knew what we were doing here, and what was at stake." Rafa drew a deep breath. He jutted his chin forward. "She was an employee at one time. One small part—"

"I'd like to see her. I need to clear Alex Cole of the charges against him, and I believe she has information that will help me do so."

He closed his mouth. His expression hardened. "You're becoming very tedious again, Miss Kimball."

"I'm interested in what you're doing, and I do think it will make you immortal. I'd definitely like to help you. But I made a promise to a friend and to my bosses, and I must honor that. Surely you, of all people, understand." Jess flattered him shamelessly. If it got Alex Cole out from under these false charges, the flattery would be well worth her effort. "A man's life is at stake, and I believe the police may have the wrong person in custody."

"I'm certain they do have the wrong man, Miss Kimball."

Lopez glared and his blue eyes flashed against tanned skin that made him look more menacing than she'd seen him before. "Because the man responsible was killed in Johannesburg."

Jess shifted her weight. Franco Olivetti, the fake Marco Benito, had planted the bomb. She was close to the truth now. She could feel it. "How do you know that?"

He turned to face her directly. His nostrils flared like an angry bull. "Because I sent him there to do it. Kelso had to be stopped."

Jess suppressed a shiver as the truth finally found its way to her heart in a flash of clarity.

She was standing four floors underground in a secure facility with an armed guard prepared to shoot on command. Lopez did not intend to release her. He was willing to maim and kill to achieve his immortality. He'd done it before. He'd do it again. He'd spend less than a nanosecond mourning her when she died.

She took a breath, thinking furiously. Was there any way out of here? "So you had someone plant a bomb at Kelso Products to distract them."

"Distract them? No, my dear." He smirked and shook his head. "Kelso was ahead of us in the research when they stopped the work. They could not be allowed to restart. Grupo Lopez was close. Very close. Biological research is as much luck as skill. Simply put, Kelso could not get lucky before Grupo Lopez succeeded."

"You worried they would get there before you. Solve the big problem. Mosquitoes and malaria."

He gestured to the building. "I have invested heavily. I found the best scientists in the world. I've risked everything. I won't be denied what should rightfully be mine."

"Fame? Like Newton and Darwin?"

He breathed hard. "There's nothing wrong with reaching for a prize."

"But how you get there matters."

He laughed, contemptuously. "What if I perform an experiment, and one person dies and one person lives? What does that tell you?"

"What you were doing was dangerous."

"But what if I perform the same experiment on a thousand other people, and they all live? What then?" He paused for a moment. "History is littered with examples of people who didn't do enough. People who fell short of greatness because they were too timid to reach further."

Jess stared at him. For the first time, she fully accepted that he was evil to his very soul.

He leaned toward Jess. "That is why you need the courage to do big experiments. That is why how you reach your goal does not matter."

"Of course, it matters." Jess widened her eyes. "It matters to the person who dies. It matters to his family and the people who love him. It matters to all of us. You can't just experiment on humans without regard to the consequences."

He glared, his mouth half open. The air conditioner buzzed in the background.

She had gone too far. She'd pushed him over the edge, and he didn't want to see what was below.

He took a deep breath, turned his back to her, and stared down at the labs below. "Take her away."

The guard grabbed Jess's arm and twisted it behind her back. She leaned forward to ease the pain.

"Get rid of her?" Sánchez said.

"Yes. But first, tell Tebogo to get the aircraft on the way. Now." He scowled. "Get the product sprayed immediately."

CHAPTER SEVENTY-FOUR

SÁNCHEZ DIRECTED THE GUARD to keep Jess's arm
twisted behind her back as they crossed the compound from the
research building to another. The sight of Jess in pain seemed to
please her, based on that gleeful smile.

The guard kicked open the door to the second building.

The noise hit Jess immediately. Animals were going wild,
grunting and screeching. The smell came next. It was rancid and
as primal as the noise.

The guard pushed her past cages of monkeys of all kinds.
Most of them shrunk back into the corner of their tiny prison
cells, but some of them hopped around, their arms reaching out
between the bars.

The walkway between the cells was barely wide enough to
keep away from the clutching hands.

Larger cells came next. Here, the dividing walls were solid,
but the fronts were iron bars like in an old-time Wild West
movie.

From her doubled over position, Jess saw Debora Elden in
one of the larger cells. She was curled up in a far corner with her

arms crossed, staring through the bars. Her eyes followed Jess as she passed.

Hadlow was in the next cell. He was leaning over, holding onto the bars, his head hung down. He swayed from side to side, groaning.

Sánchez unlocked the cell opposite Hadlow. She stepped behind the guard holding Jess.

Jess braced herself as the guard put one more pound of pressure into twisting her arm. He pulled her backward, and put his boot on her ass to shove her headlong into the cell.

Instead of toppling to the ground, Jess was yanked backward. The pain in her arm ratcheted up a notch. She yelped as she was thrown sideways. Which was when she saw Hadlow.

He had one hand wrapped around the guard's throat and the man pinned against the bars.

In his other hand, Hadlow held the guard's gun pointed directly at Sánchez's face. "Don't even think about it."

Hadlow pounded the guard's head twice against the bars. The guard dropped to the ground unconscious.

Lightning fast, Sánchez drew a knife and moved between Jess and Hadlow.

"You're surrounded. Pull that trigger, and a dozen mercenaries will be here in seconds. You'll seal your own death warrant." She smiled as she adjusted her grip on the knife. "Let's see how good you are without the gun. Better than your Johannesburg friend, I assume."

"Jess, throw me the keys," Hadlow said, eyes narrowed, the gun never wavering.

Jess unclipped a ring of keys from the guard's belt. She hefted them in her hand, judging the weight before tossing them to Hadlow.

Her judgment was good. The keys landed in his hand.

He snapped his fingers closed, but the ring twisted in his hand and looped into the air.

Sánchez stepped forward.

Hadlow grabbed at the flying metal.

His second attempt was good.

"Back up." He inched the gun forward toward Sánchez's face. "A dozen mercenaries may kill me, but you'll still be dead either way."

She stepped back, breathing hard.

Hadlow worked his way through three keys before his cell door opened. The hinges creaked as he stepped forward.

All in one fast, smooth motion, Sánchez lunged, rammed her shoulder into the bars of the cell door, grabbed the gun, and yanked Hadlow's arm upward against the edge of the door and over the lock's bolt.

He grunted once and wrenched his arm free.

The gun spun down the walkway behind Sánchez.

He rammed the door back at Sánchez and stepped into the corridor.

He held his arms forward, fists clenched. He rolled his shoulders.

Sánchez speared forward, knife first. She swept the blade in a tightly controlled arc, her movements like lightning.

Hadlow was heavier and slower. He jerked his arm sideways, catching hers.

He deflected the knife's path over his head.

Sánchez stepped to one side as she whipped the knife back.

Hadlow kicked her knee.

She rotated fast, folding her arm.

She smashed her elbow into the side of his head.

He punched at her gut.

She arched backward, but not far enough.

She grunted as he made contact, and lashed out with the knife.

The blade scored across his forearm.

Jess grabbed a flashlight from the guard's belt. It was a light aluminum cylinder, but the batteries gave it weight.

Hadlow's fists were up. Blood dripped from his forearm.

Sánchez was laser focused on him.

She darted left, swinging the knife.

Jess lunged forward, swinging the flashlight down toward Sánchez's head.

The flashlight missed her head, smacking hard on the woman's shoulder.

Sánchez turned and growled like one of the feral animals in the cages.

Jess kept the flashlight moving, using its momentum to bring it around in a circle.

Her second blow struck the back of Sánchez's head with a sickening crunch.

Sánchez crumpled to her knees.

Jess swung again and connected a second time.

Sánchez dropped the knife to the floor.

A moment later Hadlow had the gun pointed at her, but she toppled backward.

"Is she dead?" Jess asked, breathing hard.

Hadlow growled, "We should be so lucky."

Hadlow grabbed her feet and dragged her into his cell, banging her head against the door on the way.

He handed Jess the gun. Coldly, he said, "Shoot her if she moves."

He dragged the guard into the same cell as Sánchez and took back the gun.

He glared at Sánchez and spat.

Jess said nothing. Given his feelings for his friend in Johannesburg, if Sánchez survived, she'd be lucky.

Elden eyed them suspiciously.

"We're here to get you out," Jess said.

"Who sent you?" Elden stepped back. "I don't know who you are. And I've had enough surprises for today."

"I've come all the way from Chatham to Spain and now here to find you." Jess stepped up to the bars to Elden's cell. "We know about you and Alex Cole, Local World Action, mosquito control, and the sepsis outbreak."

"What do you mean?" Elden frowned. "What are you talking about?"

"We're wasting time." Hadlow opened Elden's cell. "You can come with us, or you can stay here."

She swallowed and stepped forward. "But there are armed guards everywhere. Mercenaries. And Rafa Lopez is here. He's insane."

"Good of you to mention it," Hadlow said. "Are you coming or not?"

Something seemed to click with her and Elden's demeanor changed instantly. She stepped out of her cell. She looked at Sánchez and the guard. "Wait here."

She ran down the corridor and returned with a pair of syringes. She snapped off the protective covers from the needles and gave Sánchez and the guard a shot each. "They'll be out for hours."

"You said Lopez is insane. Why?" Hadlow said.

Elden took a deep breath. "At first, I thought he was really trying to do some good. He was investing heavily. We had great facilities. I reported back that our guys were on the wrong track."

"Reported back to who?" Jess asked.

Elden cocked her head. "Aren't you two of ours?"

"What do you mean?" Jess asked, feeling bewildered. She looked at Hadlow.

He shrugged.

Jess waited, but he said nothing, so she pushed on. "What changed your mind about Lopez?"

"I found a bio sample. An extremely dangerous one." Elden swallowed. "I recognized the sample because it was one I'd worked with at Kelso Products. The sample had disappeared from the Kelso labs. We were all panicked. We conducted a company-wide search."

Jess remembered that Kelso's CEO seemed to be hiding something at that press conference. "Kelso kept that a secret at the time, didn't they?"

Elden nodded. "Kelso was struggling to stay afloat. This was an unstable biological sample. It could have harmed a lot of people if it was used right away. But by the time we had finished searching everywhere for it, it should have been inactive and harmless."

"But that's not how it turned out, is it?" Hadlow practically snarled.

"Lopez stole it. He kept it alive." Elden shook her head miserably. "He had people working on it here. Then he recruited me to continue the work, which suited our guys just fine."

"What does this stuff do?" Hadlow said.

"It was intended for mosquito control. Kelso and Lopez, separately, were trying to develop something cheap with widespread effectiveness. Most pesticides kill quickly, and then they're useless. No staying power. But we found a fungus that slowly penetrates the body of the mosquito. It kills slowly, so the insects can spread the pesticide, resulting in much more complete coverage."

"That doesn't sound like such a bad idea," Jess said.

"It's a brilliant idea. It has significant potential to solve one of the greatest health issues in the world."

"I hear a but coming," Hadlow joked.

Elden nodded. "We couldn't restrict it to mosquitoes. It attacked a lot of different species. Which is a huge downside. We were making improvements, but there's a long way to go. And when I got here this time, Lopez wanted to go straight to a live trial on humans without the proper interim testing. I tried to stop him."

Hadlow grimaced. "Which is why he tossed you into these cages."

"Exactly," Elden replied.

Jess nodded. "He told me the same. And he wanted me to cover his work and give him good world-wide press."

"I just wanted to help," Elden shook her head. "That's why I agreed to work with the authorities when they wanted me to come here."

"What authorities? What the hell are you talking about?" Jess frowned and shook her head.

Hadlow peered at Elden briefly and then his face cleared. He smiled. "You're not one of ours. You're American. So you're working with the FBI or the CIA or one of the other three-letters on all of this, aren't you?"

"And that's why you had a security access card to Kelso. So you could go back into the files while you were working with Lopez. To look like you were on Grupo Lopez's side in all this.

Keep your covert operation going," Jess said.

"Of course. And maybe do some good, too, since Lopez was funding the research." Elden grimaced. "You know how many people die every year from malaria?"

Hadlow started for the door. "Yeah, we know. Save your questions, Jess. Let's go. If we don't get out of here, we could be three of the million who die this year."

CHAPTER SEVENTY-FIVE

HADLOW STOPPED AT THE main door out of the building and turned to Elden. "How many guards does this place have?"

"Five guards normally. But more mercenaries arrived by aircraft from Zambia last night, and Lopez seemed really thrilled about it," she replied.

One of the Antonovs revved its engines.

Hadlow shook his head. "They're prepping those aircraft to spray the insecticide."

Elden looked pained. "He doesn't care how many could die. He just wants to get there first."

"Anything we can use as a weapon in here?" Hadlow said.

Elden shook her head. "Tranquilizer syringes, but the sedative takes minutes to work."

Hadlow hefted his gun. "Oh, joy."

"A back door?" Jess said.

Elden shook her head then stopped. "Wait." She grabbed a set of keys from a hook on the wall, raced down the corridor, and unlocked a cell.

Jess and Hadlow arrived at her side as the door swung open.

A monkey's wide eyes stared at them. The monkey edged along the wall, closer to the open door. Elden stepped into the cage, shooing it into the far corner.

On the back wall was a three-foot-high hatch.

Jess and Hadlow stepped into the cell.

"Close the door," Elden said. "If the monkeys get out they'll be shot."

Hadlow closed the door and secured the latch.

Elden unlocked the hatch. "There was a cage outside, but it was removed."

Hadlow eased the hatch open a fraction. The sound of aircraft engines grew louder.

"No one in the immediate area," he said, closing the hatch. "This is a small island. They'll find us pretty quickly. Once we're out, head for the trees and keep going. You need to put as much distance between you and this place as you can."

"What are you going to do?" Jess said with a sinking feeling.

"Go the other way. They might find all of us, but we can make it harder. And if we can stop them getting this stuff airborne for a while, the navy will get here."

"You really think they're going to arrive in time? They're a long way out."

"It's the only chance we have. Regardless," Hadlow held up his hand, "this is why I'm here. You can do the most good if you stay alive to tell the world what happened here, Jess. That's ultimately why we allowed you to come along. Do your job. I'll do mine. The navy will do theirs. And maybe we'll all live to tell about it."

Jess opened her mouth. Hadlow turned back to the hatch and flipped the safety off the gun. "Ready?"

"But—"

"Good," he said as he opened the hatch and darted through.

Jess went next, and Elden brought up the rear and locked the hatch.

Hadlow waved them toward the trees as he walked casually for the corner of the building.

Her stomach churned at the idea of separating from him, but he was right. They headed for a gap and disappeared into the foliage.

Jess knelt and watched as he stood checking around the corner. By his side of the building was a long stretch of open ground that led to the hulking Antonovs. Hadlow looked tiny next to them.

Several mercenaries were loading equipment up the rear ramp onto the aircraft. On the other end of the building, a jeep was parked at an angle.

Hadlow was right about the strategy. Delaying the aircraft was the smart thing to do. But the only weapons he had to accomplish the job were a gun and a knife. The odds were heavily stacked against him.

There had to be something Jess could do besides watch and report later. If Rafa Lopez's mercenaries succeeded, there might not even be a later.

Armed men jogged between the aircraft. The last plane closed its ramp. They were prepping to leave.

She rocked on her haunches. Her adrenaline was getting to her. Elden must have sensed what she meant to do.

"He told us to go." Elden reached out to grab Jess's arm. "It's the smart play."

"We have to stop them." Jess shook her head, and Elden released her arm. "You've been working with the FBI or something. Are you an agent?"

"Not exactly." Elden shook her head. "You might call me a resource. When they need someone with my specialty, I've been," she paused, searching for the right word, "*asked* to help."

"By which you mean coerced in some way, right? Probably has something to do with the bombing of that whaling boat in the Far East, doesn't it?"

Elden didn't reply.

"That's why you still have an apartment in Chatham, too. Why you didn't tell your parents or anyone else. And why you've got that security access card to Kelso. You were stringing Lopez along. It's all part of your cover, isn't it?"

Elden still said nothing.

"Well, you've had some training, I assume?" Jess said.

"Yes, but—"

"Now's the time to use it or lose it." Jess rocked one more time. "Stay here if you want. Up to you."

She abandoned stealth and ran for the jeep parked behind the building and mostly hidden from the men loading the aircraft.

She dove into the driver's seat. The keys dangled from the ignition.

Elden followed and jumped into the rear.

Jess twisted around, only mildly surprised to see her.

"I said I wanted to stop Lopez, remember?" Elden said.

Jess started the jeep and reversed around the building. She kept the revs low as she drove up to Hadlow.

He pulled his gun and started looking in all directions.

"Get in," Jess said.

"Dammit, Jess! Can't you follow orders just once?" Hadlow said.

"We can block the runway," she replied.

He jumped into the passenger seat. "With this? Not a chance."

Elden pointed to the second aircraft. "Straight up the ramp."

"Good thinking," Hadlow said and waved his gun at the second aircraft. "Straight up the ramp. Fast."

"Everybody hold on!" Jess took a deep breath, put the jeep in gear, turned around the edge of the building, and raced for the second aircraft.

CHAPTER SEVENTY-SIX

JESS RACED FOR THE aircraft. Two men near the aircraft stared at the jeep. One of them shouted and raised his gun. Hadlow fired. The men scattered.

The ramp looked too steep to hit at full speed. Jess slowed a fraction. The jeep's suspension crashed into the ramp, bottoming out. Jess was thrown hard against the steering wheel. She hung on, guiding the vehicle into the belly of the plane as she stomped on the brakes with both feet.

A man stood in the center of the fuselage, hidden by the dark interior. The Jeep was almost stationary when she hit him. He toppled over the hood.

Hadlow jumped out before the Jeep stopped. He hit a switch, and the rear ramp started to close. He ran down the length of the aircraft. "Wedge anything you can find behind the side doors!"

Jess leaped out, grabbing several wooden blocks and securing the aircraft's two doors.

The man Jess had hit lay on the floor, clutching his leg. Elden found a metal bar and held it menacingly over him.

The pilot emerged from the cockpit. Hadlow hit him with a

punch so hard that Jess heard it over the rapidly growing engine noise.

The aircraft was moving.

Bullet holes appeared in the fuselage behind her. She ran forward to the cockpit.

Hadlow was in the pilot's seat. He had the throttle levers at max and steered the aircraft with the pedals. "Get down," he yelled.

He steered left, but there was no way he could miss the aircraft in front.

The wings clipped.

The Antonov shook on impact.

The propeller chewed through the first aircraft's wing. A storm of debris flew everywhere.

Hadlow crouched low as chunks of metal hammered into their aircraft. Jess crouched between the engineer and navigator stations.

Hadlow kept the throttles at max, driving sideways into the first aircraft. It tilted. Its opposite propellers hit the ground, churning up dust and earth.

Moments later the far wing exploded. Flames shot from the engines.

Hadlow adjusted their path, separating from the first aircraft, and veering around the growing fire.

A jeep sped into view on the left-hand side.

Hadlow weaved the aircraft, bringing the propellers close enough to the jeep to scare the driver off.

The plane gained speed. Hadlow pushed the throttle to max. The engines were straining. One of the outboard engines caught fire.

Hadlow flipped several switches.

Jess gawked. "What are you doing? This thing won't fly now!"

He jerked his thumb toward the engines. Liquid sprayed from under the wings. "Fuel dump."

A moment later, the fuel mixed with the engine fire.

Flames raced across the width of the runway. The aircraft roared on, laying a carpet of fire behind it.

"Tell Elden to be ready to make a run for it," he shouted.

The airspeed indicator showed seventy knots. Jess stared, wide-eyed.

He laughed. "I'm going to stop first."

Jess managed to breathe again. "Of course you will."

CHAPTER SEVENTY-SEVEN

JESS HAD JUST ENOUGH time to warn Elden before Hadlow used reverse-thrust to slow the aircraft. Elden grabbed a handhold and said something, but the engines roared too loudly to hear further conversation.

The brakes squealed a long time as the giant machine finally came to a stop.

Hadlow appeared from the cockpit and checked one of the side doors. "Too much fire." He opened the door on the opposite side and carried the man with the damaged leg from the Antonov.

The carpet of fire had spread across the runway and into the trees. They kept moving up the runway's slope out of the path of the flames.

By the time the fire engulfed the aircraft, they'd reached a safe enough distance. They left the injured mercenary by a tree and continued on to the island's peak.

Jess looked back at the black smoke billowing into the sky.

Her heart stopped when a large helicopter approached from the ocean, missiles hanging from stubby wings on either side and dropped down to the buildings, out of sight.

Hadlow smiled. "Westland One-oh-one. The Marines got here early."

So, not one of Rafa Lopez's mercenaries. She released her breath. "I thought the navy was still hours away."

He shrugged. "I guess when I stopped updating them they sent their helicopter ahead."

"One helicopter?"

"Only one helicopter." Hadlow grinned. "Two dozen rockets, half a dozen machine guns and thirty heavily armed Royal Marines, none of who will be in a happy mood after being cooped up for an hour or two. Trust me, that's plenty."

She hoped he was right. "Should we go back?"

"We did our bit." He gestured to the fire and shook his head. "Give them a while to get everything sorted. They'll come when they're ready."

The trio sat on the ground to watch and wait.

The Westland took off and flew along the line of the burning runway. In a matter of seconds, half a dozen Marines fast roped to the ground, and the helicopter was on the move again.

Over the next few minutes, sporadic gunfire erupted. Jess kept watching the way they had come. Five minutes later she saw the Royal Marines approaching.

Hadlow stood. "Put your hands up until they know who we are."

Jess and Elden followed his lead.

Several Marines in camouflage and face paint arrived, machine guns ready. "Down," yelled the man on point.

They lay down.

Hadlow called out.

The Marine on point moved closer to Hadlow. "We've been looking for you. What happened?"

"Got caught. Took my phone. We had to bug out." He nodded down the hill. "Things under control?"

The Marine lowered his weapon. "Better believe it. You start the fire?"

Hadlow nodded. "Got out of hand."

The Marine grunted. "It happens."

He held out his hand and yanked Jess and Elden to their feet. "Come on, we've got to walk back."

CHAPTER SEVENTY-EIGHT

Monday, August 22
11 p.m. WAT
HMS Buckland, off Gloriana, Africa

JESS LEANED ON THE metal railing that ringed the deck of the *HMS Buckland*. The ship barely rocked as it rode the waves to keep its station, a quarter mile from the coast of Gloriana.

The salt breeze was refreshing against her face. The last eighteen hours had been a whirlwind. And she'd had plenty of time alone to think things through.

The Marines had quickly rounded up the mercenaries and gained control of Lopez's facility. After a couple of small firefights, most of the resistance had crumbled when they realized there was no way they could escape.

HMS Buckland had arrived at Gloriana two hours after the helicopter. It brought a small flotilla of support ships and more helicopters as well. Very quickly, a steady flow of personnel and equipment had deployed onto the island.

Elden quickly advised on the dangers the site posed. The

Royal Navy was well-equipped to handle biological contaminants. Sailors in nuclear, biological, and chemical gear secured forty drums of the agent Lopez had planned to release.

The fire Hadlow had started was brought under control. The Antonovs were identified as Zambian. After several hours the Zambian government finally admitted the aircraft were stolen.

Jess took hundreds of photographs of the Antonovs equipped with insecticide spraying modifications, the laboratory facilities, and Rafa Lopez's yacht.

Lopez had attempted a getaway on his yacht, claiming immunity when he reached international waters. The Royal Navy officers were not swayed.

Jess snapped pictures of the giant Westland 101 helicopter hovering a mere twenty feet from the bow of the yacht, its missile load at the ready.

Minutes later, the yacht's passengers and crew were face down on the deck being cuffed by a boarding party.

By the time the sun set over the horizon, Rafa Lopez's grand plan was reduced to little more than the ramblings of his overactive imagination.

Hadlow had been busy, but as the light faded, he'd shepherded Jess into a helicopter and onboard the *Buckland*. Although the ship's crew couldn't possibly know him, he was treated with great deference.

She had been allocated a small room and allowed to roam above decks.

Later, two women and a man in unmarked flight suits questioned her for an hour. She answered as many questions as she could. She was assured that her whereabouts would be communicated to the US State Department, but they took her phone and pictures.

She hadn't slept well and the morning dragged. She'd been cut off from the outside world, and twelve hours later she was more than ready to go home.

Hadlow came through a bulkhead hatch and stood beside her, staring at the sea. "Beautiful day."

"I suppose," she said.

"You had dinner?"

"Yes."

"Wasn't as good as Rooibank."

"No."

He looked at her. "Typical military operation. Everyone's just a cog. Come on."

He walked back through the bulkhead hatch. She followed him to a small room with a conference table. Half a dozen men and women in uniform stood up immediately.

The man at the head of the table stepped forward, his hand out. "Captain Rudolph Perry. Good to meet you."

His grip was predictably firm. Jess wasn't sure of the protocol for addressing a Royal Navy captain, so she settled for, "Good to meet you, too."

He gestured to an empty chair. Jess sat, and so did the crew. Hadlow remained standing by the door.

Perry cleared his throat. "Mr...." He looked at Hadlow.

"Hadlow," Hadlow said.

"Right. Mr. Hadlow has filled us in on your activities. As I understand it, if you hadn't driven that jeep onto the aircraft, we would have had a massive multination operation on our hands."

Jess shrugged. "Perhaps."

"I'm sure of it."

"What's happened to Debora Elden and Rafa Lopez?"

"Ms. Elden is already on her way back to the States for debriefing. Lopez is in the brig. He will be handed over to the Spanish authorities."

"The guy who tried to kill Cantor back in Zorita?"

"He's in custody, on his way to prison. You don't need to worry about him."

Jess nodded. "And Sánchez?"

"The Angolans, the Spanish, and Her Majesty's Government all want her for murder. So I think we can safely say she won't be assassinating anyone else in our lifetime." He offered a reassuring smile.

"I'm glad to hear it."

Perry nodded. "The last twelve hours have probably been very frustrating for you. It was essential to round up this operation as quickly as possible. Once others learn about the situation, everything gets exponentially more difficult."

"And has the operation been rounded up?"

"It has," he replied. "The biological agent has been secured. The Spanish authorities have taken control of Grupo Lopez. Arrests have been made. There will be more. The Angolan Army is now on the island. They will ensure the laboratories are properly guarded until decisions are made about the future."

She looked at Hadlow. "What about Alex Cole?"

Hadlow smiled. "Someone is on the line waiting to fill you in on that."

She frowned.

Perry rose, and the crew around the table stood immediately. Perry held his hand out. "Thank you, Ms. Kimball."

She shook his hand.

"Your phone and camera will be returned to you, and you're free to publish your story. I do ask that you refrain from using real names and photographs of my men, and," Perry gestured to Hadlow, "other people."

She nodded. The request was more than reasonable.

The captain left, followed by his crew.

Hadlow said, "Just so you know, Cole's been released. He'd been working with Elden as an activist, but he's done nothing illegal in this case. The Kelso Products CEO, Claire Winter, is being questioned about the lost biological sample and why it wasn't reported. Whether or not she'll be charged is a decision for your government."

"Good. I'm glad about Alex. Thank you." She cocked her head and looked at him. "Now that this is over, I don't suppose you're going to tell me your real name."

"Wouldn't help you. It'll be a different name next week." He grinned.

She shook her head and smiled in return.

He picked up a remote control. "Anyway, make the most of what counts as privacy onboard a warship."

She frowned.

He clicked a button, and a television on the wall sprang into life. It showed a teleconference picture of another room.

"See you when I see you." Hadlow waved as he left the room. Jess never expected to cross paths with him again.

The television screen sprang to life. Henry Morris sat in the chair directly in front of the camera.

She smiled. He smiled back with what she interpreted as both relief and pleasure.

He leaned into the camera. "You're a hard woman to find."

"All the best ones are." She grinned.

Because he deserved to squirm at least a little, she said,

"You might want to keep that in mind the next time you withhold vital information from me."

His smile wobbled. "I didn't know about Elden at first. And when I found out, I couldn't tell you, Jess. Everything was classified. Lopez would have killed her if he'd found out."

"Oh, so you're suggesting I can't keep a secret now?" she challenged.

"No." He shook his head several times. "I thought she and Hadlow could help you if you got into trouble. Since I couldn't be there."

"You think I need someone to take care of me? That I can't handle myself?" she pushed.

"Not at all. I mean, I…" He was both speechless and miserable.

And she did understand his reasoning. Sort of. So she let him off the hook. "It's okay, Henry. I get it."

He broke into a big grin that reached all the way to his eyes. "When will you be home?"

"As soon as I can get there," she replied, her own smile widening. "Tell me what's been going on since I left."

As he talked, her mind wandered back to Debora Elden. All the time Jess was searching for Elden, Henry had known where she was and why. Information he had not shared with her. Even though most of it was classified, he could have found a way to help her if he'd wanted to. But he didn't.

Of course, no one knew that Rafa Lopez was responsible for the sepsis outbreak. Or his grand plan for testing his mosquito killer on thousands of humans.

Elden was one of many field operatives covering one of many possibilities. Hadlow, too, was one of many. A multi-national operation intended to find and bring down the source of that sepsis outbreak. Just like Hadlow said.

While dozens of unanswered questions remained, Marcia McAllister had to be pleased with the result, although she'd worried for too long. A single moment's worry was too long. Solving the Alex Cole problem was a good start. But Marcia deserved to know what had happened to her daughter, too.

Jess shrugged. There was nothing more she could do here. Time to go home and get back to her own life.

All's well that ends well, perhaps.

But she had learned important things about Henry Morris she hadn't fully understood before. He cared about her, for sure. She could trust him.

Up to a point.

When Henry Morris was forced to choose between her and his job, the job came first.

Good to know.

And one more lesson she'd finally absorbed.

She could easily have died during this whole situation. She'd been lucky. And she might not be so lucky in the future.

It was time she put one hundred percent of her energy into the things closest to her heart. Because life was too precious to waste even one moment of it.

ABOUT THE AUTHORS

DIANE CAPRI is an award-winning *New York Times*, *USA Today*, and worldwide bestselling author. She's a recovering lawyer and snowbird who divides her time between Florida and Michigan. An active member of Mystery Writers of America, Author's Guild, International Thriller Writers, Alliance of Independent Authors, and Sisters in Crime, she loves to hear from readers and is hard at work on her next novel.

Please connect with Diane online:
http://www.DianeCapri.com
Twitter: http://twitter.com/@DianeCapri
Facebook: http://www.facebook.com/Diane.Capri1
http://www.facebook.com/DianeCapriBooks

NIGEL BLACKWELL was born in rural Oxfordshire in England. He has a love of books, a Ph.D. in Physical Chemistry, and a black belt in pointing out the obvious. He has driven trains, crashed single-seat racecars, and traveled much of the world.

He now lives in Texas with his wife and daughter, and a sixty-pound Siberian husky called Sindei, who apparently owns the house even though she refuses to pay the mortgage. Together, they enjoy the sunshine and listen to the coyotes howl at night.

Please connect with Nigel online:
http://www.NigelBlackwell.com
Twitter: http://www.twitter.com/Nigel_Blackwell
Facebook: http://www.facebook.com/authorNigelBlackwell